Blossom Whitt,

Clashmore,

Dornoch,

Sutherland

From Aileen E. Smart.

at Waverley, 17th Dec 1941

THE DINNER CLUB

SAPPER

THE
DINNER CLUB

HODDER AND STOUGHTON

FIRST PRINTED 1923
THIRTY-FIRST EDITION . . . JULY 1941

Made and Printed in Great Britain.
Hazell, Watson & Viney, Ltd., London and Aylesbury.

Contents

On a certain day in the year of grace 1920, there came into being a special and very select club. There was no entrance fee and no subscription, in which respect it differed from all other clubs. Its membership was limited to six: the *Actor*, the *Barrister*, the *Doctor*, the *Ordinary Man*, the *Soldier*, and the *Writer*. And since each in his own particular trade had achieved what the world calls fame, except the Ordinary Man, who was only ordinary, it was decided that for purposes of convenience they should be entered in the list of members alphabetically according to their trade, and further that they should carry out the only rule of the club in the order of that entry. And the only rule of the club was, that on certain nights, to be mutually agreed on, the member whose turn it was should give to the remaining members an exceedingly good dinner, after which he should tell them a story connected with his own trade, that should be of sufficient interest to keep them awake.

And the only penalty of the club was that if the story was not of sufficient interest to keep the audience awake, the offending member should pay a sum of ten pounds to a deserving charity.

No rule was deemed necessary as to the quality of the dinner : the members had elected themselves with discretion.

"The trouble in my game," he began, "is that the greatest plays can never be staged. There would be no money in them. The public demand a plot—a climax : after that the puppets cease strutting, the curtain rings down. But in life—in real life—there's no plot. It's just a series of anti-climaxes strung together like a patchwork quilt, until there comes the greatest anti-climax of all and the quilt is finished."

He passed his hand through his fast-greying hair, and stared for a moment or two at the fire. The Soldier was filling his pipe ; the Writer, his legs stretched in front of him, had his hands thrust deep in his trouser pockets.

"It's one of the patches in one of the quilts that my story is about," continued the actor thoughtfully. "Just an episode in the life of a woman—or shall I say, just the life of a woman in an episode ?

"You remember that play of mine—'John Pendlesham's Wife'?" He turned to the Barrister, who nodded.

"Very well," he answered. "Molly Travers was your leading lady."

"I was out of England," said the Soldier. "Never saw it."

9

" It's immaterial." The Actor lit a cigarette. " The play itself has nothing to do with my story, except indirectly. But as you didn't see it, I will just explain this much. I, of course, was John Pendlesham—Molly was my wife, and the third act constituted what, in my opinion, was the finest piece of emotional acting which that consummate actress has ever done in her career."

The Writer nodded. " I agree. She was superb."

" Night after night the fall of the curtain found her nearly fainting ; night after night there was that breathless moment of utter silence followed by a perfect crash of applause. I am mentioning these old facts because her marvellous perform-ance does concern my story directly—even though the play does not.

" We had been running about a month, I suppose, when my story begins. I had just come off after the third act, and was going to my dressing-room. For some reason, instead of going by the direct door which led into it from the stage, I went outside into the passage. There were some hands moving furniture or something. . . .

" I think you've all of you been behind at my theatre. First you come to the swing doors out of the street, inside which the watch dog sits demanding callers' business. Then there is another door, and beyond that there are three steps down to my room. And it was just as I was opening my door on that night that I happened to look round.

" Standing at the top of the three stairs was a woman who was staring at me. I only saw her for a moment : then the watch dog intervened, and I went into my room. But I *had* seen her for a moment : I had seen her for long enough to get the look in her eyes.

" We get all sorts and conditions of people behind, as you'd expect—stage-struck girls, actors out of a shop, autograph hunters, beggars. And the watch dog knew my invariable rule : only personal friends and people who had made an appointment by letter were allowed inside the second door. But a rule cannot legislate for every case.

" Gad ! you fellows, it's many years now since that night, but I can still feel, as clearly as if it were yesterday, the message in that girl's eyes. There had been hope and fear and pitiful entreaty : the look of one who had staked everything on a last desperate throw : the look of a mother who is fighting for her child. It was amazing : I couldn't understand it. As I stood just inside my door I couldn't have told you whether she was old or young, plain or pretty. And yet in that one fleeting second this vivid, jumbled message had reached me." The Actor pressed out his cigarette, and there was silence while he lit another one.

" For a moment I hesitated," he continued after a while ; " then I rang the bell for the watch dog.

" ' Who is that lady I saw outside there ? ' I asked, as he came in.

" ' Won't give no name, sir,' he answered. ' Wants to see you, but I told her the rules.'

" Once again I hesitated; probably I'd exaggerated—put a totally false construction on her expression, probably she was looking for a job like the rest of them. And then I knew that I'd got to see that woman, and that I should have no peace of mind until I'd heard what she had to say. The watch dog was regarding me curiously; plainly he could see no reason whatever for my hesitation. He was a matter-of-fact fellow, was the guardian of the door.

" ' Show her in, I'll see her now.' I had my back to him, but I could feel his virtuous indignation. After all, rules are rules.

" ' Now, sir ? ' he echoed.

" ' Now; at once.'

" He went out, and I heard him go up the steps.

" ' Mr. Trayne will see you. Come this way.'

" And then the door opened again, and I turned to face the woman. She was young— quite young, dressed in a kind of cheap suburban frock. Her shoes had been good ones—once, now—well, however skilfully a patch is put on it is still a patch. Her gloves showed traces of much needle and cotton; the little bag she carried was rubbed and frayed. And over the cheap suburban frock she had on a coat which was worn and threadbare.

" ' It was good of you to see me, Mr. Trayne.'

" She was nervous and her voice shook a little, but she faced me quite steadily.

" ' It's a very unusual thing for me to do,' I said. ' But I saw you at the top of the stairs, and . . .'

" ' I know it's unusual,' she interrupted. ' The man outside there told me your rule. But believe me '—she was talking with more assurance now—' my reason for coming to see you is very unusual also.'

" I pulled up a chair for her. What is your reason ? ' I asked.

" She took a deep breath and began fumbling with her handkerchief.

" ' I know you will think me mad,' she began, ' but I don't want to tell you my reason now. I want to wait until after the play is over, and I know you go on at once in the fourth act.'

" ' You've seen the play, then ? ' I remarked.

" ' I've seen the play,' was her somewhat astonishing answer, ' every night since the first.'

" ' Every night ! ' I stared at her in surprise. ' But . . .'

" I must have glanced at her clothes or something and she saw what was in my mind.

" ' I suppose you think that I hardly look as if I could afford such luxuries.' She smiled faintly. ' I've only seen it from the gallery and pit, you know. And even that has meant that I've had to go without lunch. But—you see—

it was necessary for me to see it : I had to. It was part of my plan—a necessary part.'

"'I don't want to seem dense,' I said gently, 'but I'm afraid I don't quite follow. How can seeing my play thirty odd times be a necessary part of your plan ?'

"'That's what I don't want to tell you now,' she repeated, and once more her hands began twisting nervously. 'I want to wait till afterwards, when perhaps you'll—of your kindness—do as I ask you. Oh! Mr. Trayne—for God's sake, don't fail me!' She leant forward beseechingly in her chair.

"'My dear child,' I answered quietly—I don't think she can have been much more than twenty, 'you haven't told me yet what you want me to do.'

"'I want you to come to a house in Kensington with me,' she said steadily."

Once again the Actor paused, and stared at the fire. Then he gave a short laugh.

"When she said that, I looked at her pretty sharply. Without appearing conceited or anything of that sort, one has occasionally in the course of one's career, received certain flattering attentions from charming women—attentions which—er—one is tempted to conceal from one's wife."

"Precisely," murmured the Ordinary Man. "Precisely."

"And for a moment, I must confess that the thought passed through my mind that this was one of those occasions. And it wasn't until the colour rose to her face and stained it scarlet, that I realised that not only had I made a mistake, but that I had been foolish enough to let her see that I had.

" ' My God ! ' she whispered, ' you don't think—you couldn't think—that I meant . . .'

" She rose and almost cowered away from me. ' Why, I'm married.'

" I refrained from remarking that the fact was hardly such a conclusive proof of the absurdity of my unspoken thought as she seemed to imagine. I merely bowed, and said a little formally : ' Please don't jump to conclusions. May I ask why you wish me to come to a house in Kensington with you ? '

" The colour ebbed away from her cheeks, and she sat down again.

" ' That's the very thing I don't want to tell you, until you come,' she answered very low. ' I know it sounds absurd—it must do, it seems as if I were being unnecessarily mysterious. But I can't tell you, Mr. Trayne, I can't tell you . . . Not yet. . . .'

" And then the call boy knocked, and I had to go on for the last act. In a way I suppose it was absurd of me—but life is made up of impulses. I confess that the whole thing intrigued me. When a woman comes and tells you that she has seen your play every night since it started ; that she's had to go without her lunch to do so ; that it was a necessary part of some wonderful plan, and that she wants you to go to a house in Kensington, the least curious man would be attracted. And from my earliest infancy I've always been engrossed in other people's business.

" ' All right,' I said briefly. 'I'll come with you.'

" And then I had to put out my hand to steady her, I thought she was going to faint. Reaction, I thought at the time ; later, it struck me that the reason was much more prosaic—lack of food.

" I stopped for a moment till she seemed herself again ; then I told her to wait outside.

" ' I shall be about half an hour,' I said, ' and then we'll take a taxi, and go down to Kensington. Tell them to give you a chair. . . .'

" And my last impression as I went on to the stage was of a white-faced girl clutching the table, staring at me with great brown eyes that held in them a dawning triumph.

" I think," went on the Actor thoughtfully, " that that is where the tragedy of it all really lay. Afterwards she told me that the part of her plan which had seemed most difficult to her was getting my consent to go with her to Kensington. Once that was done, she knew all would be well, she was absolutely and supremely confident. And when I went on to the stage for the fourth act, she felt that success had crowned her efforts, that what was to come after was nothing compared to that which she had already done. The

inaccessible stronghold had been stormed, the
ogre had proved to be a lamb.

" Well, we went to Kensington. I sent my
own car home, and we took a taxi. During
the drive she was very silent, and I didn't try
to make her talk. Evidently no inkling of the
mysterious plan was to be revealed until we arrived at the address she had given the driver.
It was some obscure street that I had never
heard of and the name of which I have completely forgotten. I know it was somewhere not
far from Barker's.

" The door was opened by a repulsive-looking
woman who peered at me suspiciously. And
then the girl took her on one side and whispered
something in her ear. Apparently it had the
desired effect, as the Gorgon retired grumbling
to an odoriferous basement, leaving us alone in
the hall.

" When she had shut the door the girl turned
to me.

" ' Will you come upstairs, Mr. Trayne. I
want you to meet my husband.'

" I bowed. ' Certainly,' I said, and she led
the way.

" ' So the husband was in the plan,' I reflected
as I followed her. Was he a genius with a play
that he proposed to read to me ? I had suffered
from the plays of genius before. Or was he some
actor down on his luck ? If so, why all the
mystery ? And then, when I'd made up my
mind that it was a mere begging case, we arrived at

2

the room. Just before she turned the handle of the door she again looked at me.

" ' My husband is ill, Mr. Trayne. You'll excuse his being in bed.'

" Then we went in. Good Lord ! you fellows," the Actor leant forward in his chair. " I've been pretty hard up in the old days, but as I stood inside that door I realised for the first time what poverty—real poverty—meant. Mark you, the girl was a lady ; the weak, cadaverous-looking fellow propped up in bed with a tattered shawl round his shoulders was a gentleman. And beyond the bed, and one chair, and a rackety old chest-of-drawers there wasn't a stick of furniture in the room. There was a curtain in the corner with what looked like a washstand behind it, and a shelf by the bed with two cups and some plates on it. And nothing else except an appalling oleograph of Queen Victoria on the wall.

" ' This is Mr. Trayne, dear.' She was bending over her husband, and after a moment he looked up at me.

" ' It was good of you to come, sir,' he said. ' Very good.' And then he turned to his wife and I heard him say : ' Have you told him yet, Kitty ? '

" She shook her head. ' Not yet, darling, I will now.' She left his side and came over to me.

" ' Mr. Trayne, I know you thought me very peculiar at the theatre. But I was afraid that if I told you what I really wanted you'd have refused to come. You get hundreds and hundreds of people coming to see you who think they can act. Asking you to help them get a job and that sort of thing. Well, I was afraid that if I told you that that was what I wanted, you'd have told me to go away. Perhaps you'd have given me a straw of comfort—taken my address—said you'd let me know if anything turned up. But nothing would have turned up. . . . And, you see, I was rather desperate.'

"The big brown eyes were fixed on me pleadingly, and somehow I didn't feel quite as annoyed as I should have done at what was nothing more nor less than a blatant trick to appeal to my sympathy.

"'Perhaps nothing would have turned up,' I said gently, 'but you must remember that to-day the stage is a hopelessly overstocked profession. There are hundreds of trained actors and actresses unable to obtain a job.'

"'I know that,' she cried eagerly, 'and that's why I—why I thought out this plan. I thought that if I could *really* convince you that I could act above the average . . .'

"'And she can, Mr. Trayne,' broke in her husband. 'She's good, I know it.'

"'We must leave Mr. Trayne to be the judge of that, Harry,' she smiled. 'You see,' she went on to me, 'what I felt was that there is an opening for real talent. There is, isn't there?'

"'Yes,' I agreed slowly. 'There is an opening for *real* talent. But even that is a small one. . . . Have you ever acted before?'

" ' A little.   In amateur theatricals ! '

" I turned away.   Amateur theatricals ! More heart-burning and disappointment has been caused by those abominable entertainments than their misguided originators will ever realise.

" ' But don't think I'm relying on that.'   The girl was speaking again, and I almost laughed. ' I want you to judge me to-night.'

" I swung round and looked at her.   So this was the mysterious plan : I was to witness an impromptu performance, which was to convince me that the second Sarah Bernhardt had been discovered.

" ' I couldn't have shown you, you see, in your dressing-room.   I shouldn't have had time. That's why I asked you to come here.'

" ' You have the courage of your convictions anyway,' I said quietly.   ' I am perfectly ready to be convinced.'

" ' Then will you sit there.'   She took off her hat and coat as I sat down on the only available chair, and from underneath his pillow the man produced a paper-covered book.

" ' You'll forgive me if I read my lines, Mr. Trayne,' he said.   ' I find I can't learn them— I can't concentrate.' He passed a thin, emaciated hand over his forehead.   ' And it's her you want to see.'

" He turned over the pages weakly ; then he began to read.   And I—I sat up as if I'd been stung.   At last everything was clear : the continual visits to the theatre—everything.   The part of all others which they had selected to prove her ability, was the love-scene between Molly Travers and myself in the third act of ' John Pendlesham's Wife. . . .' "

For a while there was silence, while the Actor thoughtfully lit another cigarette.

" This unknown child," he went on after a moment, " who had acted a little in amateur theatricals, had deliberately challenged London's greatest emotional actress in her most marvellous success before, Heaven help us, *me*—of all people. I suppose if I was writing a story I should say that she triumphed ; that as I sat in that bare and hideous room I realised that before me was genius—a second and greater Molly ; that from that moment her foot was set on the ladder of fame, and there was no looking back."

The Actor laughed a little sadly. " Unfortunately, I'm not writing a story, I'm telling the truth. I don't know how I sat through the next twenty minutes. It was the most ghastly caricature of Molly that I have ever thought of ; the more ghastly because it was so intensely unintentional. Every little gesture was faithfully copied ; every little trick and mannerism had been carefully learnt by heart. And this, as I say, to me who acted with that divine genius every night. God ! it was awful. That marvellous line of Molly's, when, standing in the centre of the stage facing me across the table, she said : ' Then you don't want me back ? ' that line which was made marvellous merely through the consummate restraint with which she said it, sounded from this poor child like a parlour-maid giving notice.

"And then, at last it was over, and I realised I had to say something. They were both staring at me, hope shining clear in the girl's eyes and pride in the man's.

"'She's great, isn't she, Mr. Trayne?' he said. 'I've not had the privilege of seeing you and Miss Travers in the part—but I feel that now—why,' he gave a little shaky laugh, 'that it's hardly necessary.'

"You see," said the Actor slowly, "that was the devil of it all. They were both so utterly certain, especially the man. The difficulty had been to get me there; after that it had been easy. I glanced at the poor fellow in the bed, and his thoughts were plain to read. No more grinding poverty, no more unfurnished bed-sitting rooms, and—fame for the woman he loved! And then he spoke again.

"I'm such a hopeless crock, Mr. Trayne, and she'—he took one of her hands in both his own—' she's had to do all the work. Beastly, grinding work in an office, when she was capable of this.'

"The girl bent over him, and I looked away. It seemed to me that the ground on which I stood was holy."

The Actor gave a short laugh which deceived no one. "I suppose I was an ass," he went on, "but I'd do it again to-day. 'It was wonderful,'

I said, ' quite wonderful.' And because I'm an
actor they believed me. Not that he, at any
rate, required much convincing—he only wanted
his knowledge confirmed. Of course, when I
spoke I didn't realise what I was letting myself
in for. I should have done, I suppose, but—I
wasn't left long in doubt. If she was wonderful
—and had not I, Herbert Trayne, said so—what
about a job? At once . . . With my backing
it was easy. . . . Which was all quite true
except for the one vital fact of my having
lied. But, hang it, you fellows! " he exploded,
" could you have told 'em it was the most
appalling exhibition of utter futility you'd ever
witnessed ? "

" No, I couldn't," said the Soldier. " What
happened ? "

" I can see them now," continued the Actor.
" He was holding her hand, and looking up into
her face—as a dog looks at the being it adores.
And she was smiling a little, and crying a little—
tears of pure joy. The strain was over, the
lunches had not been missed in vain. And I
stood there like a dumb idiot racking my brains
for something to say. They thought I was
wondering what job to offer her ; they were
right, I was.' The Actor laughed shortly.

" But I'd gone into the morass, and there was
nothing for it but to blunder in deeper. The one
vital essential was that in no circumstances must
the poor child ever be allowed to act. The other
was money—and at once. So I offered her then

and there a job as Molly Travers' understudy at
five pounds a week."

"Great Scott!" The Doctor sat up with a
jerk. "Understudy Molly?"

"I explained, of course," went on the Actor,
"that there was an understudy already, and that
to save unpleasantness it would be better if she
didn't come to the theatre, unless I sent for her.
That, of course, it was more than likely that Miss
Travers wouldn't be ill during the run of the play,
and that in those circumstances I didn't want
to offend the present understudy. And when
another play came along, we must see what we
could do. That, thank Heaven, I knew was some
way off yet! It gave me breathing space.

"I gave her a week's salary in advance, and
I got away—somehow. I think they were both a
little dazed with the wonder of it, and they
wanted to be alone. I heard his voice—weak
and quavering—as I shut the door.

"'Oh! my very dear girl,' he was whispering
—and she was on her knees beside the bed. And
I blundered my way downstairs, cursing myself
for a sentimental fool. There's whisky on the
table, you fellows. Help yourselves."

But no one moved, and the Actor lit another
cigarette.

"I saw her occasionally during the next two
or three months," he continued, "though I never
went to their rooms again. They had moved—I
knew that—because I used to post the cheque
every week. But the few times I did see her, I

gathered that her husband was not getting any better. And one day I insisted on Lawrence, the specialist, going to see him. I couldn't have one of my company being worried, I told her, over things of that sort. I can see her face now as I said ' one of my company.' I don't know what Lawrence said to her, but he rang me up at the theatre that night, and he did not mince his words to me.

" ' I give him a month,' he said. ' It's galloping consumption.'

" It was just about a month later that the thing happened which I had been dreading. Molly went down with 'flu. Her understudy—the real one—was Violet Dorman, who was unknown then. And, of course it was her chance."

" One moment," interrupted the Barrister. " Did anyone at the theatre know about this girl ? "

" Good God ! no," cried the Actor. " Not a soul. In this censorious world actions such as mine in that case are apt to be misconstrued, which alone was sufficient to make me keep it dark. No one knew.

" The first night—all was well. Molly went down in the afternoon, and it didn't come out in any of the evening papers. Violet acted magnificently. She wasn't Molly, of course—she isn't now. But it was her chance, and she took it—and took it well. Next morning the papers, naturally, had it in. ' Temporary indisposition of Miss Molly Travers. Part filled at a moment's notice with great credit by Miss Violet Dorman.' She had a press agent and he boomed her for all he was worth. And I read the papers and cursed. Not that I grudged her her success in the slightest, but I was thinking of the afternoon. It was matinée day and the girl must read it in the papers.

" There was only one thing for it—to go round and see her. Whatever happened I had to prevent her coming to the theatre. How I was going to do it without giving the show away I hadn't an idea, but somehow or other it had got to be done. My blundering foolishness—even though it had been for the best—had caused the trouble ; it was up to me to try and right it. So I went round and found her with a doctor in the sitting-room. He was just going as I came in, and his face was grave.

" ' Harry's dying,' she said to me quite simply, and I glanced at the doctor, who nodded.

" Poor child ! I crossed over to her side, and though it seems an awful thing to say, my only feeling was one of relief. After what Lawrence had said I knew it was hopeless, and since the poor devil had to go he couldn't have chosen a more opportune moment from my point of view. It solved the difficulty. If he was dying she couldn't come to the theatre, and by the time the funeral was over Molly would be back. I didn't realise that one doesn't get out of things quite as easily as that.

" ' I've only just realised how bad he was,' she went on in a flat, dead voice.

" ' Does he know ? ' I asked.

" ' No. He thinks he's going to get better. Why didn't you send for me last night, Mr. Trayne ? '

" It was so unexpected, that I hesitated and stammered.

" ' I couldn't get at you in time,' I said finally. ' Miss Travers only became ill late in the afternoon.'

" With a strange look on her face she opened a paper—some cursed rag I hadn't seen.

" ' It says here,' she went on slowly, ' that she was confined to her bed all yesterday. Oh ! it doesn't matter much, does it ? ' She put the paper down wearily, and gave the most heartrending little sobbing laugh I've ever heard.

" ' What do you mean ? ' I stammered out.

" ' I suppose you did it for the best, Mr. Trayne. I suppose I ought to be grateful. But you lied that night—didn't you ? '

" I was fingering a book on the table and for the life of me I couldn't think of anything to say. ' He doesn't know,' she went on. ' He still thinks I'm a God-sent genius. And he mustn't know.'

" ' Why should he ? ' I said. And then I put my hand on her arm. ' Tell me, how did you find out ? '

" ' You admit it then ? '

" ' Yes,' I said quietly, ' I admit that I lied. I was so desperately sorry for you.'

" ' I mentioned it to someone—a man who knew the stage—about a week ago. He looked at me in blank amazement, and then he laughed. I suppose he couldn't help it : it was so ridiculous. I was furious—furious. But afterwards I began to think, and I asked other people one or two questions—and then that came,' she pointed to the paper, ' and I knew. And now—oh! thank God—he's dying. He mustn't know, Mr. Trayne, he mustn't.'

" And at that moment he came into the room— tottered in is a better word.

" ' Boy,' she cried in an agony, ' what are you doing ? '

" ' I thought I heard Mr. Trayne's voice,' he whispered, collapsing in the chair. ' I'm much better to-day, much. Bit weak still——'

" And then he saw the paper, and he leant forward eagerly.

" ' Ill,' he cried. ' Molly Travers ill. Why, my dear—but it's your chance.' He read on a bit, and she looked at me desperately. ' But why weren't you there last night ? Who is this woman, Violet Dorman ? '

" ' You see, Tracy,' I said, picking up the paper and putting it out of his reach, ' it was so sudden, Miss Travers' illness, that I couldn't get at your wife in time.'

" ' Quite,' he whispered. ' Of course. But there's a matinée this afternoon, isn't there ?

Oh! I wonder if I'm well enough to go. I'm so much better to-day.' And then he looked at his wife. ' My dear! my dear—at last! '

" I don't think I've ever seen such pathetic pride and love shining in a man's face before or since.

" ' I'm afraid you won't be quite well enough to go,' I muttered.

" ' Perhaps it would be wiser not to,' he whispered. ' But to think I shall miss her first appearance. Have you come to fetch her now, Mr. Trayne ? '

" ' Yes, darling,' the girl replied, and her voice sounded as steady as a rock. ' Mr. Trayne has come to fetch me. But it's early yet and I want you to go back to bed now. . . . '

" Without a glance at me she helped him from the room and left me standing there. I heard their voices—hers clear and strong, his barely audible. And not for the first time in my life I marvelled at the wonder of a woman who loves. I was to marvel more in a moment or two.

" She came back and shut the door. Then she stood facing me.

" ' There's only one way, Mr. Trayne, though I think it's going to break my heart. I must go to the theatre.

" ' But—your husband . . .' I stammered.

" ' Oh! I'm not really going. I shall be here—at hand—the whole time. Because if the end did come—why then—I *must* be with him. But he's got to think I've gone ; I've got to hide

from him until after the matinée is over.   And
then I must tell him '—she faltered a little—' of
my success.   I'll keep the papers from him—if
it's necessary. . . .'   She turned away and I
heard her falter :   ' Three hours away from him
—when he's dying.   Oh, my God ! ' "

The Actor paused, and the Soldier stirred
restlessly in his chair.   " I left shortly after,"
he went on at length, " I saw she wanted me to.

" All through the play that afternoon it
haunted me—the pathos of it—aye, the horror of
it.   I pictured that girl hiding somewhere, while
in the room above the sands were running out.
Longing with all the power of her being to go to
him—to snatch every fleeting minute with him—
and yet condemned by my stupidity to forfeit
her right.   And then at last the show was over,
and I went to her room again.

" She was by his side, kneeling on the floor,
as I came in.   As he saw me he struggled up on
his elbow, and one could see it was the end.

" ' Dear fellow,' I said, ' she was wonderful—
just wonderful ! '

" And the girl looked up at me through her
blinding tears.

" ' Just wonderful,' I said again.   Five minutes
later he died. . . .' "

The Actor fell silent.

" Did you ever see her again ? " asked the
Soldier thoughtfully.

" Never : she disappeared.   Just a patch on
the quilt as I said.   But there was one thread

missing. Three years later I received a registered envelope. There was no letter inside, no word of any sort. Just these." He fumbled in his pocket. "There are twenty of them."

He held out his hand, and the Soldier leaning forward saw that it contained a little bundle of five-pound notes.

"This morning," he began, leaning back in his chair and crossing his legs, " I mislaid my cigarette-case. I knew it was somewhere in the study, but find it I could not. Finally, having searched all over my writing table, I rang the bell, and somewhat irritably demanded its immediate production. The butler stepped forward and lifted it up from the centre of the blotting pad, where it had been the whole time, literally under my nose. What peculiar temporary kink in the brain had prevented my noticing the very thing I was looking for, when it was lying in the most conspicuous place in which it could possibly have been, I don't know. I leave that to the Doctor. But the point of my parable is this—it decided in my mind the story with which I should bore you fellows to-night."

He paused to light a cigar, then he glance round at the faces of the other five.

"And if, as I get on with it, you think y recognise the real characters under the fictio names I shall give them, I can't prevent yo But don't ask me to confirm your thoughts."

"Exactly," murmured the Actor. "F ahead."

" It was about four years before the war," commenced the Barrister, " that I was stopping for a few nights at a certain house in Park Lane. It was in the middle of the season—June, to be accurate—and I was waiting to get in here. My wife was in the country, and, as I was more or less at a loose end, I accepted the offer of staying at this house. My hostess—shall we call her Granger, Ruth Granger—had been an old school pal of my wife's ; in later years she had become a real, intimate friend of us both.

" At the time of which I speak she was a lovely girl of twenty-six, with the suffering of six years of hell in her eyes. At the age of twenty she had married Sir Henry Granger, and that fatal mistake had been the cause of the hell. Henry Granger was one of the most loathsome brutes it has ever been my misfortune to run across. He had not one single instinct of a gentleman in him, though he did happen to be the tenth baronet. How her parents had ever allowed the marriage beat me completely. Perhaps it was money, for Granger was rich ; but whatever it was she married him, and her hell began.

" Granger was simply an animal, a coarse and vicious animal. He drank heavily without getting drunk, which is always a dangerous sign, and he possessed the morals—or did not possess the morals, whichever you prefer—of a monkey. He was unfaithful to her on their honeymoon— my wife told me that ; and from then on he made

3

not the slightest attempt to conceal his mode of life."

The Barrister carefully removed the ash from his cigar. " I won't labour the point," he went on with a faint smile. " We have all of us met the type, but I'd like to emphasise the fact that I, at any rate, have never met any member of that type who came within a mile of him. Most of 'em have some semblance of decency about 'em— make some attempt to conceal their affairs. Granger didn't ; he seemed to prefer that they should be known. Sometimes since then I have wondered whether he was actuated by a sort of blind rage—by a mad desire to pierce through the calm, icy contempt of his wife ; to make her writhe and suffer, because he realised she was so immeasurably his superior." He paused thoughtfully. " He made her suffer right enough."

" Did she never try for a divorce ? " asked the Soldier

" No, never. We discussed it once—she, and my wife and I ; and I had to explain to her our peculiar laws on the subject. His adultery by itself was, of course, not sufficient, and for some reason she flatly refused to consider a mere separation. She wouldn't face the scandal and publicity for only that. I said to her then : ' Why not apply for a restitution of conjugal rights. Get your husband to leave the house, and if he doesn't return in fourteen days——'

" She stopped me with a bitter laugh.

" ' It seems rather fatuous,' she said slowly,

' getting a lawyer to ask my husband to do what he is only too ready to do—return to me.'

" ' But surely,' I began, not quite taking her meaning.

" ' You see, Bill,' she answered in a flat, dead voice, ' my husband is very fond of me—as a stopgap. After most of his episodes he honours me with his attentions for two or three days.'

" That was the devil of it—he didn't intend to let her divorce him. She formed an excellent hostess for his house, and for the rest there were always *les autres*. And he wanted her, too, because he couldn't get her, and that made him mad."

The Barrister leant forward, and the firelight flickered on his thin, ascetic face.

" Such was the state of affairs when I went to stay. The particular lady at the time who was being honoured by Henry Granger was a shining light in musical comedy—Nelly Jones, shall we call her ? It is very far from her real name. If possible, he had been more open over this affair than usual ; everyone who knew the Grangers in London knew about it—*everyone*. He had twice dined with her at the same restaurant at which his wife was entertaining, once deliberately selecting the next table."

" What an unmitigated swine ! " cried the Ordinary Man.

" He was," agreed the Barrister briefly. " But even that was not sufficient to satisfy the gentleman. He proceeded to do a thing which

put him for ever outside the pale. He brought
this girl to a reception of his wife's at his own
house.

"It was the night that I arrived. She had
fixed up one of those ghastly entertainments
which are now, thank Heaven, practically extinct.
Somebody sings and nobody listens, and you meet
everybody you particularly want to avoid.
Mercifully I ran into an old pal, also of your
calling, Actor-man—Violet Seymour. No reason
why I should disguise her name at any rate.
She was not acting at the moment, and we sat
in a sort of alcove-place at the top of the stairs,
on the same landing as the reception-room.

"'There's going to be a break here soon,
Bill,' she said to me after a while. 'Ruth is
going to snap.'

"'Poor girl!' I answered. 'But what the
devil can one do, Violet?'

"'Nothing,' she said fiercely, 'except alter
your abominably unjust laws. Why can't she
get a divorce, Bill? It's vile—utterly vile.'

"And then—well, let's call him Sir Edward
Shoreham, joined us. He was on the Bench—
a judge, which makes the disguise of a false name
pretty thin, especially in view of what is to come.
I remember he had recently taken a murder case
—one that had aroused a good deal of popular
attention—and the prisoner had been found
guilty. We were talking about it at the time Sir
Edward arrived, with Violet, as usual, tilting
lances against every form of authority.

" I can see her now as she turned to Sir Edward with a sort of dreadful fascination on her face.

" ' And so you sentenced him to death ? '

" He nodded gravely. ' Certainly,' he answered. ' He was guilty.'

" And then she turned half-away, speaking almost under her breath.

" ' And doesn't it ever appal you ? Make you wake in the middle of the night, with your mouth dry and your throat parched. All this—life, love—and in a cell, a man waiting—a man you've sent there. Ticking off the days on his nerveless fingers—staring out at the sun. My God ! it would drive me mad.'

" Ned Shoreham smiled a little grimly.

" ' You seem to forget one unimportant factor,' he answered ; ' the wretched woman that man killed.'

" ' No, I don't,' she cried. ' But the punishment is so immeasurably worse than the crime. I don't think death would matter if it came suddenly ; but to sit waiting with a sort of sickening helplessness——''

" It was then Ruth Granger joined us. Some woman was singing in the reception-room and, for the moment, she was free from her duties as hostess.

" ' You seem very serious,' she said with her grave, sweet smile, holding out her hand to Sir Edward.

" ' Miss Seymour is a revolutionary,' he answered lightly, and I happened at that moment to glance at Ruth. And for the moment she had let the mask slip as she looked at Ned Shoreham's face. Then it was replaced, but their secret was out, as far as I was concerned, though on matters of affection I am the least observant of mortals. If they weren't in love with one another, they were as near to it as made no odds. And it gave me a bit of a shock.

" Shoreham was young—young, at any rate, for the Bench—and he was unmarried. And somehow I couldn't fit Shoreham into the situation of loving another man's wife. There had never been a breath of scandal that I had heard ; if there had been, it would have finished him for good. A judge must be like Cæsar's wife. And Shoreham, even then, had established a reputation for the most scrupulous observance of the law. His enemies called him cruel and harsh ; those who knew him better realised that his apparent harshness was merely a cloak he had wrapped tightly round himself as a guard against a naturally tender heart. I don't know any man that I can think of who had such an undeviating idea of duty as Shoreham, and without being in the least a prig, such an exalted idea of the responsibilities of his position. And to realise suddenly that he was in love with Ruth Granger, as I say, came as a shock.

" ' What was the argument about ? ' she said, sitting down beside me.

" ' Morality *versus* the Law,' chipped in Violet.

" ' The individual *versus* the community,'

amended Sir Edward. ' Justice—real justice—against sickly sentimentality, with all due deference to you, Miss Seymour. There are hard cases, one knows, but hard cases make bad laws. There's been far too much lately of men taking matters into their own hands—this so-called Unwritten Law. And it has got to stop.'

" ' You would never admit the justification,' said Ruth slowly.

" ' Never—in any circumstances,' he answered. ' You have the law—then appeal to the law. Otherwise there occurs chaos.'

" ' And what of the cases where the law gives no redress ? ' demanded Violet, and even as she spoke Granger came up the stairs with this girl on his arm.

" Ruth Granger rose, deathly white, and gazed speechlessly at her husband's coarse, sneering face. I don't think for a moment she fully grasped the immensity of the insult; she was stunned. The footmen were staring open-mouthed ; guests passing into the supper-room stopped and smirked. And then it was over; the tension snapped.

" ' Have you had any supper, Sir Edward ? ' said Ruth calmly, and with her hand on his arm she swept past her husband, completely ignoring both him and the girl, who flushed angrily.

" ' I suppose,' said Violet Seymour to me, as Granger and the girl went into the reception-room, ' that had Ruth shot that filthy black-guard dead on the stairs, Sir Edward would have

piously folded his hands and, in due course,
sentenced her to death.'

"And at the moment I certainly sympathised
with her point of view."

The Barrister got up and splashed some soda-
water into a glass. Then he continued :

"I won't weary you with an account of the
rest of the reception. You can imagine for yourselves the covert sneers and whisperings. I want
to go on two or three hours to the time when the
guests had gone, and a white-faced, tight-lipped
woman was staring at the dying embers of a fire
in her sitting-room, while I stood by the mantelpiece wondering what the devil to do to help.
Granger was in his study, where he had retired on
the departure of Miss Jones, and I, personally,
had seen two bottles of champagne taken to him
there by one of the footmen.

"'It's the end, Bill,' she said, looking at me
suddenly, 'absolutely the end. I can't go on—
not after to-night. How dared he bring that
woman here ?   How dared he ? '

"Violet had been right—the break had come.
Ruth Granger was desperate, and there was an
expression on her face that it wasn't good to see.
It put the wind up me all right.

"'Go to bed, Ruth,' I said quietly. 'There's
no good having a row with Granger to-night; you
can say what you want to say to-morrow.'

"And at that moment the door opened and
ner husband came in. As I said, he was a man
who never got drunk, but that night he was

unsteady on his legs. He stood by the door, swaying a little and staring at her with a sneer on his face. He was a swine sober ; in drink he was —well, words fail. But, by God ! you fellows, she got through him and into him until I thought he was going to strike her. I believe that was what she was playing for at the time, because I was there as a witness. But he didn't, and when she finished flaying him he merely laughed in her face.

" ' And what about your own damned lover, my virtuous darling ? ' he sneered. ' What about the upright judge whom you adore—dear, kind Edward Shoreham ? '

" It was unexpected ; she didn't know he had guessed—and her face gave her away for a moment. Then she straightened up proudly.

" ' Sir Edward Shoreham and I are on terms which an animal of your gross mind couldn't possibly understand,' she answered coldly, and he laughed. ' If you insinuate that he is my lover in the accepted sense of the word, you lie and you know it.'

" Without another word she walked contemptuously by him, and the door closed behind her. And after a moment or two I followed her, leaving him staring moodily at the empty grate. I couldn't have spoken to him without being rude and, after all, I was under his roof."

The Barrister leant back in his chair and crossed his legs.

" Now that was the situation," he continued,
" when I went to bed. My room was almost
opposite Lady Granger's, and at the end of the
passage, which was a cul-de-sac, was the door
leading into Granger's study. I hadn't started
to undress when I heard him come past my room
and go along the passage to his study. And I was
still thinking over the situation about ten minutes
later when Lady Granger's door opened. I knew
it was hers because I heard her speak to her maid,
telling her to go to bed. The girl said ' Good
night,' and something—I don't quite know what
—made me look through the keyhole of my door.
I was feeling uneasy and alarmed ; I suppose the
scene downstairs had unsettled me. And sure
enough, as soon as the maid's footsteps had died
away, I saw through my spy-hole Ruth Granger
go down the passage towards her husband's study.
For a moment I hesitated ; an outsider's position
is always awkward between husband and wife.
But one thing was very certain, those two were
in no condition to have another—and this time a
private—interview. I opened my door noiselessly and peered out. It struck me that if I
heard things getting too heated I should have to
intervene. She was just opening the door of
his study as I looked along the passage, and then
in a flash the whole thing seemed to happen. The
door shut behind her ; there was a pause of one—
perhaps two seconds—and a revolver shot rang
out, followed by the sound of a heavy fall. For
a moment I was stunned ; then I raced along the

passage as hard as I could, and flung open the door of the study.

" On the floor lay Henry Granger, doubled up and sprawling, while in the middle of the room stood his wife staring at him speechlessly. At her feet on the carpet was a revolver, an automatic Colt. I stood there by the door staring foolishly, and after a while she spoke.

" ' There's been an accident,' she whispered. ' Is he dead ? '

" I went up to the body and turned it over. Through the shirt front was a small hole ; underneath the left shoulder blade was another. Henry Granger had been shot through the heart from point-blank range ; death must have been absolutely instantaneous.

" ' My God, Ruth ! ' I muttered. ' How did it happen ? '

" ' Happen ? ' she answered vaguely. ' There was a man . . . the window.'

" And then she fainted. The butler, with a couple of footmen, by this time had appeared at the door, and I pulled myself together.

" ' Her ladyship's maid at once,' I said. ' Sir Henry has been shot. Ring up a doctor, and ask him to come round immediately.'

" The butler rushed off, but I kept the two footmen.

" ' Wait a moment,' I cried, picking up the revolver. ' A man did it. Pull back the two curtains by the window, and I'll cover him.'

" They did as I told them, pulled back the two

heavy black curtains that were in front of the window. It was set back in a sort of alcove, and I had the revolver ready pointed to cover the murderer. I covered empty air; there was no one there. Then I walked over to the window and looked out. It was wide open, and there was a sheer drop of forty feet to the deserted area below. I looked upwards—I looked sideways : plain brickwork without footing for a cat."

" ' Go down to the room below,' I cried ; ' he may have got in there.'

" They rushed away to come back and tell me that not only were the windows bolted, but that they were shuttered as well. And I thought they looked at me curiously."

He paused to relight his cigar; then he continued thoughtfully :

" I don't quite know when I first began to feel suspicious about this mysterious man. The thing had been so sudden that for a while my brain refused to work ; then gradually my legal training reasserted itself, and I started to piece things together. Ruth had come-to again, and I put one or two questions to her. She was still very dazed, but she answered them quite coherently :

" A man in evening clothes—at least, she thought he had on evening clothes—had been in the room as she came in. She heard a shot ; the light went out and the window was thrown up. And then she had turned on the light just before I came in to see her husband lying dead on

the floor. She knew no more. I suppose I
must have looked a bit thoughtful, for she suddenly got up from her chair and came up to me.

" ' You believe me, Bill, don't you ? ' she said,
staring at me.

" ' Of course, of course,' I answered hurriedly.
' Go and lie down now, Ruth, because we shall
have to send for the police.'

" Without another word she left the room
with her maid, and, after telling the footmen to
wait downstairs till they were wanted, I sat down
to think. Now, this isn't a detective story ; such
as it is, it concerns a more interesting study than
the mere detection of crime. It concerns the
struggle in the soul of an upright man between
love and duty. And the man was Sir Edward
Shoreham.

" Unknown to me she sent for him—asked
him to come at once—and he came. He was
shown by the butler into the study, where I was
still sitting at the desk, and he stopped motionless by the door staring at the body, which had
not been moved. I was waiting for the doctor,
and I got up surprised.

" ' The butler told me he had been shot,' he
said a little jerkily. ' How did it happen ? '

" ' I wasn't expecting you, Sir Edward,' I
answered slowly. ' But I'm glad that you've
come. I'd like another opinion.'

" ' What do you mean ? ' he cried. ' Is there
any mystery ? '

" ' I'll tell you exactly what happened as far

as I know the facts,' I said. Lady Granger
and her husband had a very bad quarrel to-night.
Then she came to bed, and so did I. Shortly
afterwards her husband came along into this room.
Now, my bedroom is in the passage you have
just come along, and about ten minutes after
Sir Henry came in here, his wife followed him.
I opened my door, because I was afraid they
might start quarrelling again, and he had been
drinking. I saw her come in ; there was a pause,
and then a revolver shot rang out.'

" ' Was this door shut ? ' he snapped.

" ' Yes,' I answered, ' it was. I rushed along
the passage and came in. I found her standing,
with the revolver at her feet, staring at her
husband, who was lying where he is now. She
said : ' There's been an accident.' And then
she muttered something about a man and
the window before she fainted. I went to the
window, and there was no one there. I looked
out ; will you do the same ? '

" I waited while he walked over and looked
out, and after what seemed an interminable time
he came back again.

" ' How long was it after the shot before you
looked out ? ' His voice was very low as he asked
the question.

" ' Not a quarter of a minute,' I answered, and
we both stood staring at one another in silence.

" ' Good God ! ' he said at length, ' what are
you driving at ? '

" ' I'm not driving at anything, Sir Edward,'

I answered. 'At least, I'm trying not to drive at it. But the man is dead, and the police must be sent for. What are we going to say?'

" ' The truth, of course,' he answered instantly.

" ' Quite,' I said slowly. ' But what is the truth?'

" He turned very white, and leant against one of the old suits of armour, of which the dead man had a wonderful collection all over the house.

" ' Did Lady Granger see this man go out of the window?' he asked at length.

" ' No, she only heard him open it. You see, she says he switched off the light. It was on when I rushed in.'

" ' A rope,' he suggested.

" ' Impossible in the time,' I said; ' utterly impossible. Such a suggestion would be laughed out of court.'

" He came over and sat down heavily in a chair, and his face was haggard.

" ' Sir Edward,' I went on desperately, ' the doctor will be here shortly; the police must be sent for. We've got to decide something. This man didn't go out by the door or I'd have seen him; only a fly could have gone out by the window. We've got to face the facts.'

" ' You don't believe there was a man here at all,' he said slowly.

" ' Heaven help me! I don't,' I answered. ' It's all so easy to reconstruct. The poor girl was driven absolutely desperate by what happened to-night, and by the last thing he said to her after their quarrel.' I looked at him for a moment before going on. 'He accused her of being in love with you.' I said it deliberately, and he caught his breath sharply.

"'Can't you see it all?' I continued. 'She came in here, and she shot him; and when she'd done it her nerves gave, and she said the first thing to me that came into her head.'

"'If you're right,' he said heavily, 'it means that Ruth will be tried for murder!' He got up with his hands to his temples. 'My God! Stratton,' he cried, 'this is awful. Premeditated murder, too—not done blindly in the middle of a quarrel, but a quarter of an hour after it was over.'

"'That's how it would strike a jury,' I answered gravely.

"'Supposing she had done it suddenly, blindly'—he was talking half to himself— 'snatched the revolver off the table as he tried to make love to her, let's say.' And then he stopped and stared at me.

"'Supposing that had happened, it would be better for her to say so at once,' I said.

"'But it didn't happen,' he answered; 'it couldn't have.'

"'No,' I agreed. 'It didn't happen; it couldn't have. But supposing it had, Sir Edward, what then?'

"'Stop, Stratton,' he cried. 'For Heaven's sake, stop!'

"'There's no good stopping,' I said. 'We haven't any time for argument. Your legal knowledge has suggested the same solution as occurred to me. If *now*, at once, when we send for the police, she says it was an accident—gives a complete story, chapter and verse——'

" ' Invents it, you mean,' he interrupted.

" ' Call it what you like,' I said, ' but, unless she does that and substantiates the story, she will be tried for the premeditated and wilful murder of her husband. She'll have to be tried anyway, but if she makes a voluntary confession—makes a story out of it that will appeal to sentiment—they will acquit her. It's the only chance.'

" ' But it's monstrous, man,' he muttered—only now his eyes were fixed on me questioningly.

" ' Look here, Sir Edward,' I said, ' let's discuss this matter calmly. Humanly speaking, we know what happened. Ruth came along that passage, opened this door, and shot her husband dead through the heart—that is the case as I should put it to the jury, the plain issue shorn of all its trappings. What is going to be the verdict ? '

" Shoreham plucked at his collar as if he were fighting for breath.

" ' If, on the other hand, the shot was not immediate—and I am the only witness as to that ; if I had heard his voice raised in anger ; if he had sprung at her, tried to kiss her, and she blindly, without thought, had snatched up the first thing that came to her hand, the revolver, not even knowing it was loaded—what then ? The servants can be squared. She was talking

4

wildly when she mentioned this man—didn't know what she was saying. And then, when she got back to her room she realised that the truth was best, and rang you up, a Judge. What better possible proof could any jury have of her desire to conceal nothing? And you with your reputation on the Bench——'

" ' Ah, don't, don't! ' he cried hoarsely. ' You're driving me mad! You're—you're——! '

" ' Why, Ned, what's the matter ? '

" We both swung round. Ruth had come in, unnoticed by us, and was staring at Shoreham with wonder in her eyes. Then, with a shudder, she stepped past her husband's body and came into the room.

" ' They've just told me you were here,' she said, and then she gave a little cry. ' Ned, why are you looking like that ? Ned! you don't think—you don't think I did it ? '

" She cowered back, looking first at him and then at me.

" ' You *can't* think I did it.' she whispered. ' I tell you there was a man here—the man who shot him. Oh! they'll believe me, won't they ? '

" ' Ruth,' I said, ' I want you to realise that we're both of us your friends.' Which is the sort of fatuous remark one does make when the tension is a bit acute. She never even glanced at me as I spoke ; with a sort of sick horror in her eyes, she was staring at Shoreham, and I blundered on : ' When you talked about this man you were unnerved—distraught ; you didn't know what you were saying. We both realise that. But now we've got to think of the best way of—of helping you. You see, the police must be sent for—we ought to have sent for them sooner—and——'

" She walked past me and went over to Shoreham.

" ' Do you believe I did it, Ned ? ' she said quietly. ' If I swear to you that I didn't— would that convince you ? '

" ' But, Ruth,' he cried desperately, ' it isn't me you've got to convince—it's the police. A man couldn't have got out of that window in the time. It's a physical impossibility. If you told it to the police, they'd laugh. Tell us the truth, my dear. I beseech you. Tell us the truth, and we'll see what can be done.'

" She stood very still, with her hands clenched by her sides. And then quite deliberately she spoke to Shoreham.

" ' If you don't believe there was a man here,' she said, ' you *must* think I shot my husband. There was no one else who could have done it. Well—supposing I did. You acknowledge no justification for such an act ? '

" I started to speak, but she silenced me with an imperative wave of her hand.

" ' Please, Bill—— Well, Ned—I'm waiting. If I did shoot him—what then ? ' "

The Barrister paused to relight his cigar, and the others waited in silence.

" She was staring at Shoreham," he went on

after a while, " with a faint, half-mocking, wholly tender smile on her lips, and if either he or I had been less dense that smile should have made us think. But at the moment I was absorbed in the problem of how to save her ; while she was absorbed in a very different one concerning the mentality of the man she cared for. And Shoreham—well, he was absorbed in the old, old fight between love and duty, and the fierceness of the struggle was showing on his face.

" There in front of him stood the woman he loved, the woman who had just shot her husband, and the woman who was now free for him to marry. He knew as well as I did that in adopting the line I had suggested lay the best chance of getting her acquitted. He knew as well as I did that the vast majority of juries would acquit if the story were put to them as we had outlined it. He could visualise as well as I the scene in court. Counsel for the defence—I'd already fixed on Grayson in my mind as her counsel—outlining the whole scene : her late husband's abominable conduct culminating in this final outrage at her reception. And then as he came to the moment of the tragedy, I could picture him turning to the jury with passionate sincerity in his face— appealing to them as men—happily married, perhaps, but men, at any rate, to whom home life was sacred.

" I could hear his voice—low and earnest—as he sketched for them that last scene. This poor, slighted, tormented woman—girl, gentlemen, for

she is little more than a girl—went in desperation
to the man—well, he is dead now, and we will
leave it at that—to the man who had made her
life a veritable hell. She pleaded with him,
gentlemen, to allow her to divorce him—pleaded
for some remnant of decent feelings in him. And
what was his answer—what was the answer of
this devil who was her husband? Did he
meet her half-way? Did he profess the slightest
sorrow for his despicable conduct?

" No, gentlemen—not one word. His sole
response was to spring at her in his drunken
frenzy and endeavour to fix his vile attentions on
her. And she, mad with terror and fright,
snatched up the revolver which was lying on the
desk. It might have been a ruler—anything ;
she was not responsible at the moment for what
she did. Do you blame her, gentlemen? You
have daughters of your own. She no more knew
what she had in her hand than a baby would.
To keep him away—that was her sole idea. And
then—suddenly—it happened. The revolver
went off—the man fell dead.

" What did this girl do, gentlemen, after that?
Realising that he was dead, did she make any
attempt to conceal what she had done—to
conceal her share in the matter? No—exactly
the reverse. Instantly she rang up Sir Edward
Shoreham, whose views on such matters are well
known to you all. And then and there she told
him everything—concealing nothing, excusing
nothing. Sir Edward Shoreham of all people,

who, with due deference to such a distinguished
public man, has at times been regarded as—
well—er—not lenient in his judgments. And
you have heard what Sir Edward said in the
box. . . ."

Once again the Barrister paused and smiled
faintly.

" I'd got as far as that, you see, before
Shoreham answered her. And he had got as far
as that, too, I think. He saw it all, built on a
foundation of lies—built on the foundation of his
dishonour. No one would ever know except us
three—but that doesn't make a thing easier for
the Edward Shorehams of the world.

" And then he spoke—in a low, tense voice :

" ' If you shot him, dear,' he said, ' nothing
matters save getting you off.'

" Some people," pursued the Barrister, " might
call it a victory—some people would call it a de-
feat. Depends on one's outlook ; depends on
how much one really believes in the ' Could not
love you half so much, loved I not honour more '
idea. But certainly the murderer himself was
very pleased.'

" The murderer ? " cried the Ordinary Man
sitting up suddenly.

" The murderer," returned the Barrister.
" That's why I mentioned about my cigarette-
case this morning. He had been standing behind
the suit of armour in the corner the whole time.
He came out suddenly, and we all stared at him
speechlessly, and then he started coughing—a

dreadful tearing cough—which stained his handkerchief scarlet.

"'I must apologise,' he said when he could speak, ' but there was another thing besides shooting Granger that I wanted to do before I died. That was why I didn't want to be caught to-night. However, a man must cough when he's got my complaint. But I'm glad I restrained myself long enough to hear your decision, Sir Edward. I congratulate you on it.'

"'You scoundrel!' began Shoreham, starting forward, ' why didn't you declare yourself sooner?'

"'Because there's another thing I wanted to do,' he repeated wearily. ' In Paris, in the Rue St. Claire, there lives a woman. She was beautiful once—to me she is beautiful now. She was *my* woman until——' And his eyes sought the dead body of Henry Granger.

"Ruth took a deep breath. ' Yes—until?' she whispered.

"'Until he came,' said the man gravely. ' And God will decide between him and me. But I would have liked to look on her once more, and hold her hand, and tell her, yet again, that I understood—absolutely.'

" It was then Ruth Granger crossed to him.

"'What is her name and the number of the house?' she said.

"'Sybil Deering is her name,' he answered slowly, ' and the number is fourteen.'

"'Will you leave it to me?' she asked.

" For a moment he stared at her in silence, then he bowed.

" ' From the bottom of my heart I thank you, Lady Granger, and I hope you will have all the happiness you deserve.' He glanced at Shoreham and smiled. 'When a man loves everything else goes to the wall, doesn't it? Remember that in the future, Sir Edward, when they're standing before you, wondering, trying to read their fate. Someone loves them, just as you love her.' "

The Barrister rose and drained his glass.

" And that is the conclusion of your suffering," he remarked.

" Was the man hanged? " asked the Soldier.

" No, he died a week later of galloping consumption."

" And what of the other two? " demanded the Actor.

" They married, and are living happily together to-day, doing fruit farming as a hobby."

" Fruit farming! " echoed the Doctor. " Why fruit farming? "

" Something to do," said the Barrister. " You see, Sir Edward has never tried another case. Some men are made that way."

" Sooner or later," began the Doctor, settling himself comfortably in his chair, " it comes to most of us. Sooner or later a man or a woman comes to consult us on what they imagine to be some trifling malady, and when we make our examination we find that it isn't trifling. And occasionally we find that not only is the matter not trifling, but that—well, you all have seen Collier's picture, ' The Sentence of Death.'

" It's a thing, incidentally, which requires careful thought—just how much you will tell. Different people take things different ways, and where it might be your duty to tell one man the half-truth, to another it might be just as much your duty to lie. But broadly speaking, I, personally, have always maintained that, unless the circumstances are quite exceptional, it is a doctor's duty to tell a patient the truth, however unpleasant it may be. What would a man say if his lawyer or his stockbroker lied to him ?

" Which brings me to the opening of my story. It was in the May before the War that a man came into my consulting-room—a man whom I will call Jack Digby. I motioned him to a chair on the other side of my desk, so placed that the light from the window fell on his face. I put him down as a man of about three-and-thirty who was used to an outdoor life. His face was bronzed, his hands were sunburnt, and the whole way he carried himself—the set of his shoulders, the swing of his arms as he walked across the room— indicated the athlete in good condition. In fact, he was an unusual type to find in a Harley Street consulting-room, and I told him so by way of opening the conversation.

"He grinned, a very pleasant, cheery grin, and put his hat on the floor.

"'Just a matter of form, Doctor,' he said, leaning back in his chair and crossing his legs. 'I'm thinking of entering for the matrimonial stakes, and before saddling-up I thought I'd just get you to certify me sound in wind and limb.'

"Now he spoke very easily and naturally, but something—I don't quite know what—made me look at him a little more closely. The study of human nature is a vital necessity if the study of human ailments is to be successful—and one gets plenty of opportunity for it if one is a consulting physician. And I suddenly wondered if it was 'just a matter of form' in his mind. The ordinary young, healthy man doesn't usually take the trouble to be overhauled by a doctor merely because he is going to be married.

"However, at that stage of the proceedings my thoughts were my own, and I answered him in the same vein. And while he was taking off his coat and shirt we talked casually on various topics. Then I started my examination. And within half a minute I knew that something was very, very wrong.

" ' I would like you to take off your vest, please, Mr. Digby,' I said, and for a moment he stared at me in silence. I was watching him quietly, and it was then I knew that my first surmise was correct. In his eyes there was a look of dreadful fear.

" He stripped his vest off, and I continued my examination. And after I'd finished I walked over to my desk.

" ' You can put on your clothes again,' I said gravely, to swing round as I felt his hand like a vice on my shoulder.

" ' What is it ? ' he muttered. ' Tell me.'

" ' It was not altogether a matter of form with you, was it, Mr. Digby ? ' I answered. ' Put on your clothes ; I want to ask you a few questions.'

" ' Hang it, man ! ' he cried. ' I can't wait. What have you found ? '

" ' I would like to have another opinion before telling you.' I was fencing for time, but he was insistent.

" ' You can have another opinion—you can have fifty other opinions,' he cried, still gripping me by the shoulder—' but I want to know what you think *now*. Can I marry ? '

" ' You cannot,' I said gravely, and his hand fell to his side. Then he slowly walked across the room and stood with his back to me, staring out of the window. Once his shoulders shook a little, but except for that he stood quite motionless.

And after a while he picked up his clothes and started to dress.

" I said nothing until he had finished ; with a man of his type talking is a mistake. It was not until he again sat down in the chair opposite me that I broke the silence.

" ' You asked me a specific question, Mr. Digby,' I said quietly, ' and I answered as a man of your type would like to be answered. But I now want to modify my reply slightly. And I will put it this way. If I had a daughter, I would not allow a man whose heart was in the condition that yours is to marry her. It would not be fair to her ; it would certainly not be fair to any possible children.'

" He nodded gravely, though he didn't speak.

" ' You feared something of this sort when you came to me ? ' I asked.

" ' My mother died of it,' he answered quietly. ' And once or twice lately, after exercise, I've had an agonising twinge of pain.' And then, under his breath, he added : ' Thank God, she doesn't know ! '

" ' But I would like another opinion,' I continued. ' There are men, as you know, who are entirely heart specialists, and I will give you the address of one.'

" ' Confirmation of the death sentence,' he laughed grimly. ' No saddling-up for me—eh, Doctor ? '

" ' Not as you are at present, Mr. Digby.' I was writing the address of the biggest heart man on a piece of paper, though I felt it was useless. It didn't require an expert to diagnose this trouble.

" ' Is there any chance of getting better ? ' he cried eagerly, and I stopped writing and looked at him. There was hope—a dawning hope in his eyes—and for a moment I hesitated.

" My own opinion was that there was no chance : that he might, with care and luck, live for two or three years—perhaps more—but that he might equally well drop dead at any moment. It was enough—that momentary hesitation ; the eager look in his eyes faded, and he sat back wearily in his chair.

" ' Don't bother,' he said slowly ; ' I see how it is.'

" ' No, you don't, Mr. Digby,' I answered. ' You see how I think it is. Which is an altogether different matter. There is always a chance.'

" ' That's juggling with words,' he said, with a twisted little smile. ' The great point is that I'm not in a position to ask this girl to marry me.'

" He glanced at the slip of paper I handed to him, then he rose.

" ' I would like you to go and see him,' I said quietly. ' You see I feel the gravity of what I've had to tell you this morning very much, and in fairness to myself as well as to you, my dear fellow, I'd like you to go to Sir John.'

" For a few seconds he stood there facing me,

then he grinned as he had done at the beginning
of the interview.

"'All right, Doctor,' he cried. 'I'll go, and
Sir John shall drive the nail right in.'

"'I'm sorry,' I said—'infernally sorry.
You've taken it, if I may say so, like a very
brave man.'

"He turned away abruptly. 'What the deuce
is the good of whining?' he cried. 'If it's the
same as in my mother's case, the end will be very
abrupt.'

"The next moment he was gone—a man under
sentence of death. And the pitiful tragedy of it
hit one like a blow. He was so essentially the
type of man who should have married some
charming girl and have children. He was just a
first-class specimen of the sporting Englishman,
but——" The Doctor paused and looked at the
Soldier. "The type that makes a first-class
squadron leader," and the Soldier nodded.

"It was in the afternoon," continued the
Doctor after a while, "that Sir John Longworth
rang me up. Digby had been to him, and the
result was as I expected. Two years, or possibly
two days, and as for marriage, out of the
question entirely. He had merely confirmed my
own diagnosis of the case, and there for a time
the matter rested. In the stress of work Jack
Digby passed from my mind, until Fate decreed
that we should meet again in what were to prove
most dramatic circumstances.

"It was two months later—about the beginning of July—that I decided to take a short holiday. I couldn't really spare the time, but I knew that I ought to take one. So I ran down for a long week-end to stop with some people I knew fairly well in Dorsetshire. They had just taken a big house a few miles from Weymouth, and I will call them the Maitlands. There were Mr. and Mrs. Maitland, and a son, Tom, up at the 'Varsity, and a daughter, Sybil. When I arrived I found they had a bit of a house-party, perhaps a dozen in all, and after tea the girl, whom I'd met once or twice before, took me round the place.

" She was a charming girl, very, very pretty, of about twenty-two or three, and we chattered on aimlessly as we strolled through the gardens.

" ' You're quite a big party,' I laughed, ' and I thought I was coming for a quiet week-end.'

" ' We've got two or three more arriving to-night,' she said. ' At least I think so. One of them is a most elusive person.' She was staring straight in front of her as she spoke, and for the moment she seemed to have forgotten my existence.

" ' Male or female—the elusive one ? ' I asked lightly.

" ' A man,' she answered abruptly, and changed the conversation.

" But being an old and wary bird, I read into her harmless remark a somewhat deeper significance than was perhaps justified, and it struck me very forcibly that if I were the man I would not be elusive in the circumstances. She surely was most amazingly pretty."

" With great deductive ability," murmured the Actor, as the Doctor paused to refill his pipe, " we place the elusive man as Jack Digby."

" You go to blazes ! " laughed the teller of the story. " I haven't got to that yet. Of course you're quite right—he was ; though when I found it out a little later it came as a complete surprise to me. I'd almost forgotten his existence.

" It was her father who first mentioned his name. I was having a sherry and bitters with him in his study before going up to dress for dinner, and the conversation turned on the girl. I think I said how extraordinarily pretty I thought she was, and remarked that I supposed somebody would soon be walking off with her.

" Joe Maitland's face clouded a little.

" ' As a matter of fact,' he said, ' both her mother and I have been expecting it for some time. A most charming man, and Sybil is in love with him, I'm sure. We all thought that he was in love with her,' and then he exploded— ' damn it, it isn't a question of thinking, I *know* he's in love with her ! And for some extraordinary reason he won't tell her so. He's kept away from her for the last two months, after having lived in her pocket. And he's not the type that monkeys round and makes a girl fond of him for no reason. He's coming here to-night, and——'

" My host, still frowning slightly, lit a cigarette.

So evidently this was the elusive man, I thought, putting down my glass. It was no business of mine, and then suddenly I stood very still as I heard him speak again.

"'Jack Digby is as white as they're made,' he was saying, but I didn't hear any more. Luckily my back was towards him, so he couldn't see my face. Jack Digby! Poor devil! With Sybil Maitland, the girl, in his mind, the blow I'd given him must have been even crueller than I'd thought. And what a strange coincidence that I should be going to meet him again in such circumstances. Maitland was still rambling on, but I was paying no attention to him. I could, of course, say nothing unless Digby gave me permission; but it struck me that if I told him how the land lay—if I told him that not only was his silence being completely misconstrued, but that it was making the girl unhappy, he might allow me to tell her father the truth. After all, the truth was far better; there was nothing to be ashamed of in having a rotten heart.

" And it was just as I had made up my mind to see Digby that night that the door opened and Tom, the boy, came in. I hadn't seen him since he was quite a child, and the first thing that struck me about him was that he was almost as good-looking as his sister. He'd got the same eyes, the same colouring, but—there was the devil of a but. Whereas his sister gave one the impression of being utterly frank and fearless, the boy struck me immediately as being the very reverse. That he was the apple of his mother's eye, I knew—but that signifies nothing. Thank God! mothers are made that way. And as I stood watching him talking to his father I recalled certain vague rumours that I'd heard recently and had paid scant attention to at the time. Rumours of wild extravagance up at Oxford—debts well into the four figures. . . . They came back to my mind, those idle bits of gossip, and they assumed a definite significance as I studied the boy's face. It was weak—utterly weak; he gave one the impression of having no mental or moral stamina whatever. He poured himself out a glass of sherry, and his hand wasn't quite steady, which is a bad sign in a boy of under twenty-one. And he was a little frightened of his father, which is bad in a boy of any age when the father is a man like Joe Maitland. And that wasn't all, either. There was something more—something much bigger on his mind : I was sure of it. There was fear in his heart ; you could see it lurking round his eyes—round his mouth. I glanced at Joe, but he seemed quite oblivious of it, and then I left them and went up to dress for dinner. I remember wondering as I turned into my room whether the boy had got into another scrape— then I dismissed him from my mind. Jack Digby was a more interesting and more pressing problem.

" I met him in the hall as I came down, and he gave a sudden start of astonishment.

" ' Why, Doctor,' he said quietly as we shook

hands, ' this is a surprise. I'd no idea you were to be here.'

" ' Nor I that you were coming,' I answered, ' until Mr. Maitland happened to mention it a little while ago.'

" ' You haven't said anything to him, have you ? ' he cried anxiously.

" ' My dear fellow,' I said, ' you ought to know that doctors don't.' He muttered an apology, and I went on : ' You know, Digby, I can't help thinking you're making a mistake in not telling the truth.'

" He shook his head vigorously. ' I'm sure I'm not,' he answered. ' The mistake I've made has been in coming here at all. I haven't seen her since the day—when you told me. And I oughtn't to have come now. It's the last— I swear that. I couldn't help it ; I had to see her once again. I'm going to Africa in August— big game shooting.'

" I stared at him gravely, and after a while he went on :

" ' No one knows better than you,' he said gravely, ' my chance of returning. And when I don't come back—she'll forget me.' I saw his hands clench at his side. ' But if I tell her now— why, she'll want me to stop in England—to go to specialists—to eke out life to the full two or three years. It'll be hell—hell ! Hell for both of us. Every day she'll be wondering if she is going to hear I'm dead ; it'll ruin her life. Whereas Africa, if she doesn't know about my heart, will be sudden.   You see, Doctor, she is the only one to be considered—the only one.'

"I drew a deep breath; truly Joe Maitland had been right. This man was white clean through. And then he gave a little choking gasp, and, turning round, I saw the girl coming towards us across the hall.

"'I didn't know you'd come, old man,' I heard her say, and then I moved away and left them. It was one of those occasions when you say it's the smoke that has got into your eyes— and you lie."

For a while the Doctor was silent; then he gave a short laugh.

"They sat next to one another at dinner, opposite me, and I'm afraid my partner must have thought I was a little wanting in intellect. They were such a perfectly ideal couple; and I noticed old Joe Maitland watching them every now and then. But gradually, as the meal progressed, a puzzled look began to creep into the girl's eyes, and once she bit her lip suddenly and turned abruptly to the man on her other side. It was then that Digby looked across the table at me, and in that moment I realised that he was right. For him to remain in England would be impossible for both of them; the end, quick and sudden in an African jungle—if he ever got as far—was the only way out.

"'My God! Doctor,' he said as he came round and sat down next to me after the ladies had gone, 'I knew I was a fool to come,

but I didn't think it was going to be as bad
as this.'

" ' When are you going to start ? ' I asked.

" ' As soon as I can get things fixed up at home,
here, and make some sort of arrangements for
carriers and people the other end. One must act,
I suppose, even though it's the last appearance.'
He gave a mirthless laugh. ' I've always wanted
to go South from Khartoum—I wonder how far
I'll get.' Then he began to drum on the table
with his fingers. ' And what I wonder still more,'
he went on slowly, ' is how in Heaven's name I'll
get through this evening. You see, though I didn't
actually propose in so many words before I came to
see you, I'd—I'd let things drift to such a position
that a proposal was hardly necessary. That's
the devil of it. . . . She knows I worship the
ground she walks on—and I know she cares too.'

" ' How long are you going to stop here ? '
I asked.

" ' I accepted for the week-end,' he said
abruptly. ' I shall go first thing to-morrow. I
can't stand it.'

" At that we left it, and I didn't speak to him
again until the thing occurred which even now—
though seven years have slipped by—is as clearly
imprinted on my brain as if it had happened
last night.

" I couldn't sleep very well that night, and at
about two I switched on my light, with the idea of
reading. I was just reaching out for a book when
I heard the sound of voices from a room almost

opposite. I listened for a moment, then I got up and went to the door. For the voices were excited and angry; something unusual was evidently happening. For a moment or two I hesitated; then I slipped on a dressing-gown and looked out. Across the passage the door of a room was open, and through it the light was streaming out. And then I heard Joe Maitland speak, and his words literally rooted me to the ground with amazement.

"'So, Mr. Digby, you're just a common damned thief. The gentleman crook—what? The amateur cracksman. That's what they call them on the stage, I believe. Sounds better. But I prefer the more homely name of thief.'

"It was then that I appeared in the door, and Maitland swung round.

"'Oh, it's you, is it, Tranton?' He had a revolver in his hand, and he lowered it when he saw who it was. 'A pretty tableau, isn't it? It appears that a second edition of—what was the gentleman's name—Raffles, wasn't it?—has been honouring me with his presence. Unfortunately Tom and I both happened to hear him.'

"But I was paying no attention to what he was saying; my eyes were fixed on Digby and—Tom. Digby, with a quiet smile on his face and his hands in his pockets, was standing beside an open safe. He was still in evening clothes, and once he glanced my way. Then he looked back again at his host, and I looked at Tom. He was in his dressing-gown, and he was shivering as if he

had the ague. He was standing close to his
father, and a little behind him—and Joe Maitland
was too engrossed with Digby to notice the condition he was in.

" ' Can you advance any reason, Mr. Digby,'
he demanded, ' why I shouldn't call up the local
police ? '

" ' None whatever, Mr. Maitland,' he answered
gravely. ' Your son caught me fair and square.'

" And it seemd to me that Tom made an effort
to speak, though no words came from his lips.

" ' You damned scoundrel ! ' cried Maitland.
' You come to my house—you make love to my
daughter—and then you abuse my hospitality by
trying to steal my wife's jewellery ! "

" It was at that moment that the girl came in.
I saw Digby catch his breath and lean against
the wall for support ; then he straightened up
and faced his host again. Just once had he
glanced at her, with her glorious hair falling over
her shoulders and a startled look of wonder in her
great eyes. Then resolutely he looked away.

" ' What's happened, Daddy ? ' she whispered. ' I heard your voice and——'

" ' This has happened, my dear,' said Maitland
grimly. ' We have been privileged to discover
Mr. Digby's method of earning a livelihood.' He
pointed to the open safe. ' He apparently
ingratiates himself with people for the express
purpose of stealing their valuables. In other
words, a common thief.'

" ' I don't believe it ! ' she flashed out

imperiously. 'Jack—a thief! How can you say such a thing?'

"'Then may I ask what he was doing when your brother discovered him by the open safe? Besides, he admits it himself.'

"'Jack!' The cry seemed to come from the very depths of her soul. 'Say it's a lie!'

"For one second he hesitated; then he spoke quite steadily, though he didn't look at her.

"'I am afraid, Miss Maitland—that I can't say it's untrue.'

"And then there fell one of those silences that can be felt. She was staring at Jack Digby, was the girl—staring at him with a great amazement dawning on her face.

"'Jack,' she whispered, 'look at me!'

"He raised his eyes and looked at her, and a little pulse was beating just above his jaw. Then, after what seemed an interminable time, she gave a little laugh that was half a sob and turned away.

"'I see,' she said below her breath. 'I see.'

"But what it was she saw, I didn't at the moment realise. It was to be made clear a little later."

The Doctor paused and threw a log on the fire.

"Yes, I found out later what she thought," he went on after a while, "and for the first and probably the last time in my life I was guilty of a breach of professional confidence. It was about half an hour later that I went round to Jack Digby's room. Maitland, after thinking it over— and it is possible that I had something to do with

his decision—had dismissed the idea of sending
for the police. Digby was to clear out by the
first train next morning, and was never to make
an attempt to communicate with the girl again.
And Jack Digby had bowed in silence and gone
to his own room. He wouldn't look at me as he
passed; I think he knew that he hadn't deceived
me.

"He was sitting by the open window when I
went in, still in his evening clothes, and he looked
round with a start as I entered. His face was
drawn and grey.

"'My dear chap,' I said, before he could speak,
'is it worth while?'

"'I don't understand what you mean, Doctor,'
he said slowly.

"'Oh, yes, you do!' I answered. 'You
deceived Mr. Maitland all right—you didn't
deceive me. It was Tom who opened the safe—
not you.'

"For a moment I thought he was going to
deny it; then he gave a little mirthless laugh.

"'Perfectly correct,' he said. 'As you say,
it was Tom who opened the safe. I caught him
absolutely in the act. And then Mr. Maitland
came.'

"'But—good God!' I cried, 'what an unutterable young waster he must be to let you
shoulder the blame!'

"Digby faced me steadily. 'I made him.
You see, I saw it was the chance I had been
looking for.'

3*

" ' You mean you told him about your heart ? '

" ' No,' he answered quietly.   ' But I told him
I was entangled with another woman, and that
the best way of saving his sister's feelings was to
let her think——'

" And then the boy broke down utterly.   With
his hands on my shoulders he stood there facing
me, and he made me swear I wouldn't tell the
girl.

" ' She must never know, Doctor.   I've done
it for her.   She must never know.'

" And even as he spoke, the words died away
on his lips, and he stood motionless, staring past
me at the door.   Without looking round I knew
what had happened—I could smell the faint scent
she used.

" ' What have you done for me, Jack, and why
must I never know ? '

" She came steadily up to him, and his hands
fell to his side.

" ' Why, you've been crying, dear,' she said.
' What's the matter ? '

" True to his purpose, he started some fantastic
story about sorrow at having been found out, but
she cut him short.

" ' Don't lie, Jack—not now,' she whispered.
' I know it wasn't you who opened the safe.   I
know it was Tom.   But what I want to know is
why you said you did it.'

" It was then I made up my mind.

" ' I'm going to tell her, Digby, whether you
like it or not,' and she looked at me quickly.   He

didn't say anything ; things had got beyond him. And very briefly I told her the truth about his heart.

" She listened to me in absolute silence, and when I'd finished she just turned round to him and held out both her arms.

" ' Thank God ! I know, my darling,' she whispered. ' I thought it was because you'd got fond of another woman. I thought—oh ! Heaven knows what I thought ! But now—oh ! you stupid, wonderful boy ! '

" I went to the window and looked out ! It must have been five minutes later that I found the girl at my side.

" ' Is it absolutely hopeless ? ' she asked.

" ' Humanly speaking,' I answered, ' yes.'

" ' How long ? ' and she put her hand on my arm.

" ' Two days ; two months ; at the utmost, two years,' I said gravely.

" ' And why shouldn't I look after him for those two years ? ' she demanded fiercely.

" ' I'm thinking of a possible child,' I said quietly, and she began to tremble a little.

" ' That's ridiculous,' she cried—' quite ridiculous.'

The Doctor was carefully cleaning out the bowl of his pipe. " In the morning Jack Digby had gone, leaving behind him a note for her. She showed it to me later.

" ' The Doctor is right, my darling,' it ran. ' It's just Fate, and there's not much use kicking.

I'm glad though that you know the truth—it helps. Good-bye, dear heart. God bless you.' "

The Doctor paused.

" Is that all ? " said the Ordinary Man.

" Very nearly," answered the Doctor. " I had been right when I said two months, only the cause of death was not what I expected. How he got across the water so soon I don't know. But he did—in a cavalry regiment. And he stopped one —somewhere up Ypres way."

" And the girl ? " asked the Soldier.

" Has not got over it yet," said the Doctor.

" And did she ever hear from him again ? " demanded the Barrister.

" Once, from France. Written just before— the end. She didn't show me *that* one. Pass the whisky, Actor-man. Talking makes one's throat infernally dry."

"Any of you know Burma?" asked the Ordinary Man, putting out his hand for the tobacco-jar.

"I've been there," grunted the Soldier. "Shooting. Years ago. West of the Irawadi from Rangoon."

"It's years since I was there, too," said the Ordinary Man. "More than a score. And if I wasn't so beastly fat and lazy I'd like to go back for a visit. Only a visit, mind you. I've got to the time of life when I find that London is quite good enough for my needs. But the story which I propose to inflict on you fellows to-night concerns Burma, and delving into the past to get the details right has brought the fascination of the place back to me.

"I was about thirty-five at the time—and my benevolent Aunt Jane had not then expired and endowed me with all her worldly goods. I was working for a City firm who had considerable interests out there—chiefly teak, with a strong side-line in rubies.

"At that time, as you may know, the ruby mines in the Mandalay area were second to none, and it was principally to give my employers a report on the many clashing interests in those mines that I went back to England after a few months in the country. And it was in their office that I met a youngster, who had just joined the firm, and who, it turned out, was going out to Burma on the same boat as myself. Jack Manderby was his name, and I suppose he must have been ten or eleven years younger than I. He was coming to my district, and somewhat naturally I was a bit curious to see what sort of a fellow he was.

" I took to him from the very first moment, and after we'd lunched together a couple of times my first impression was strengthened. He was a real good fellow—extraordinarily good-looking and straight as a die, without being in the least degree a prig.

" We ran into a good south-westerly gale the instant we were clear of the Isle of Wight, which necessitated a period of seclusion on my part. In fact, my next appearance in public was at Gibraltar.

" And the first person I saw as I came on deck was Jack Manderby. He was leaning over the side bargaining with some infernal robber below, and at his side was a girl. In the intervals of haggling he turned to her, and they both laughed ; and as I stood for a few minutes watching them, it struck me that Master Jack had made good use of the four days since we left England. Then I strolled over and joined them.

" ' Hullo, old man ! ' he cried, with a twinkle in his eyes. ' Is the rumour correct that you've been engaged in research work below, and had given orders not to be disturbed ? '

" ' Your vulgar jests leave me unmoved,' I answered with dignity. ' At any rate, I appear to have arrived in time to save you being robbed. That man is a thief and the son of a thief, and all his children are thieves.'

" Jack laughed ; then he swung round to the girl.

" ' By the way, you haven't met Mr. Walton, have you ? This is Miss Felsted, old boy, who is going out to Rangoon.'

" We shook hands, and no more was said at the time. But one thing was definitely certain. Whatever the girl was going to Rangoon for, the gain was Rangoon's. She was an absolute fizzer—looked you straight in the face with the bluest of eyes that seemed to have a permanent smile lurking in them. And then, suddenly, I noticed her left hand. On the third finger was a diamond ring. It couldn't be Jack she was engaged to, and I wondered idly who the lucky man was. Because he was lucky—infernally lucky.

" I think," continued the Ordinary Man, pulling thoughtfully at his pipe, " that I first began to scent complications at Malta. We landed there for a few hours, and the idea was that Miss Felsted, Jack, and I should explore Valetta. Now, I don't quite know how, but we got separated. I spent a pleasant two hours with a naval pal in the Union Club, while Jack and the girl apparently went up by the narrow-gauge railway to Citta Vecchia, in the centre of the island. And since no one in the full possession of their senses would go on that line for fun, I wondered. I wondered still more when they came back to the ship. Jack was far too open and above-board to be very skilful at hiding his feelings. And something had happened that day.

"Of course, it was no concern of mine. Jack's affairs were entirely his own ; so were the girl's. But a ship is a dangerous place sometimes—it affords unequalled and unending opportunities for what in those days were known as flirtations, and to-day, I believe, are known as ' pashes.' And to get monkeying round with another fellow's fiancée—well, it leads to complications generally. However, as I said, it was no concern of mine, until it suddenly became so the evening before we reached Port Said.

"I was talking to Jack on deck just before turning in. We were strolling up and down— the sea like a mill-pond, and almost dazzling with its phosphorescence.

"' Is Miss Felsted going out to get married ? ' I asked him casually.

"' Yes,' he answered abruptly. ' She's engaged to a man called Morrison.'

"' Morrison,' I repeated, stopping and staring at him. ' Not Rupert Morrison, by any chance ? '

"' Yes. Rupert is his name. Do you know him ? '

" I'd pulled myself together by this time, **and** we resumed our stroll.

" ' I know Rupert Morrison quite well,' I answered. ' As distance goes in that country, Jack, he's a near neighbour of ours '; and I heard him catch his breath a little quickly.

" ' What sort of a fellow is he ? ' asked Jack quietly, and then he went on, which saved me the trouble of a reply : ' She hasn't seen him for four years. They got engaged before he left England, and now she's going out to marry him.'

" ' I see,' I murmured non-committally, and shortly afterwards I made my excuse and left him.

" I didn't turn in at once when I got to my cabin, I wanted to try and get things sorted out in my mind. The first point, which was as obvious as the electric light over the bunk, was that if Jack Manderby was not in love with Molly Felsted he was as near to it as made no odds. The second and far more important point was one on which I was in the dark—was the girl in love with him ? If so, it simplified matters considerably ; but if not, if she was only playing the fool, there was going to be trouble when we got to Burma. And the trouble would take the form of Rupert Morrison. For the more I thought of it the more amazed did I become that such a girl could ever have become engaged to such a man.

" Of course, four years is a long time, especially when they are passed in comparative solitude. I had no idea what sort of fellow Morrison had

been when first he arrived in the country, but I
had a very shrewd idea what manner of man he
was now.   Perhaps it had been the loneliness—
loneliness takes some men worse than others—
but, whatever the cause, Morrison, after four
years in Burma, was no fit mate for such a girl
as Molly Felsted.   A brooding, sullen man,
given to fierce fits of almost animal rage, a heavy
drinker of the type who is never drunk, and——"

The Ordinary Man paused and shrugged his
shoulders.

"Well, it's unfair to mention the last point.
After all, most of us did that without thinking;
but the actual arrival of an English girl—a wife—
who was to step, blindly ignorant, into her
predecessor's shoes, so to speak, made one pause
to think.   Anyway, that was neither here nor
there.   What frightened me was the prospect of
the girl marrying the Morrison of her imagination
and discovering, too late, the Morrison of reality.
When that happened, with Jack Manderby not
five miles away, the fat was going to be in the fire
with a vengeance.

"It was after Colombo that matters came to a
head.   We left the P. & O. there, and got into
another boat going direct to Rangoon.   The
weather was glorious—hot as blazes by day, and
just right at night.   And it was after dinner one
evening a couple of days before we were due in,
that quite inadvertently I butted into the pair of
them in a secluded spot on deck.   His arms were
round her, and they both sounded a bit inco-

herent. Of course, there was no use pretending I hadn't seen—they both looked up at me. I could only mutter my apology and withdraw. But I determined, even at the risk of being told to go to hell, to have a word with young Jack that night.

" ' Look here, old man,' I said to him a bit later, ' you've got a perfect right to request me to mind my own business, but I'm going to risk that. I saw you two to-night, kissing to beat the band—confound it all, there wasn't a dog's earthly of not seeing you—and what I want to know is where Morrison comes in, or if he's gone out ? ' "

" He looked at me a bit shamefacedly, then he lit a cigarette.

" ' Hugh,' he said, with a twisted sort of smile, ' I just worship the ground that girl walks on.'

" ' Maybe you do, Jack,' I answered. ' But the point is, what are her feelings on the matter ? '

" He didn't answer, and after a while I went on.

" ' This show is not my palaver,' I said ordering two whisky pegs from the bartender. ' It's nothing to do with me, except that you and I are going to share the same bungalow, which is within easy calling distance of Morrison's. Now, Morrison is a funny-tempered fellow, but, apart from that altogether, the situation seems strained to me. If she breaks off her engagement with him and marries you, well and good. But if she isn't going to do that, if she still intends to marry

Morrison—well, then, old man, although I hold no brief for him, you're not playing the game. I'm no sky pilot, but do one thing or the other. Things are apt to happen, you know, Jack, when one's at the back of beyond and a fellow gets playing around with another fellow's wife—things which might make an English court of justice sit up and scratch its head.'

"He heard me out in silence, then he nodded his head.

"'I know it must seem to you that I wasn't playing the game,' he said quietly. 'But, believe me, it's not for want of asking on my part that Molly won't marry me. And I believe that she's as fond of me—almost—as I am of her.'

"'Then why the——?' I began, but he stopped me with a weary little gesture of his hand.

"'She feels that she's bound to him in honour,' he went on. 'I've told her that there can't be much question of honour if she doesn't love him any more, but she seems to think that, as he has waited four years for her, she can't break her bargain. And she's very fond of him; if it hadn't been for fate chucking us together she would never have thought of not marrying him. To-night we both forgot ourselves, I suppose; it won't occur again.'

"He sat back staring out of the port-hole. The smoke-room was empty, and I fairly let myself go.

"'You very silly idiot,' I exploded, 'do you

imagine I've been delivering a homily on the sins of kissing another man's fiancée. What I want to get into your fat head is this. You're going to a place where the only white woman you'll see from year's end to year's end is that girl, if she marries Morrison. You can prattle about honour, and forgetting yourselves, and not letting it occur again, and it's worth the value of that used match. Sooner or later it will occur again, and it won't stop at kissing next time. And then Morrison will probably kill you, or you'll kill him, and there'll be the devil to pay. For Heaven's sake, man, look the thing square in the face. Either marry the girl, or cut her right out of your life. And you can only do that by cabling the firm—or I'll cable them for you from Rangoon—asking to be posted to another district. I shall be sorry, but I'd far rather lose you than sit on the edge of a young volcano.'

" I left him to chew over what I'd said and went to bed, feeling infernally sorry for both of them. But the one fact over which there was no doubt whatever in my mind was that if Morrison married Molly Felsted, then Jack Manderby would have to be removed as far as geographically possible from temptation.

" My remarks apparently had some effect, because the next day Jack buttonholed me on deck.

" ' I've told Molly what you said last night, old man, and we've been talking it over. Morrison is meeting her apparently at Rangoon, and she has agreed to tell him what has happened. And when he knows how the land lies it's bound to be all right. Of course, I'm sorry for him, poor devil, but——' and he went babbling on in a way common to those in love.

"I'm afraid I didn't pay much attention; I was thinking of Morrison and wondering whether Jack's optimism was justified. Apart from his moroseness and drinking, there were other stories about the man—stories which are not good to hear about a white man. I'd never paid any heed to them before, but now they came back to me—those rumours of strange things, which only the ignorant sceptic pretends to scorn; strange things done in secret with native priests and holy men; strange things it is not well for the white man to dabble in. And someone had it that Rupert Morrison did more than dabble."

The Ordinary Man paused and sipped his whisky.

"He met the boat at Rangoon," he continued after a while, "and came on board. Evidently the girl wasted no time in telling him what had occurred, because it was barely ten minutes before I saw him coming towards Jack and myself. There was a smouldering look in his eyes, but outwardly he seemed quite calm. He gave me a curt nod, then he addressed himself exclusively to Jack.

"'Miss Felsted has just made a somewhat unexpected announcement to me,' he remarked.

"Jack bowed gravely. 'I am more than sorry,

Mr. Morrison,' he said, ' if it should appear to you that I have acted in any way caddishly.' He paused a little constrainedly and I moved away. The presence of a third person at such an interview helps nobody. But once or twice I glanced at them during the next quarter of an hour, and it seemed to me that, though he was trying to mask it, the look of smouldering fury in Morrison's eyes was growing more pronounced. From their attitude it struck me that Jack was protesting against some course of action on which the other was insisting, and I turned out to be right.

" ' Morrison has made the following proposal,' he said irritably to me when their conversation had finished. ' That Molly should be left here in Rangoon with the English chaplain and his wife—apparently he'd fixed that already—and that we—he and I—should both go up country for a month or six weeks. Neither of us to see her during that time, and at the end of it she to be free to choose. As he pointed out, I suppose quite rightly, he had been engaged to her for more than four years, and it was rather rough on him to upset everything for what might prove only a passing fancy, induced by being thrown together on board ship. Of course, I pointed out to him that this was no question of a passing fancy—but he insisted.'

" ' And you agreed ? ' I asked.

" ' What else could I do ? ' he cried. ' Heaven knows I didn't want to—it's such awful rot and waste of time. But I suppose it is rather rough luck on the poor devil, and if it makes it any easier for him to have the agony prolonged a few weeks, it's up to me to give him that satisfaction.'

" He went off to talk to the girl, leaving me smoking a cigarette thoughtfully ; for, try as I would, I could not rid my mind of the suspicion that there was something behind this suggestion of Morrison's—something sinister. Fortunately, Jack would be under my eye—in my bungalow ; but even so, I felt uneasy. Morrison had been too quiet for safety, bearing in mind what manner of man he was.

" We landed shortly after and I went round to the club. I didn't see Morrison—he seemed to have disappeared shortly after his interview with Jack ; but he had given the girl full directions as to how to get to the chaplain's house. Jack took her there, and I'd arranged with him that he should come round after and join me.

" The first man I ran into was McAndrew—a leather-faced Scotsman from up my part of the country—who was down in Rangoon on business.

" ' Seen the bridegroom ? ' he grunted as soon as he saw me.

" ' Travelled out with the bride,' I said briefly, not over-anxious to discuss the matter.

" ' And what sort of a lassie is she ? ' he asked curiously.

" ' Perfectly charming,' I answered, ringing the bell for a waiter.

" ' Is that so ? ' he said slowly, and our eyes met. ' Man,' he added still more slowly, ' it should not be, it should not be. Poor lassie! Poor lassie ! '

" And then Jack Manderby came in, and I introduced him to two or three other fellows. I'd arranged to go up country that evening— train to Mandalay, and ride from there the following morning—and Jack, of course, was coming with me. He had said good-bye to the girl ; he wasn't going to see her again before he went up country, and we spent the latter part of the afternoon pottering round Rangoon. And it was as we were strolling down one of the native bazaars that he suddenly caught my arm.

" ' Look—there's Morrison ! ' he muttered. ' I distinctly saw his face peering out of that shop.'

" I looked in the direction he was pointing. It was an ordinary native shop where one could buy ornaments and musical instruments and trash like that—but of Morrison I could see no sign.

" ' I don't see him,' I said ; ' and anyway there is no reason why he shouldn't be in the shop if he wants to.'

" ' But he suddenly vanished,' persisted Jack, ' as if he didn't want to be seen.' He walked on with me slowly. ' I don't like that man, Hugh ; I hate the swine. And it's not because of Molly, either.'

" He shut up at that, and I did not pursue the

topic. It struck me that we should have quite enough of Morrison in the next few weeks."

The Ordinary Man paused and lit a cigarette; then he smiled a little grimly.

"I don't know what I expected," he continued thoughtfully: "I certainly never said a word to Jack as to my vague suspicions. But all the time during the first fortnight, while he was settling down into the job, I had the feeling that there was danger in the air. And then, when nothing happened, my misgivings began to go.

"After all, I said to myself, what could happen, anyway? And perhaps I had misjudged Rupert Morrison. On the two or three occasions that we met him he seemed perfectly normal; and though, somewhat naturally, he was not over effusive to Jack, that was hardly to be wondered at.

"And then one morning Jack came to breakfast looking as if he hadn't slept very well. I glanced at him curiously, but made no allusion to his appearance.

"'Did you hear that music all through the night?' he said irritably, half-way through the meal. 'Some infernal native playing a pipe or something just outside my window.'

"'Why didn't you shout at him to stop?' I asked.

"'I did. And I got up and looked.' He took a gulp of tea; then he looked at me as if he were puzzled.

"'There was no one there that I could see.

Only something black that moved over the compound, about the size of a kitten.'

" ' He was probably just inside the jungle beyond the clearing,' I said. ' Heave half a brick at him if you hear it again.'

" We said no more, and I dismissed the matter from my mind. I was on the opposite side of the bungalow, and it would take more than a native playing on a pipe to keep me awake. But the following night the same thing happened—and the next, and the next.

" ' What sort of a noise is it ? ' I asked him. ' Surely to Heaven you're sufficiently young and healthy not to be awakened by a bally fellow whistling ? '

" ' It isn't that that wakes me, Hugh,' he answered slowly. ' I wake before it starts. Each night about the same time I suddenly find myself wide awake—listening. Sometimes it's ten minutes before it starts—sometimes almost at once ; but it always comes. A faint, sweet whistle—three or four notes, going on and on—until I think I'll go mad. It seems to be calling me.'

" ' But why the devil don't you go and see what it is ? ' I cried peevishly.

" ' Because '—and he stared at me with a shamefaced expression in his eyes—' because I daren't.'

" ' Rot ! ' I said angrily. ' Look here, young fellow, nerves are bad things anywhere—here they're especially bad. You pull yourself together.'

" He flushed all over his face, and shut up like an oyster, which made me rather sorry I'd spoke so sharply. But one does hear funny noises in the jungle, and it doesn't do to become fanciful.

"And then one evening McAndrew came over to dinner. It was during the meal that I mentioned Jack's nocturnal serenader, expecting that Mac would treat it as lightly as I did.

"'Seven times you've heard him, Jack, haven't you,' I said, 'and always the same tune?'

"'Always the same tune,' he answered quietly.

"'Can you whistle it now?' asked McAndrew, laying down his knife and fork and staring at Jack.

"'Easily,' said Jack. 'It goes like this'— and he whistled about six notes. 'On and on it goes—never varying—— Why, McAndrew, what the devil is the matter?'

"I glanced at McAndrew in amazement; then out of the corner of my eye I saw the native servant, who was shivering like a jelly.

"'Man—are you sure?' said Mac, and his face was white.

"'Of course I'm sure,' answered Jack quietly. 'Why?'

"'That tune you whistled—is not good for a white man to hear.' The Scotsman seemed strangely uneasy. 'And ye've heard it seven nights? Do you know it, Walton?'

"'I do not,' I said grimly. 'What's the mystery?'

" But McAndrew was shaking his head dourly, and for a while he did not answer.

" ' Mind ye,' he said at length, ' I'm not saying there's anything in it at all, but I would not care to hear that whistled outside my window. I heard it once—years ago—when I was 'way up in the Arakan Mountains. Soft and sweet it was— rising and falling in the night air, and going on ceaselessly. 'Way up above me was a monastery, one into which no white man has ever been. And the noise was coming from there. I had to go ; my servants wouldn't stop. And when I asked them why, they told me that the priests were calling for a sacrifice. If they stopped, they told me, it might be one of us. That no one could tell how Death would come, or to whom, but come it must—when the Pipes of Death were heard. And the tune you whistled, Manderby, was the tune the Pipes of Death were playing.'

" ' But that's all bunkum, Mac,' I said angrily. ' We're not in the Arakans here.'

" ' Maybe,' he answered doggedly. ' But I'm a Highlander, and—I would not care to hear that tune.'

" I could see Jack was impressed ; as a matter of fact I was myself—more than I cared to admit. Sounds rot here, I know, but out there, with the dim-lit forest around one, it was different.

" McAndrew was stopping with us that night. Jack, with the stubbornness of the young, had flatly refused to change his room, and turned in early, while Mac and I sat up talking. And it was not till we went to bed ourselves that I again alluded to the whistle.

" ' You don't really think it meant anything, Mac, do you ? ' I asked him, and he shrugged his shoulders.

" ' Maybe it is just a native who has heard it,' he said guardedly, and further than that he refused to commit himself.

" I suppose it was about two o'clock when I was awakened by a hand being thrust through my mosquito curtains.

" ' Walton, come at once ! '   It was Mc-Andrew's voice, and it was shaking. ' There's devil's work going on, I tell you—devil's work.'

" I was up in a flash, and together we crept along the passage towards Jack's room. Almost instinctively I'd picked up a gun, and I held it ready as we paused by the door.

" ' Do you hear it ? ' whispered Mac a little fearfully, and I nodded. Sweet and clear the notes rose and fell, on and on and on in the same cadence. Sometimes the whistler seemed to be far away, at others almost in the room.

" ' It's the tune,' muttered McAndrew, as we tiptoed towards the bed. ' The Pipes of Death. Are ye awake, boy ? '

" And then he gave a little cry and gripped my arm.

" ' In God's name,' he whispered, ' what's that on the pillow beside his head ? '

" For a while in the dim light I couldn't make

out. There was something big and black and
motionless on the white pillow, and I crept
nearer to see what it was. And then suddenly
seemed to stand still. I saw two beady, un-
winking eyes staring at Jack's face close by;
I saw Jack's eyes wide open and sick with terror,
staring at the thing which shared his bed. And
still the music went on outside.

" ' What is it? ' I muttered through dry lips.

" ' Give me your gun, man,' whispered Mc-
Andrew hoarsely. ' If the pipes stop, the boy's
doomed.'

" Slowly he raised the gun an inch at a time,
pushing the muzzle forward with infinite care
towards the malignant, glowing eyes, until at
last the gun was almost touching its head. And at
that moment the music died away and stopped
altogether. I had the momentary glimpse of two
black feelers shooting out towards Jack's face—
then came the crack of the gun. And with a little
sob Jack rolled out of bed and lay on the floor
half-fainting, while the black mass on the pillow
writhed and writhed and then grew still.

" We struck a light, and stared at what was
left of the thing in silence. And it was Jack who
spoke first.

" ' I woke,' he said unsteadily, ' to feel something crawling over me on the bed. Outside that
infernal whistling was going on, and at last I
made out what was—what was—— My God ! '
he cried thickly, ' what was it, Mac—what was
it ? '

" ' Steady, boy ! ' said McAndrew. ' It's dead now, anyway. But it was touch and go. I've seen 'em bigger than that up in the Arakans. It's a bloodsucking, poisonous spider. They're sacred to some of the sects.'

Suddenly out of the jungle came one dreadful, piercing cry.

" ' What was that ? ' Jack muttered, and McAndrew shook his head.

" ' We'll find out to-morrow,' he said. ' There are strange things abroad to-night.'

" We saw the darkness out—the three of us—round a bottle of whisky.

" ' They've been trying to get you for a week, Manderby,' said the Scotsman. ' To-night they very near succeeded.'

" ' But why ? ' cried Jack. ' I've never done 'em any harm.'

" McAndrew shrugged his shoulders.

" ' Don't ask me that,' he answered. ' Their ways are not our ways.'

" Has that brute been in my room every night ? ' the boy asked.

" ' Every night,' answered McAndrew gravely. ' Probably two of them. They hunt them in pairs. They starve 'em, and then, when the music stops, they feed.' He thoughtfully poured out some more whisky.

" And then at last came the dawn, and we went out to investigate. It was Jack who found him. The face was puffed and horrible, and as we approached, something black, about the size of a big kitten, moved away from the body and shambled sluggishly into the undergrowth.

" ' You're safe, boy,' said McAndrew slowly. ' It was not the priests at all. Just murder—plain murder.'

" And with that he took his handkerchief and covered the dreadful, staring eyes of Rupert Morrison."

" You can set your minds at rest about one thing, you fellows," began the Soldier, with a grin. " My yarn isn't about the war. There have been quite enough lies told already about that performance without my adding to the number. No; my story concerns peace soldiering, and, strangely enough, I had an ocular demonstration when dining at the Ritz two nights ago that everything had finished up quite satisfactorily, in the approved story-book manner. At least, when I say quite satisfactorily—there was a price, and it was paid by one of the principal actors. But that is the unchangeable rule : one can but shrug one's shoulders and pay accordingly.

" The regiment—I was a squadron-leader at the time—was quartered at Murchester. Not a bad station at all : good shooting, very fair hunting, especially if you didn't scorn the carted stag, polo, and most excellent cricket. Also some delightful houses in the neighbourhood ; and as we'd just come home from our foreign tour we found the place greatly to our liking. London was an hour and a bit by train ; in fact, there are many worse stations in England than the spot I have labelled Murchester.

"The only fly in the ointment when we first arrived was a fairly natural one, and a thing which only time could cure. The men were a bit restive. We'd been abroad, don't forget, for more than ten years—India, Egypt, South Africa—and the feel of the old country under their feet unsettled 'em temporarily. Nothing very bad, but an epidemic of absence without leave and desertion broke out, and the officers had to settle down to pull things together. Continual courts-martial for desertion don't do a regiment any good with the powers that be, and we had to stop it.

"Of course, one of the first things to look to, when any trouble of that sort is occurring, is the general type and standard of your N.C.O.'s. In my squadron they were good, though just a little on the young side. I remember one day I discussed the matter pretty thoroughly with the squadron sergeant-major—an absolute top-notcher.

"'They're all right, sir,' he said. 'In another two or three years there will be none better in the British Army. Especially Trevor.'

"'Ah! Sergeant-Major,' I said, looking him straight in the face, 'you think Trevor is a good man, do you?'

"'The best we've got, sir,' he answered quietly, and he stared straight back at me.

"'You weren't so sure when he first came,' I reminded him.

"'Well, I reckon there was a bit of jealousy,

sir,' he replied, ' his coming in from the link
regiment over a good many of the chaps' heads.
But he's been with us now three months—and we
know him better.'

" ' I wish I could say the same,' I answered.
' He defeats me, does Sergeant Trevor.'

" The Sergeant-Major smiled quietly. ' Does
he, sir ?   I shouldn't have thought he would
have.   That there bloke Kipling has written
about the likes of Trevor.'

" ' Kipling has written a good deal about the
Army,' I said, with an answering smile. ' Mulvaney and Co. are classics.'

" ' It's not Mulvaney I'm meaning, sir,' he
answered.   ' But didn't he write a little bit of
poetry about " Gentlemen-rankers out on the
spree " ? '

" ' Why, yes, he did.' I lit a cigarette
thoughtfully. ' I'd guessed that much, Manfield.
Is Trevor his real name ? '

" ' I don't know, sir,' and at that moment
the subject of our discussion walked past and
saluted.

" ' Sergeant Trevor,' I called after him, on the
spur of the moment, and he came up at the
double.   I hadn't anything really to say to him,
but ever since he'd joined us he'd puzzled me, and
though, as the sergeant-major said, the other
non-commissioned officers might know him
better, I certainly didn't.

" ' You're a bit of a cricketer, aren't you ? '
I said, as he came up.

" A faint smile flickered across his face at my question. ' I used to play quite a lot, sir,' he answered.

" ' Good; we want to get games going really strong.' I talked with them both—squadron ' shop '—a bit longer, and all the time I was trying to probe behind the impassive mask of Trevor's face. Incidentally, I think he knew it; once or twice I caught a faint gleam of amusement in his eyes—a gleam that seemed to me a little weary. And when I left them and went across the parade ground towards the mess, his face haunted me. I hadn't probed—not the eighth of an inch; he was still as much a mystery as ever. But he'd got a pair of deep blue eyes, and though I wasn't a girl to be attracted by a man's eyes, I couldn't get his out of my mind. They baffled me; the man himself baffled me—and I've always disliked being baffled.

" It was a few nights after, in mess, that the next piece in the puzzle came along. We had in the regiment—he was killed in the war, poor devil! —a fellow of the name of Blenton, a fairly senior captain. He wasn't in my squadron, and his chief claim to notoriety was as a cricketer. Had he been able to play regularly he would have been easily up to first-class form—as it was he periodically turned out for the county; but he used to go in first wicket down for the Army. So you can gather his sort of form.

" It was over the port that the conversation cropped up, and it interested me because it was about Trevor. As far as cricket was concerned I hardly knew which end of a bat one held.

"'Dog-face has got a winner,' I heard Blenton say across the table. I may say that I answered to that tactful sobriquet, for reasons into which we need not enter. 'One Sergeant Trevor in your squadron, old boy,' he turned to me. 'I was watching him at the nets to-night.'

"'Is he any good?' I said.

"'My dear fellow,' answered Blenton, deliberately, 'he is out and away the best bat we've had in the regiment for years. He's up to Army form!'

"'Who's that?' demanded the commanding officer, sitting up and taking notice at once.

"'Sergeant Trevor in B squadron, Colonel,' said Blenton. 'I was watching him this evening at nets. Of course, the bowling was tripe, but he's in a completely different class to the average soldier cricketer.'

"'Did you talk to him?' I asked, curiously.

"'I did. And he struck me as being singularly uncommunicative. Asked him where he learnt his cricket, and he hummed and hawed, and finally said he'd played a lot in his village before joining the Army. I couldn't quite make him out, Dog-face. And why the devil didn't he play for us out in Jo'burg?'

"'Because he only joined a couple of months before we sailed,' I answered. 'Came with that last draft we got.'

" ' Well, I wish we had a few more trained in his village,' said Blenton. ' We could do with them.'

" After mess, I tackled Philip Blenton in the ante-room.

" ' What's your candid opinion of Trevor, Philip ? ' I demanded.

" He stopped on his way to play bridge, and bit the end off his cigar.

" ' As a cricketer,' he said, ' or as a man ? '

" ' Both,' I answered.

" ' Well, my candid opinion is that he learned his game at a first-class public school,' he replied. ' And I am further of the opinion, from the few words I spoke to him, that one would have expected to find him here and not in the Sergeants' Mess. What's his story ? Do you know ? '

" ' I don't.' I shook my head. ' Haven't an idea. But you've confirmed my own impressions.'

" And there I had to leave it for some months. Periodically I talked to Trevor, deliberately tried to trap him into some admission which would give me a clue to his past, but he was as wary as a fox and as close as an oyster. I don't know why I took the trouble—after all, it was his business entirely, but the fellow intrigued me. He was such an extraordinarily fine N.C.O., and there was never a sign of his hitting the bottle, which is the end of a good many gentlemen-rankers. Moreover, he didn't strike me as a fellow who had come a cropper, which is the usual cause of his kind.

"And then one day, when I least expected it, the problem began to solve itself. Philip Blenton rang me up in the morning after breakfast, from a house in the neighbourhood, where he was staying for a couple of two-day matches. Could I possibly spare Sergeant Trevor for the first of them ? Against the I Z., who had brought down a snorting team, and Carter—the Oxford blue—had failed the local eleven at the last moment. If I couldn't they'd have to rake in one of the gardeners, but they weren't too strong as it was.

So I sent for Trevor, and asked him if he'd care to play. I saw his eyes gleam for a moment; then he shook his head.

"'I think not, thank you, sir,' he said, quietly.

"It's not quite like you to let Captain Blenton down, Trevor,' I remarked. 'He's relying on you.'

"I knew it was the right note to take with him, and I was very keen on his playing. I was going out myself that afternoon to watch, and I wanted to see him in different surroundings. We argued for a bit—I knew he was as keen as mustard in one way to play—and after a while he said he would. Then he went out of the office, and as it happened I followed him. There was an old cracked mirror in the passage outside, and as I opened the door he had just shut behind him, I had a glimpse of Sergeant Trevor examining his face in the glass. He'd got his hand so placed that it blotted out his moustache, and he seemed very intent on his reflection. Then he saw me, and for a moment or two we stared at one another in silence. Squadron-leader and troop-sergeant had gone; we were just two men, and the passage was empty. And I acted on a sudden impulse, and clapped him on the back.

"'Don't be a fool, man,' I cried. 'Is there any reason why you shouldn't be recognised?'

"'Nothing shady, Major,' he answered, quietly. 'But if one starts on a certain course, it's best to go through with it!'

"At that moment the pay-sergeant appeared, and Trevor pulled himself together, saluted smartly, and was gone.

"I suppose these things are planned out beforehand," went on the Soldier, thoughtfully. "To call it all blind chance seems a well-nigh impossible solution to me. And yet the cynic would assuredly laugh at connecting a child eating an orange in a back street in Oxford, and the death while fishing in Ireland of one of the greatest-hearted men that ever lived. But unless that child had eaten that orange, and left the peel on the pavement for Carter, the Oxford blue, to slip on and sprain his ankle, the events I am going to relate would, in all probability, never have taken place. However, since delving too deeply into cause and effect inevitably produces insanity, I'd better get on with it.

" I turned up about three o'clock at Crosby Hall, along with four or five other fellows from the regiment. Usual sort of stunt—marquee and lemonade, with whisky in the background for the hopeless cases. The I Z. merchants were in the field, and Trevor was batting. There was an Eton boy in with him, and the score was two hundred odd for five wickets. Philip Blenton lounged up as soon as he saw me, grinning all over his face.

" ' Thank Heaven you let him come, old man ! He's pulled eighty of the best out of his bag already, and doesn't look like getting out.'

" ' He wouldn't come at first, Philip,' I said, and he stared at me in surprise. ' I think he was afraid of being recognised.'

" A burst of applause greeted a magnificent drive past cover-point, and for a while we watched the game in silence, until another long round of cheering announced that Sergeant Trevor had got his century. As I've said before, I'm no cricketer, but there was no need to be an expert to realise that he was something out of the way. He was treating the by-no-means-indifferent I Z. bowling with the utmost contempt, and old Lord Apson, our host, was beside himself with joy. He was a cricket maniac ; his week was an annual fixture ; and for the first time for many years he saw his team really putting it across the I Z. And

it was just as I was basking in a little reflected
glory that I saw a very dear old friend of mine
arrive in the enclosure, accompanied by a perfectly charming girl.

" ' Why, Yeverley, old man ! ' I cried, ' how
are you ? '

" ' Dog-face, as I live ! ' he shouted, seizing
me by both hands. ' Man-alive, I'm glad to
see you. Let me introduce you to my wife ;
Doris, this is Major Chilham—otherwise Dog-
face.'

" I shook hands with the girl, who was standing
smiling beside him, and for a while we stopped
there talking. He was fifteen years or so older
than I, and had left the service as a Captain, but
we both came from the same part of the country,
and in days gone by I'd known him very well
indeed. His marriage had taken place four
years previously while I was abroad, and now,
meeting his wife for the first time, I recalled bit by
bit the gossip I'd heard in letters I got from home.
How to everyone's amazement he'd married a girl
young enough to be his daughter ; how everybody had prophesied disaster, and affirmed that
she was not half good enough for one of the elect
like Giles Yeverley ; how she'd been engaged to
someone else and thrown him over. And yet
as I looked at them both it struck me that the
Jeremiahs had as usual been completely wrong :
certainly nothing could exceed the dog-like
devotion in Giles's eyes whenever he looked at his
wife.

" We strolled over to find some easy chairs, and he fussed round her as if she was an invalid. She took it quite naturally and calmly with a faint and charming smile, and when he finally bustled away to talk to Apson, leaving me alone with her, she was still smiling.

" ' You know Giles well ? ' she said.

" ' Awfully well,' I answered. 'And having now returned from my sojourn in the wilds, I hope I shall get to know his wife equally well.'

" ' That's very nice of you, Dog-face '—she turned and looked at me—and, by Jove, she was pretty. ' If you're anything like Giles—you must be a perfect dear.'

" Now I like that sort of a remark when it's made in the right way. It establishes a very pleasant footing at once, with no danger of misconstruction—like getting on good terms with a new horse the moment you put your feet in the irons, instead of messing around for half the hunt. Anyway, for the next ten minutes or so I didn't pay very much attention to the cricket. I gathered that there was one small son—Giles junior—who was the apple of his father's eye ; and that at the moment a heavy love affair was in progress between the young gentleman aged three and the General's daughter, who was as much as four, and showed no shame over the matter whatever. Also that Giles and she were stopping with the General and his wife for a week or ten days.

" And it was at that stage of the proceedings that a prolonged burst of applause made us look at the cricket. Sergeant Trevor was apparently out—how I hadn't an idea—and was half-way between the wickets and the tent next to the one in which we were sitting, and which Apson always had erected for the local villagers and their friends. I saw them put up one hundred and twenty-five on the board as Trevor's score, and did my share in the clapping line.

" ' A fine player—that fellow,' I said, following him with my eyes. ' Don't know much about the game myself, but the experts tell me——" And at that moment I saw her face, and stopped abruptly. She had gone very white, and her knuckles were gleaming like the ivory on the handle of her parasol.

" ' Major Chilham,' she said—and her voice was the tensest thing I've ever heard—' who is that man who has just come out ? '

" ' Trevor is his name,' I answered, quietly. ' He's one of the troop-sergeants in my squadron.' I was looking at her curiously, as the colour slowly came back to her face. ' Why ? Did you think you knew him ? '

" ' He reminded me of someone I knew years ago,' she said, sitting back in her chair. ' But of course I must have been mistaken.'

" And then rather abruptly she changed the conversation, though every now and then she glanced towards the next tent, as if trying to see Trevor. And sitting beside her I realised that

there was something pretty serious in the wind.
She was on edge, though she was trying not to
show it—and Trevor was the cause, or the man
who called himself Trevor. All my curiosity
came back, though I made no allusion to him;
I was content to await further developments.

"They weren't long in coming. The house
team, with the respectable total of three hundred
and fifty odd, were all out by tea-time, and both
elevens forgathered in the tent behind. All,
that is, except Trevor, who remained in the other
until Apson himself went and pulled him out. I
watched the old man, with his cheery smile, take
Trevor by the elbow and literally drag him out
of his chair; I watched Trevor in his blue undress
jacket, smart as be damned, coming towards us
with our host. And then very deliberately I
looked at Giles Yeverley's wife. She was staring
over my head at the two men; then she lowered
her parasol.

"'So you weren't mistaken after all, Mrs.
Giles,' I said, quietly.

"'No, Dog-face, I wasn't,' she answered.
'Would you get hold of Giles for me, and tell him
I'd like to get back. Say I'm not feeling very
well.'

"I got up at once and went in search of her
husband. I found him talking to the Zingari
captain and Sergeant Trevor. He seemed quite
excited, appealing as he spoke to the I Z. skipper,
while Trevor stood by listening with a faint
smile.

"'What he says is quite right, Sergeant Trevor,' remarked the Zingari man as I came up. 'If you cared to consider it—you are absolutely up to the best county form. Of course, I don't know about your residential qualifications, but that can generally be fixed.'

"'Dog-face,' cried Yeverley, as soon as he saw me, 'he's in your squadron, isn't he? Well, it's so long since I left the Army that I've forgotten all about discipline—but I tell you here—right now in front of him—that Sergeant Trevor ought to chuck soldiering and take up professional cricket. Bimbo here agrees with me.'

"'Giles, you'll burst your waistcoat if you get so excited,' I remarked, casually. 'And, incidentally, Mrs. Yeverley wants to go home.'

"As I said the name I looked at Trevor, and my last doubt vanished. He gave a sudden start, which Giles, who had immediately torn off to his wife, didn't see, and proceeded to back into the farthest corner of the tea-tent. But once again old Apson frustrated him. Not for him the endless pauses and waits of first-class cricket ; five minutes to roll the pitch and he was leading his team into the field. Trevor had to go from his sanctuary, and there was only one exit from the enclosure in front of the tent.

"They met—Mrs. Giles and Trevor—actually at that exit. By the irony of things, I think it was Giles who caused the meeting. He hurried forward as he saw Trevor going out, and caught him by the arm ; dear old chap !—he was cricket mad if ever a man was. And so blissfully unconscious of the other, bigger thing going on right under his nose.

" ' Don't you forget what I said, Trevor,' he said, earnestly. ' Any county would be glad to have you. I'm going to talk to Major Chilham about it seriously.'

" And I doubt if Trevor heard a word. Over Giles's shoulder he was staring at Giles's wife— and she was staring back at him, while her breast rose and fell in little gasps, and it seemed to me that her lips were trembling. Then it was over ; Trevor went out to field—Giles bustled back to his wife. And I, being a hopeless case, went in search of alcohol."

The Soldier paused to light another cigar.

" He carried out his threat, did Giles with regard to me. Two or three days later I lunched with the General, and it seemed to me that we never got off the subject of Trevor. It wasn't only his opinion ; had not Bimbo Lawrence, the I Z. captain, and one of the shrewdest judges of cricket in England, agreed with him ? And so on without cessation about Trevor, the cricketer, while on the opposite side of the table, next to me, sat his wife, who could not get beyond Trevor, the man. Once or twice she glanced at me appealingly, as if to say : ' For God's sake, stop him ! '—but it was a task beyond my powers. I made one or two abortive attempts, and then I gave it up. The situation was beyond me; one could only let him ramble on and pray for the end of lunch.

"And then he left the cricket and came to personalities.

"'Know anything about him, Dog-face?' he asked. 'Up at old Apson's place he struck me as being a gentleman. Anyway, he's a darned nice fellow. Wonder why he enlisted?'

"'Oh, Giles, for goodness' sake, let's try another topic?' said his wife, suddenly. 'We've had Sergeant Trevor since lunch began.'

"Poor old Giles looked at her in startled surprise, and she gave him a quick smile which robbed her words of their irritability. But I could see she was on the rack, and though I didn't know the real facts, it wasn't hard to make a shrewd guess as to the cause.

"It was just before we rose from the table, I remember, that she said to me under the cover of the general conversation: 'My God! Dog-face—it's not fair.'

"'Will you tell me?' I answered. 'I might help.'

"'Perhaps I will some day,' she said, quietly. 'But you can't help; no one can do that. It was my fault all through, and the only thing that matters now is that Giles should never know.'

"I don't quite know why she suddenly confided in me, even to that extent. I suppose with her woman's intuition she realised that I'd guessed something, and it helps to get a thing

8

off one's chest at times. Evidently it had been
an unexpected meeting, and I cursed myself for
having made him play. And yet how could
one have foretold ? It was just a continuation
of the jig-saw started by that damned bit of
orange peel. As she said, all that mattered,
was that Giles—dear old chap!—should never
know."

The Soldier smiled a little sadly. " So
do the humans propose ; but the God that moves
the pieces frequently has different ideas. He
did—that very afternoon. It was just as I was
going that two white-faced nurses clutching two
scared children appeared on the scene and babbled
incoherently. And then the General's groom
hove in sight—badly cut across the face and
shaky at the knees—and from him we got the
story.

"They'd started off in the General's dogcart
to go to some children's party, and something
had frightened the horse, which had promptly
bolted. I knew the brute—a great raking black,
though the groom, who was a first-class whip,
generally had no difficulty in managing him. But
on this occasion apparently he'd got clean away
along the road into the town. He might have
got the horse under control after a time, when, to
his horror, he saw that the gates were closed at
the railway crossing in front. And it was at that
moment that a man—one of the sergeants from
the barracks—had dashed out suddenly from the
pavement and got to the horse's head. He was

trampled on badly, but he hung on—and the horse had ceased to bolt when they crashed into the gates. The shafts were smashed, but nothing more. And the horse wasn't hurt. And they'd carried away the sergeant on an improvised stretcher. No ; he hadn't spoken. He was unconscious.

" ' Which sergeant was it ? ' I asked, quietly— though I knew the answer before the groom gave it.

" ' Sergeant Trevor, sir,' he said. ' B squadron.'

" ' Is he—is he badly hurt ? ' said the girl, and her face was ashen.

" ' I dunno, mum,' answered the groom. ' They took 'im off to the 'orspital, and I was busy with the 'orse.'

" ' I'll ring up, if I may, General,' I said, and he nodded.

" I spoke to Purvis, the R.A.M.C. fellow, and his voice was very grave. They'd brought Trevor in still unconscious, and, though he wouldn't swear to it at the moment, he was afraid his back was broken. But he couldn't tell absolutely for certain until he came to. I hung up the receiver and found Mrs. Giles standing behind me. She said nothing—but just waited for me to speak.

" ' Purvis doesn't know for certain,' I said, taking both her hands in mine. ' But there's a possibility, my dear, that his back is broken.'

" She was a thoroughbred, that girl. She

didn't make a fuss or cry out; she just looked me straight in the face and nodded her head once or twice.

"'I must go to him, of course,' she said, gravely. 'Will you arrange it for me, please?'

"'He's unconscious still,' I told her.

"'Then I must be beside him when he comes to,' she answered. 'Even if there was nothing else—he's saved my baby's life.'

"'I'll take you in my car,' I said, when I saw that she was absolutely determined. 'Leave it all to me.'

"'I must see him alone, Dog-face.' She paused by the door, with her handkerchief rolled into a tight little ball in her hand. 'I want to know that he's forgiven me.'

"'You shall see him alone if it's humanly possible,' I answered gravely, and at that she was gone.

"I don't quite know how I did it, but somehow or other I got her away from the General's house without Giles knowing. Giles junior was quite unhurt, and disposed to regard the entire thing as an entertainment got up especially for his benefit. And when she'd made sure of that, and kissed him passionately to his intense disgust, she slipped away with me in the car.

"'You mustn't be disappointed,' I warned her as we drove along, 'if you can't see him alone. He may have been put into a ward with other men.'

' Then they must put some screens round him,'
she whispered. ' I must kiss him before—
before——' She didn't complete the sentence ;
but it wasn't necessary.

" We didn't speak again until I turned in at
the gates of the hospital. And then I asked her
a question which had been on the tip of my
tongue a dozen times.

" ' Who is he—really ? '

" ' Jimmy Dallas is his name,' she answered.
quietly. ' We were engaged. And then his
father lost all his money. He thought that was
why—why I was beastly to him—but oh !
Dog-face, it wasn't at all. I thought he was
fond of another girl—and it was all a mistake.
I found it out too late. And then Jimmy had
disappeared—and I'd married Giles. Up at
that cricket match was the first time I'd seen
him since my wedding.'

" We drew up at the door, and I got out.
It's the little tragedies, the little misunder-
standings, that are so pitiful, and in all conscience
this was a case in point. A boy and a girl—
each too proud to explain, or ask for an explanation ; and now the big tragedy. God ! it seemed
so futile.

" I left her sitting in the car, and went in
search of Purvis. I found him with Trevor
—I still thought of him under that name—
and he was conscious again. The doctor
looked up as I tiptoed in, and shook his head
at me warningly. So I waited, and after a

while Purvis left the bed and drew me out into the passage.

"'I'm not sure,' he said. 'He's so infernally bruised and messed about. His left arm is broken in two places, and three ribs—and I'm afraid his back as well. He seems so numb. But I can't be certain.'

"'Mrs. Yeverley is here,' I said. 'The mother of one of the kids he saved. She wants to see him.'

"'Out of the question,' snapped Purvis. 'I absolutely forbid it.'

"'But you mustn't forbid it, Doctor.' We both swung round, to see the girl herself standing behind us. 'I've got to see him. There are other reasons besides his having saved my baby's life.'

"'They must wait, Mrs. Yeverley,' answered the Doctor. 'In a case of this sort the only person I would allow to see him would be his wife.'

"'If I hadn't been a fool,' she said deliberately, 'I should have been his wife,' and Purvis's jaw dropped.

"Without another word she swept past him into the ward, and Purvis stood there gasping.

"'Well, I'm damned!' he muttered, and I couldn't help smiling. It was rather a startling statement to come from a woman stopping with the G.O.C. about a sergeant in a cavalry regiment.

" And then, quite suddenly and unexpectedly, came the final turn in the wheel. I was strolling up and down outside with Purvis, who was a sahib as well as a Doctor and had asked no questions.

" ' If his back is broken it can't hurt him,' he had remarked, ' and if it isn't it will do him good.'

" At that we had left it, when suddenly, to my horror, I saw Giles himself going into the hospital.

" ' Good Lord, Doc ! ' I cried, sprinting after him, ' that's her husband. And he doesn't know she's here.'

" But a lot can happen in a few seconds, and I was just a few seconds too late. As I got to the door I saw Giles in front of me—standing at the entrance to the ward as if he had been turned to stone. A big screen hid the bed from sight—but a screen is not sound proof. He looked at me as I came up, and involuntarily I stopped as I saw his face. And then quite clearly from the room beyond came his wife's voice.

" ' My darling, darling boy !—it's you and only you for ever and ever ! '

" I don't quite know how much Giles had guessed before. I think he knew about her previous engagement, but I'm quite sure he had never associated Trevor with it. A year or two later she told me that when she married him she had made no attempt to conceal the fact that she had loved another man—and loved him still.

And Giles had taken her on those terms.   But at the time I didn't know that : I only knew that a very dear friend's world had crashed about his head with stunning suddenness.   It was Giles who pulled himself together first—Giles, with a face grey and lined, who said in a loud voice to me : ' Well, Dog-face, where is the invalid ? '

" And then he waited a moment or two before he went round the screen.

" ' Ah ! my dear,' he said, quite steadily, as he saw his wife, ' you here ? '

" He played his part for ten minutes, stiff-lipped and without a falter ; then he went, and his wife went with him to continue the play in which they were billed for life.   Trevor's back was not broken—in a couple of months he was back at duty.   And so it might have continued for the duration, but for Giles being drowned fishing in Ireland."

The Soldier stared thoughtfully at the fire.

" He was a first-class fisherman and a wonderful swimmer, was Giles Yeverley, and sometimes —I wonder. They say he got caught in a bore— that perhaps he got cramp. But, as I say, sometimes—I wonder.

" I saw them—Jimmy Dallas, sometime Sergeant Trevor, and his wife—at the Ritz two nights ago. They seemed wonderfully in love, though they'd been married ten years, and I stopped by their table.

" ' Sit down, Dog-face,' she ordered, ' and have a liqueur.'

"So I sat down and had a liqueur. And it was just as I was going that she looked at me with her wonderful smile, and said, very softly: 'Thank God! dear old Giles never knew; and now, if he does, he'll understand.'"

The Soldier got up and stretched himself.

"A big result for a bit of yellow peel."

"I'M not certain, strictly speaking, that my story can be said to concern my trade," began the Writer, after he had seen his guests were comfortable. "But it happened—this little adventure of mine—as the direct result of pursuing my trade, so I will interpret the rule accordingly.

"My starting-point is the Largest Pumpkin Ever Produced in Kent. It was the sort of pumpkin which gets a photograph all to itself in the illustrated papers—the type of atrocity which is utterly useless to any human being. And yet that large and unpleasant vegetable proved the starting-point of the most exciting episode in my somewhat prosaic life. In fact, but for very distinct luck, that pumpkin would have been responsible for my equally prosaic funeral." The Writer smiled reminiscently.

"It was years ago, in the days before a misguided public began to read my books and supply me with the necessary wherewithal to keep the wolf from the door. But I was young and full of hope, and Fleet Street seemed a very wonderful place. From which you can infer that I was a journalist, and candour compels me to admit—a jolly bad one. Not that I realised it at the time. I regarded my Editor's complete lack of appreciation of my merits as being his misfortune, not my fault. However, I pottered around, doing odd jobs and having the felicity of seeing my carefully penned masterpieces completely obscured by blue pencil and reduced to two lines.

" Then one morning I was sent for to the inner sanctuary. Now, although I had the very lowest opinion of the Editor's abilities, I knew sufficient of the office routine to realise that such a summons was unlikely to herald a rise of screw with parchment certificate of appreciation for services rendered. It was far more likely to herald the order of the boot—and the prospect was not very rosy. Even in those days Fleet Street was full of unemployed journalists who knew more than their editors.

" The news editor was in the office when I walked in, and he was a kindly man, was old Andrews. He looked at me from under his great bushy eyebrows for a few moments without speaking; then he pointed to a chair.

" ' Graham,' he remarked in a deep bass voice, ' are you aware that this paper has never yet possessed a man on its staff that writes such unutterable slush as you do ? '

" I remained discreetly silent; to dissent seemed tactless, to agree, unnecessary.

" ' What do you propose to do about it ? ' he continued after a while.

" I told him that I hadn't realised I was as bad as all that, but that I would do my best to improve my style and give satisfaction in the future.

" ' It's not so much your style,' he conceded. ' Years ago I knew a man whose style was worse. Only a little—but it was worse. But it's your nose for news, my boy—that's the worst thing that ever came into Fleet Street. Now, what were you doing yesterday ? '

" ' I was reporting that wedding at the Brompton Oratory, sir,' I told him.

" ' Just so,' he answered. ' And are you aware that in a back street not three hundred yards from the church a man died through eating a surfeit of winkles, as the result of a bet ? Actually while you were there did that man die by the winkle-barrow—and you knew nothing about it. I'm not denying that your report on the wedding isn't fair—but the public is entitled to know about the dangers of winkle-eating to excess. Not that the rights of the public matter in the least, but it's the principle I want to impress on you—the necessity of keeping your eyes open for other things beside the actual job you're on. That's what makes the good journalist.'

" I assured him that I would do so in future, and he grunted non-committally. Then he began rummaging in a drawer, while I waited in trepidation.

" ' We ll give you a bit longer, Graham,' he announced at length, and I breathed freely again. ' But if there is no improvement you'll have to go. And in the meantime I've got a job for you this afternoon. Some public-spirited benefactor has inaugurated an agricultural fête in Kent, somewhere near Ashford. From what I can gather, he seems partially wanting in intelligence, but it takes people all ways. He is giving prizes for the heaviest potato and the largest egg —though I am unable to see what the hen's activity has to do with her owner. And I want you to go down and write it up. Half a column. Get your details right. I believe there is a treatise on soils and manures in the office somewhere. And put in a paragraph about the paramount importance of the Englishman getting back to the land. Not that it will have any effect, but it might help to clear Fleet Street.'

" He was already engrossed in something else, and dismissed me with a wave of his hand. And it was just as I got to the door that he called after me to send Cresswill to him—Cresswill, the star of all the special men. His reception, I reflected a little bitterly as I went in search of him, would be somewhat different from mine. For he had got to the top of the tree, and was on a really big job at the time. He did all the criminal work— murder trials and so forth, and how we youngsters envied him ! Perhaps, in time, one might reach those dazzling heights, I reflected, as I sat in my third-class carriage on the way to Ashford. Not for him mammoth tubers and double-yolkers— but the things that really counted.

" I got out at Ashford, where I had to change.

My destination was Appledore, and the connection on was crowded with people obviously bound, like myself, for the agricultural fête. It was a part of Kent to which I had never been, and when I got out at Appledore station I found I was in the flat Romney Marsh country which stretches inland from Dungeness. Houses are few and far between, except in the actual villages themselves—the whole stretch of land, of course, must once have been below sea-level—and the actual fête was being held in a large field on the outskirts of Appledore. It was about a mile from the station, and I proceeded to walk.

" The day was warm, the road was dusty— and I, I am bound to admit, was bored. I felt I was destined for better things than reporting on bucolic flower shows, much though I loved flowers. But I like them in their proper place, growing—not arranged for show in a stuffy tent and surrounded by perspiring humanity. And so when I came to the gates of a biggish house and saw behind them a garden which was a perfect riot of colour, involuntarily I paused and looked over.

" The house itself stood back about a hundred yards from the road—a charming old place covered with creepers, and the garden was lovely. A little neglected, perhaps—I could see a respectable number of weeds in a bed of irises close to the drive—but then it was quite a large garden. Probably belonged to some family that could not afford a big staff, I reflected, and that moment

I saw a man staring at me from between some shrubs a few yards away.

" There was no reason why he shouldn't stare at me—he was inside the gate and presumably had more right to the garden than I had—but there was something about him that made me return the stare, in silence, for a few moments. Whether it was his silent approach over the grass and unexpected appearance, or whether it was that instinctively he struck me as an incongruous type of individual to find in such a sleepy locality, I can't say. Or, perhaps, it was a sudden lightning impression of hostile suspicion on his part, as if he resented anyone daring to look over his gate.

" Then he came towards me, and I felt I had to say something. But even as I spoke the thought flashed across my mind that he would have appeared far more at home in a London bar than in a rambling Appledore garden.

" ' I was admiring your flowers,' I said as he came up. ' Your irises are wonderful.'

" He looked vaguely at some lupins, then his intent gaze came back to me.

" ' The garden is well known locally,' he remarked. ' Are you a member of these parts ? '

" ' No,' I answered, ' I come from London,' and it seemed to me his gaze grew more intent.

" ' I am only a bird of passage, too,' he said easily. ' Are you just down for the day ? '

" I informed him that I had come down to write up the local fête ; being young and foolish,

I rather think I implied that only the earnest request of the organiser for me in particular had persuaded the editor to dispense with my invaluable services even for a few hours. And all the time his eyes, black and inscrutable, never left my face.

" ' The show is being held in a field about a quarter of a mile farther on,' he said when I had finished. ' Good morning.'

" He turned abruptly on his heels and walked slowly away towards the house, leaving me a little annoyed, and with a feeling that not only had I been snubbed, but, worse still, had been seen through. I felt that I had failed to convince him that editors tore their hair and bit their nails when they failed to secure my services; I felt, indeed, just that particular type of ass that one does feel when one has boasted vaingloriously, and been listened to with faintly amused boredom. I know that as I resumed my walk towards the agricultural fête I endeavoured to restore my self-respect by remembering that he was merely a glorified yokel, who probably knew no better."

The Writer leant back in his chair with a faint smile.

" That awful show still lives in my memory," he continued after a while. " There were swing boats, and one of those ghastly shows where horses go round and round with a seasick motion and ' The Blue Bells of Scotland ' emerges without cessation from the bowels of the machine.

There were coco-nut shies and people peering through horse-collars to have their photographs taken, and over everything an all-pervading aroma of humanity unsuitably clad in its Sunday best on a warm day. However, the job had to be done, so I bravely plunged into the marquees devoted to the competing vegetables. I listened to the experts talking around me with the idea of getting the correct local colour, but as most of their remarks were incomprehensible, I soon gave that up as a bad job and began looking about me.

" There were potatoes and carrots and a lot of things which I may have eaten, but completely failed to recognise in a raw state. And then suddenly, through a gap in the asparagus, I saw a vast yellowy-green object. It seemed about four times the size of an ordinary Rugby football, and a steady stream of people circled slowly round it and an ancient man, who periodically groomed it with a vast coloured handkerchief. So I steered a zigzag course between a watery-eyed duck on my right and a hand-holding couple on my left, and joined the stream. At close quarters it seemed even vaster than when viewed from the other side of the tent, and after I'd made the grand tour twice, I thought I'd engage the ancient man in conversation. Unfortunately, he was stone deaf, and his speech was a little indistinct owing to a regrettable absence of teeth, so we managed between us to rivet the fascinated attention of every human being in the tent. In return for the information that it was the largest

9

pumpkin ever produced in Kent, I volunteered
that I had come from London specially to write
about it. He seemed a bit hazy about London,
but when I told him it was larger than Appledore
he appeared fairly satisfied that his pumpkin
would obtain justice.

" He also launched into a voluble discourse,
which was robbed of much of its usefulness by
his habit of holding his false teeth in position with
his thumb as he spoke. Luckily a local interpreter was at hand, and from him I gathered that
the old man was eighty-five, and had never been
farther afield than Ashford, forty-eight years
ago. Also that he was still gardener at Cedarlime, a house which I must have passed on my
way from the station. Standing well back it
was : fine flower gardens—' but not what they
was. Not since the new gentleman come—a
year ago. Didn't take the same interest—not
him. A scholard, they said 'e was ; crates and
crates of books had come to the house—things
that 'eavy that they took three and four men to
lift them.'

" He rambled on did that interpreter, while the
ancient man polished the pumpkin in the time-
honoured manner, and wheezed spasmodically.
But I wasn't paying much attention, because it
had suddenly come back to me that Cedarlime
was the name of the house where I had spoken to
the inscrutable stranger. Subconsciously I had
noticed it as I crossed the road ; now it was
brought back to my memory.

" ' Is the owner of Cedarlime a youngish man ? ' I asked my informant. ' Dark hair; rather sallow face ? '

" He shook his head. The owner of Cedarlime was a middle-aged man with grey hair, but he often had friends stopping with him who came from London, so he'd heard tell—friends who didn't stop long—just for the week-end, maybe, or four or five days. Probably the man I meant was one of these friends.

" My informant passed on to inspect a red and hairy gooseberry, and I wandered slowly out of the stuffy tent. Probably a friend—in fact, undoubtedly a friend. But try as I would to concentrate on that confounded flower show, my thoughts kept harking back to Cedarlime. For some reason or other, that quiet house and the man who had come so silently out of the bushes had raised my curiosity. And at that moment I narrowly escaped death from a swing boat, which brought me back to the business in hand.

" I suppose it was about three hours later that I started to stroll back to the station. I was aiming at a five o'clock train, and intended to write my stuff on the way up to Town. But just as I was getting to the gates of the house that interested me, who should I see in front of me but the venerable pumpkin polisher. He turned as I got abreast of him and recognised me with a throaty chuckle. And he promptly started to talk. I gathered that he had many other priceless treasures in his garden—wonderful sweet peas, more pumpkins of colossal dimensions. And after a while I further gathered that he was suggesting I should go in and examine them for myself.

"For a moment I hesitated. I looked at my watch—there was plenty of time. Then I looked over the gates and made up my mind. I would introduce this ancient being into my account of the fête; write up, in his own setting, this extraordinary old man who had never left Appledore for forty-eight years. And, in addition, I would have a closer look at the house— possibly even see the scholarly owner.

"I glanced curiously round as I followed him up the drive. We went about half-way to the house, then turned off along a path into the kitchen garden. And finally he came to rest in front of the pumpkins—he was obviously a pumpkin maniac. I should think he conducted a monologue for five minutes on the habits of pumpkins while I looked about me. Occasionally I said ' Yes '; occasionally I nodded my head portentously; for the rest of the time I paid no attention.

"I could see half the front and one side of the house—but there seemed no trace of any occupants. And I was just going to ask the old man who lived there, when I saw a man in his shirt-sleeves standing at one of the windows. He was not the man who had spoken to me at the gate; he was not a grey-headed man either, so presumably not the owner. He appeared to be engrossed in something he was holding in his hands, and after a while he held it up to the light in the same way one holds up a photographic plate. It was then that he saw me.

"Now, I have never been an imaginative person, but there was something positively uncanny in the way that man disappeared. Literally in a flash he had gone and the window was empty. And my imagination began to stir. Why had that man vanished so instantaneously at the sight of a stranger in the kitchen garden?

"And then another thing began to strike me. Something which had been happening a moment or two before had abruptly stopped—a noise, faint and droning, but so steady that I hadn't noticed it until it ceased. It had been the sort of noise which, if you heard it to-day, you would say was caused by an aeroplane a great way off—and quite suddenly it had stopped. A second or two after the man had seen me and vanished from the window, that faint droning noise had ceased. I was sure of it, and my imagination began to stir still more.

"However, by this time my venerable guide had exhausted pumpkins, and, muttering strange words, he began to lead me towards another part of the garden. It was sweet-peas this time, and I must say they were really magnificent. In fact, I had forgotten the disappearing gentleman at the window in my genuine admiration of the flowers, when I suddenly saw the old man straighten himself up, take a firm grip of his false teeth with his one hand and touch his cap with the other. He was looking over my shoulder, and I swung round.

"Three men were standing behind me on the path. One was the man I had spoken to that morning; one was the man I had seen at the window; the other was grey-haired, and, I assumed, the owner of the house. It was to him I addressed myself.

"'I must apologise for trespassing,' I began, 'but I am reporting the agricultural fête down here, and your gardener asked me in to see your sweet-peas. They are really magnificent specimens.'

"The elderly man stared at me in silence.

"'I don't quite see what the sweet-peas in my garden have to do with the fête,' he remarked coldly. 'And it is not generally customary, when the owner is at home, to wander round his garden at the invitation of his gardener.'

"'Then I can only apologise and withdraw at once,' I answered stiffly. 'I trust that I have not irreparably damaged your paths.'

"He frowned angrily and seemed on the point of saying something, when the man I had spoken to at the gate took his arm and whispered something in his ear. I don't know what it was he said, but it had the effect of restoring the grey-haired man to a better temper at once.

"'I must apologise,' he said affably, 'for my brusqueness. I am a recluse, Mr.—ah—Mr.——'

"'Graham is my name,' I answered, partially mollified.

"He bowed. 'A recluse, Mr. Graham—and my garden is a hobby of mine. That and my books. I fear I may have seemed a little irritable when I first spoke, but I have a special system of my own for growing sweet-peas, and I guard it jealously. I confess that for a moment I was unjust and suspicious enough to think you might be trying to pump information from my gardener.'

"I looked at old Methuselah, still clutching his false teeth, and smiled involuntarily. The elderly man guessed my thoughts and smiled, too.

"'I am apt to forget that it takes several months to interpret old Jake,' he continued. 'Those false teeth of his fascinate one, don't they? I shall never forget the dreadful occasion he dropped them in the hot bed. We had the most agonising search, and finally persistence triumphed. They were rescued unscathed and restored to their rightful place.'

"And so he went on talking easily, until half-unconsciously I found myself strolling with him towards the house. Every now and then he stopped to point out some specimen of which he was proud, and, without my realising it, twenty minutes or so slipped by. It was the sound of a whistle at the station that recalled me to the passage of time, and I hurriedly looked at my watch.

"'Good Heavens!' I cried, 'I've missed my train. When is the next?'

" ' The next, Mr. Graham. I'm afraid there isn't a next till to-morrow morning. This is a branch line, you know.'

" Jove! how I swore inwardly. After what old Andrews had said to me only that morning, to go and fail again would finally cook my goose. You must remember that it was before the days of motor-cars, and, with the fête in progress, the chance of getting a cart to drive me some twelve miles to Ashford was remote—anyway for the fare I could afford to pay.

" I suppose my agitation showed on my face, for the grey-haired man became quite upset.

" ' How stupid of me not to have thought of the time,' he cried. ' We must think of the best thing to do. I know,' he said suddenly—' you must telegraph your report. Stop the night here and telegraph.'

" I pointed out to him rather miserably that newspapers did not like the expense of wiring news unless it was important, and that by no stretch of imagination could the Appledore Flower Show be regarded as coming under that category.

" ' I will pay the cost,' he insisted, and waved aside my refusal. ' Mr. Graham,' he said, ' it was my fault. I am a wealthy man; I would not dream of letting you suffer for my verbosity. You will wire your article, and I shall pay.' "

The Writer smiled reminiscently.

" What could have been more charming," he continued—" what more considerate and courteous ? My stupid, half-formed suspicions, which had been growing fainter and fainter as I strolled round the garden with my host, had by this time vanished completely, and when he found me pens, ink, and paper, as they say in the French exercise book, I stammered out my thanks. He cut me short with a smile, and told me to get on with my article. He would send it to the telegraph office, and tell his servants to get a room ready for me. And with another smile he left me alone, and I saw him pottering about the garden outside as I wrote.

" I don't know whether it has ever happened to any of you fellows "—the Writer lit a cigarette —" to harbour suspicions which are gradually lulled, only to have them suddenly return with redoubled force. There was I, peacefully writing my account of the Appledore fête, while outside my host, an enthusiastic gardener, as he had told me, pursued his hobby. Could anything have been more commonplace and matter of fact ? He was engaged on the roses at the moment, spraying them with some solution, presumably for green fly, and unconsciously I watched him. No, I reflected, it couldn't be for green fly, because he was only spraying the roots, and even I, though not an expert, knew that green fly occur round the buds. And at that moment I caught a momentary glimpse of the two other men. They were roaring with laughter, and it seemed to me that my host was the cause of the merriment. He looked up and saw them, and the hilarity ceased abruptly. The next moment they had disappeared, and my host was continuing the spraying. He went on industriously for a few minutes, then he crossed the lawn towards the open window of the room where I was writing.

" ' Nearly finished ? ' he asked.

" ' Very nearly,' I answered. ' Green fly bad this year ? '

" ' Green fly ? ' he said a little vaguely. ' Oh ! so-so.'

" ' I thought you must be tackling them on the roses,' I pursued.

" ' Er, quite—quite,' he remarked. ' Nasty things, aren't they ? '

" ' Is it a special system of yours to go for the roots ? ' I asked.

" He gave me one searching look, then he laughed mysteriously.

" ' Ah, ha ! my young friend,' he answered. ' Don't you try and get my stable secrets out of me.'

" And I felt he was lying. Without thinking something made me draw a bow at a venture, and the arrow went home with a vengeance.

" ' Wonderful delphiniums you've got,' I remarked, leaning out of the window and pointing to a bed underneath.

" ' Yes,' he said. ' I'm very proud of those.'

" And the flowers at which I was pointing were irises. So this enthusiastic gardener did not know the difference between a delphinium and an iris. Back in an overwhelming wave came all my suspicions; I knew there was a mystery somewhere. This man wasn't a gardener; and, if not, why this pretence? I remember now that every time he had drawn my attention to a specimen he had taken the attached label in his hand. Quite unobtrusive it had been, unnoticeable at the time, now it suddenly became significant. Why was he playing this part—pretending for my benefit? Futilely spraying the roots of roses, making me miss my train. I was convinced now that that had been part of the plan— but why? Why the telegraphing? Why the invitation to stop the night?

" The old brain was working pretty quickly by this time. No one, whatever his business, would object to a *bona fide* journalist writing an account of a fête, and if the business were crooked, the people engaged on it would be the first to speed that journalist on his way. People of that type dislike journalists only one degree less than the police. Then why—why? The answer simply stuck out—they suspected me of not being a journalist, or, even if they did not go as far as that, they were taking no chances on the matter.

" In fact, I was by this time definitely convinced in my own mind that I had quite unwittingly stumbled into a bunch of criminals, and it struck me that the sooner I stumbled out again the better for my health. So I put my article in my pocket and went to the door. I would wire it off, and I would not return.

"The first hitch occurred at the door, which had thoughtfully been locked. Not being a hero of fiction, I confess it gave me a nasty shock— that unyielding door. And as I stood there taking a pull at myself I heard the grey-haired man's voice outside the window :

" ' Finished yet, Mr. Graham ? '

"I walked across the room, and in as steady a voice as I could muster I mentioned the fact that the door was locked.

" ' So that you shouldn't be disturbed, Mr. Graham '—and I thought of the Wolf in ' Red Riding Hood,' with his satisfactory answers to all awkward questions.

" ' If someone would open it, I'll get along to the telegraph office,' I remarked.

" ' I wouldn't dream of your going to so much trouble,' he said suavely. ' I've a lazy boy I employ in the garden ; he'll take it.'

"For a moment I hesitated, and a glint came into his eyes, which warned me to be careful.

"It was then that I had my brainstorm. If I hadn't had it I shouldn't be here now ; if the powers that be in the newspaper world were not the quickest people on the uptake you can meet in a day's march, I shouldn't be here now either. But like a flash of light there came to my mind the story I had once been told of how a war correspondent in the South African War, at a time when they were tightening the censorship, got back full news of a battle by alluding to the rise and fall of certain stock. And the editor in

England read between the lines—substituted troops for stocks, Canadians for C.P.R., and so on—and published the only account of the battle.

" Could I do the same ? I hesitated.

" ' Oh ! there's one thing I've forgotten,' I remarked. ' I'll just add it if the boy can wait.'

" So I sat down at the table, and to my report I added the following sentences :

" ' There was also some excellent mustard and cress. Will come at once, but fear to-morrow morning may be too late for me to be of further use over Ronaldshay affair.'

" And then I handed it to the grey-haired man through the window."

The Writer leant back in his chair, and the Soldier stared at him, puzzled.

" It's a bit too cryptic for me," he confessed.

" Thank God ! it wasn't too cryptic for the office," said the Writer. " There was no Ronaldshay affair, so I knew that would draw their attention. And perhaps you've forgotten the name of our star reporter, who dealt in criminal matters. It was Cresswill. And if you write the word cress with a capital C and leave out the full stop after it, you'll see the message I got through to the office."

" It's uncommon lucky for you his name wasn't Snooks," remarked the Actor with a grin. " What happened ? "

" Well, we had dinner, and I can only suppose

that my attempts to appear at ease had failed to convince my companions.

"The last thing I remember that night was drinking a cup of coffee—the old trick—and suddenly realising it was drugged. I staggered to my feet, while they remained sitting round the table watching me. Then, with a final glimpse of the grey-haired man's face, I passed into oblivion.

"When I came to I was in a strange room, feeling infernally sick. And I shall never forget my wild relief when the man by the window turned round and I saw it was Cresswill himself. He came over to the bed and smiled down at me.

"'Well done, youngster,' he said, and a glow of pride temporarily replaced my desire for a basin. 'Well done, indeed. We've got the whole gang, and we've been looking for 'em for months. They were bank-note forgers on a big scale, but we were only just in time to save you.'

"'How was that?' I asked weakly.

"'I think they had decided that your sphere of usefulness was over,' he remarked with a grin. 'So after having removed suspicion by telegraphing your report, they gave you a very good dinner, when, as has been known to happen with young men before, you got very drunk.'

"'I was drugged,' I said indignantly.

"'The point is immaterial,' he answered quietly. 'Drunk or drugged, it's much the same after you've been run over by a train. And we found two of them carrying you along a lane towards the line at half-past eleven. The down goods to Hastings passes at twenty to twelve.'

"And at that moment Providence was kind. I ceased to *feel* sick. I was."

I

I DON'T pretend to account for it; I am merely giving the plain unvarnished tale of what took place to my certain knowledge at Jack Drage's house in Kent during the week-end which finished so disastrously. Doubtless there is an explanation: maybe there are several. The believers in spiritualism and things psychic will probably say that the tragedy was due to the action of a powerful influence which had remained intact throughout the centuries; the materialists will probably say it was due to indigestion. I hold no brief for either side: as the mere narrator, the facts are good enough for me. And, anyway, the extremists of both schools of thought are quite irreconcilable.

There were six of us there, counting Jack Drage and his wife. Bill Sibton in the Indian Civil, Armytage in the Gunners, and I—Staunton by name, and a scribbler of sorts—were the men: little Joan Neilson—Armytage's fiancée—supported Phyllis Drage. Ostensibly we were there to shoot a few pheasants, but it was more than a mere shooting party. It was a reunion after long years of us four men who had been known at

school as the Inseparables. Bill had been in
India for twelve years, save for the inevitable gap
in Mesopotamia; Dick Armytage had soldiered
all over the place ever since he'd left the Shop.
And though I'd seen Jack off and on since our
school-days, I'd lost touch with him since he'd
married. Wives play the deuce with bachelor
friends though they indignantly deny it—God
bless 'em. At least, mine always does.

It was the first time any of us had been inside
Jack's house, and undoubtedly he had the most
delightful little property. The house itself was
old, but comfortably modernised by an expert,
so that the charm of it still remained. In fact,
the only room which had been left absolutely
intact was the dining-room. And to have
touched that would have been sheer vandalism.
The sole thing that had been done to it was to
install central heating, and that had been carried
out so skilfully that no trace of the work could
be seen.

It was a room by itself, standing apart from the
rest of the house, with a lofty vaulted roof in
which one could just see the smoky old oak
beams by the light of the candles on the dinner-
table. A huge open fireplace jutted out from one
of the longer walls; while on the opposite side a
door led into the garden. And then, at one end,
approached by the original staircase at least six
centuries old, was the musicians' gallery.

A wonderful room—a room in which it seemed
almost sacrilege to eat and smoke and discuss

10

present-day affairs—a room in which one felt that history had been made. Nothing softened the severe plainness of the walls save a few mediæval pikes and battleaxes. In fact, two old muskets of the Waterloo era were the most modern implements of the collection Of pictures there was only one—a very fine painting of a man dressed in the fashion of the Tudor period— which hung facing the musicians' gallery.

It was that that caught my eye as we sat down to dinner, and I turned to Jack.

" An early Drage ? " I asked.

" As a matter of fact—no relation at all," he answered. " But a strong relation to this room. That's why I hang him there."

" Any story attached thereto ? "

" There is ; though I can't really do it justice. The parson here is the only man who knows the whole yarn.—By the way, old dear," he spoke to his wife across the table, " the reverend bird takes tea with us to-morrow. But he is the only man who has the thing at his finger tips. The previous owner was a bit vague himself, but having a sense of the fitness of things, he gave me a chance of buying the picture. Apparently it's a painting of one Sir James Wrothley who lived round about the time of Henry VIII. He was either a rabid Protestant or a rabid Roman Catholic—I told you I was a bit vague over details—and he used this identical room as a secret meeting-place for himself and his pals to hatch plots against his enemies."

" Jack *is* so illuminating, isn't he ? " laughed his wife.

" Well, I bet you can't tell it any better yourself," he retorted with a grin. " I admit my history is weak. But anyway, about that time, if the jolly old Protestants weren't burning the R.C.'s, the R.C.'s were burning the Protestants. A period calling for great tact, I've always thought. Well, at any rate, this Sir James Wrothley—when his party was being officially burned—came here and hatched dark schemes to reverse the procedure. And then, apparently, one day somebody blew the gaff, and the whole bunch of conspirators in here were absolutely caught in the act by the other crowd, who put 'em all to death on the spot. Which is all I can tell you about it."

" I must ask the padre to-morrow," I said to his wife. " I'd rather like to hear the whole story. I felt when I first came into this room there was history connected with it."

She looked at me rather strangely for a moment ; then she gave a little forced laugh.

" Do you know, Tom," she said slowly, " at times I almost hate this room. All my friends gnash their teeth with envy over it—but sometimes, when Jack's been away, and I've dined in here by myself—it's terrified me. I feel as if— I wasn't alone : as if—there were people all round me—watching me. Of course, it's absurd, I know. But I can't help it. And yet I'm not a nervy sort of person."

" I don't think it's at all absurd," I assured her. " I believe I should feel the same myself. A room of this size, which, of necessity, is dimly lighted in the corners, and which is full of historical associations, must cause an impression on the least imaginative person."

" We used it once for a dance," she laughed ; " with a ragtime band in the gallery."

" And a great show it was, too," broke in her husband. " The trouble was that one of the musicians got gay with a bottle of whisky, and very nearly fell clean through that balustrade effect on to the floor below. I haven't had that touched—and the wood is rotten."

" I pray you be seated, gentlemen." A sudden silence fell on the table, and everybody stared at Bill Sibton.

" Is it a game, Bill ? " asked Jack Drage. " I rather thought we were. And what about the ladies ? "

With a puzzled frown Bill Sibton looked at him. " Did I speak out loud, then ? " he asked slowly.

" And so early in the evening too ! " Joan Neilson laughed merrily.

" I must have been day-dreaming, I suppose. But that yarn of yours has rather got me, Jack ; though in the course of a long and evil career I've never heard one told worse. I was thinking of that meeting—all of them sitting here. And then suddenly that door bursting open." He was staring fixedly at the door, and again a silence fell on us all.

" The thunder of the butts of their muskets on the woodwork." He swung round and faced the door leading to the garden. " And on that one, too. Can't you hear them ? No escape—none. Caught like rats in a trap." His voice died away to a whisper, and Joan Neilson gave a little nervous laugh.

" You're the most realistic person, Mr. Sibton. I think I prefer hearing about the dance."

I glanced at my hostess—and it seemed to me that there was fear in her eyes as she looked at Bill. Sometimes now I wonder if she had some vague premonition of impending disaster : something too intangible to take hold of—something the more terrifying on that very account.

It was after dinner that Jack Drage switched on the solitary electric light of which the room boasted. It was so placed as to show up the painting of Sir James Wrothley, and in silence we all gathered round to look at it. A pair of piercing eyes set in a stern aquiline face stared down at us from under the brim of a hat adorned with sweeping plumes ; his hand rested on the jewelled hilt of his sword. It was a fine picture in a splendid state of preservation, well worthy of its place of honour on the walls of such a room, and we joined in a general chorus of admiration. Only Bill Sibton was silent, and he seemed fascinated—unable to tear his eyes away from the painting.

" As a matter of fact, Bill," said Dick Army-tage, studying the portrait critically, " he might

well be an ancestor of yours. Wash out your
moustache, and give you a fancy-dress hat, and
you'd look very much like the old bean."

He was quite right : there was a distinct
resemblance, and it rather surprised me that I
had not noticed it myself. There were the same
deep-set piercing eyes, the same strong, slightly
hatchet face, the same broad forehead. Even
the colouring was similar : a mere coincidence
that, probably—but one which increased the
likeness. In fact, the longer I looked the more
pronounced did the resemblance become, till it
was almost uncanny.

"Well, he can't be, anyway," said Bill
abruptly. "I've never heard of any Wrothley
in the family." He looked away from the
picture almost with an effort and lit a cigarette.
"It's a most extraordinary thing, Jack," he
went on after a moment, "but ever since we
came into this room I've had a feeling that I've
been here before."

"Good Lord, man, that's common enough in
all conscience. One often gets that idea."

"I know one does," answered Bill. "I've had
it before myself ; but never one-tenth as strongly
as I feel it here. Besides, that feeling generally
dies—after a few minutes : it's growing stronger
and stronger with me every moment I stop in
here."

"Then let's go into the drawing-room," said
our hostess. "I've had the card-table put in
there."

We followed her and Joan Neilson into the
main part of the house ; and since neither of the
ladies played, for the next two hours we four
men bridged. And then, seeing that it was a
special occasion, we sat yarning over half-for-
gotten incidents till the room grew thick with
smoke and the two women fled to bed before
they died of asphyxiation.

Bill, I remember, waxed eloquent on the
subject of politicians, with a six weeks' experience of India, butting in on things they knew less
than nothing about ; Dick Armytage grew melan-
choly on the subject of the block in promotion.
And then the reminiscences grew more personal,
and the whisky sank lower and lower in the
tantalus as one yarn succeeded another.

At last Jack Drage rose with a yawn and
knocked the ashes out of his pipe.

" Two o'clock, boys. What about bed ? "

" Lord ! is it really ? " Dick Armytage
stretched himself. " However, no shooting to-
morrow, or, rather, to-day. We might spend
the Sabbath dressing Bill up as his nibs in the
next room."

A shadow crossed Bill's face.

" I'd forgotten that room," he said, frowning.
" Damn you, Dick ! "

" My dear old boy," laughed Armytage, " you
surely don't mind resembling the worthy Sir
James ! He's a deuced sight better-looking
fellow than you are."

Bill shook his head irritably.

"It isn't that at all," he said. "I wasn't thinking of the picture." He seemed to be on the point of saying something else—then he changed his mind. "Well—bed for master."

We all trooped upstairs, and Jack came round to each of us to see that we were all right.

"Breakfast provisionally nine," he remarked. "Night-night, old boy."

The door closed behind him, and his steps died away down the passage as he went to his own room.

.   .   .   .   .

By all known rules I should have been asleep almost as my head touched the pillow. A day's rough shooting, followed by bed at two in the morning should produce that result if anything can, but in my case that night it didn't. Whether I had smoked too much, or what it was, I know not, but at half-past three I gave up the attempt and switched on my light. Then I went over, and pulling up an armchair, I sat down by the open window. There was no moon, and the night was warm for the time of year. Outlined against the sky the big dining-room stretched out from the house, and, as I lit a cigarette, Jack Drage's vague story returned to my mind. The conspirators, meeting by stealth to hatch some sinister plot; the sudden alarm as they found themselves surrounded; the desperate fight against overwhelming odds—and then, the end. There should be a story in it, I reflected; I'd get the parson to tell me the whole thing

accurately next day. The local colour seemed
more appropriate when one looked at the room
from the outside, with an occasional cloud
scudding by over the big trees beyond. Savoured
more of conspiracy and death than when dining
inside, with reminiscences of a jazz band in the
musicians' gallery.

And at that moment a dim light suddenly
filtered out through the windows. It was so dim
that at first I thought I had imagined it ; so dim
that I switched off my own light in order to make
sure. There was no doubt about it : faint but
unmistakable the reflection showed up on the
ground outside. A light had been lit in the old
dining-room : therefore someone must be in
there. At four o'clock in the morning !

For a moment or two I hesitated : should I go
along and rouse Jack ? Someone might have
got in through the garden door, and I failed to
see why I should fight another man's burglar in
his own house. And then it struck me it would
only alarm his wife—I'd get Bill, whose room was
opposite mine.

I put on some slippers and crossed the landing
to rouse him. And then I stopped abruptly.
His door was open ; his room was empty.
Surely it couldn't be he who had turned on the
light below ?

As noiselessly as possible I went downstairs,
and turned along the passage to the dining-room.
Sure enough the door into the main part of the
house was ajar, and the light was shining

through the opening. I tiptoed up to it and looked through the crack by the hinges.

At first I could see nothing save the solitary electric light over the portrait of Sir James. And then in the gloom beyond I saw a tall figure standing motionless by the old oak dining-table. It was Bill—even in the dim light I recognised that clean-cut profile; Bill clad in his pyjamas only, with one hand stretched out in front of him, pointing. And then, suddenly, he spoke.

" You lie, Sir Henry!—you lie! "

Nothing more—just that one remark; his hand still pointing inexorably across the table. Then after a moment he turned so that the light fell full on his face, and I realised what was the matter. Bill Sibton was walking in his sleep.

Slowly he came towards the door behind which I stood, and passed through it—so close that he almost touched me as I shrank back against the wall. Then he went up the stairs, and as soon as I heard him reach the landing above, I quickly turned out the light in the dining-room and followed him. His bedroom door was closed : there was no sound from inside.

There was nothing more for me to do : my burglar had developed into a harmless somnambulist. Moreover, it suddenly struck me that I had become most infernally sleepy myself. So I did not curse Bill mentally as much as I might have done. I turned in, and my nine o'clock next morning was very provisional.

So was Bill Sibton's : we arrived together for

breakfast at a quarter to ten. He looked haggard and ill, like a man who has not slept, and his first remark was to curse Dick Armytage.

"I had the most infernal dreams last night," he grumbled. "Entirely through Dick reminding me of this room. I dreamed the whole show that took place in here in that old bird's time."

He pointed to the portrait of Sir James.

"Did you?" I remarked, pouring out some coffee. "Must have been quite interesting."

"I know I wasn't at all popular with the crowd," he said. "I don't set any store by dreams myself—but last night it was really extraordinarily vivid." He stirred his tea thoughtfully.

"I can quite imagine that, Bill. Do you ever walk in your sleep?"

"Walk in my sleep? No." He stared at me surprised. "Why?"

"You did last night. I found you down here at four o'clock in your pyjamas. You were standing just where I'm sitting now, pointing with your hand across the table. And as I stood outside the door you suddenly said, 'You lie, Sir Henry!—you lie!'"

"Part of my dream," he muttered. "Sir Henry Brayton was the name of the man—and he was the leader. They were all furious with me about something. We quarrelled—and after that there seemed to be a closed door. It was opening slowly, and instinctively I knew there was something dreadful behind it. You know the terror of a dream ; the primordial terror of the mind that cannot reason against something hideous—unknown——" I glanced at him : his forehead was wet with sweat. " And then the dream passed. The door didn't open."

" Undoubtedly, my lad," I remarked lightly, " you had one whisky too many last night."

" Don't be an ass, Tom," he said irritably. " I tell you—though you needn't repeat it—I'm in a putrid funk of this room. Absurd, I know : ridiculous. But I can't help it. And if there was a train on this branch line on Sunday, I'd leave to-day."

" But, good Lord, Bill," I began—and then I went on with my breakfast. There was a look on his face which it is not good to see on the face of a man. It was terror : an abject, dreadful terror.

II

He and Jack Drage were out for a long walk when the parson came to tea that afternoon—a walk of which Bill had been the instigator. He had dragged Jack forth, vigorously protesting, after lunch, and we had cheered them on their way. Bill had to get out of the house—I could see that. Then Dick and the girl had disappeared, in the way that people in their condition *do* disappear, just before Mr. Williams arrived. And so only Phyllis Drage was there, presiding at the tea-table, when I broached the subject of the history of the dining-room.

" He spoils paper, Mr. Williams," laughed my hostess, " and he scents copy. Jack tried to tell the story last night, and got it hopelessly wrong."

The clergyman smiled gravely.

" You'll have to alter the setting, Mr. Staunton," he remarked, " because the story is quite well known round here. In my library at the vicarage I have an old manuscript copy of the legend. And indeed, I have no reason to believe that it is a legend : certainly the main points have been historically authenticated. Sir James Wrothley, whose portrait hangs in the dining-room, lived in this house. He was a staunch Protestant—bigoted to a degree ; and he fell very foul of Cardinal Wolsey, who you may remember was plotting for the Papacy at the time. So bitter did the animosity become, and so high did religious intoleration run in those days, that Sir James started counter-plotting against the Cardinal ; which was a dangerous thing to do. Moreover, he and his friends used the dining-room here as their meeting-place."

The reverend gentleman sipped his tea ; if there was one thing he loved it was the telling of this story, which reflected so magnificently on the staunch no-Popery record of his parish.

" So much is historical certainty ; the rest is not so indisputably authentic. The times of the meetings were, of course, kept secret—until the fatal night occurred. Then, apparently, some-

one turned traitor. And, why I cannot tell you,
Sir James himself was accused by the others—
especially Sir Henry Brayton. Did you say
anything, Mr. Staunton ? "

"Nothing," I remarked quietly. " The name
surprised me for a moment. Please go on."

"Sir Henry Brayton was Sir James's next-
door neighbour, almost equally intolerant of
anything savouring of Rome. And even while,
so the story goes, Wolsey's men were hammering
on the doors, he and Sir Henry had this dreadful
quarrel. Why Sir James should have been
suspected, whether the suspicions were justified
or not I cannot say. Certainly, in view of what
we know of Sir James's character, it seems hard
to believe that he could have been guilty of such
infamous treachery. But that the case must
have appeared exceedingly black against him is
certain from the last and most tragic part of
the story."

Once again Mr. Williams paused to sip his
tea ; he had now reached that point of the
narrative where royalty itself would have failed
to hurry him.

"In those days, Mrs. Drage, there was a door
leading into the musicians' gallery from one of
the rooms of the house. It provided no avenue
of escape if the house was surrounded—but its
existence was unknown to the men before whose
blows the other doors were already beginning to
splinter. And suddenly through this door
appeared Lady Wrothley. She had only re-

cently married Sir James : in fact, her first baby
was then on its way. Sir James saw her, and
at once ceased his quarrel with Sir Henry. With
dignity he mounted the stairs and approached
his girl-wife—and in her horror-struck eyes he
saw that she, too, suspected him of being the
traitor. He raised her hand to his lips ; and
then as the doors burst open simultaneously and
Wolsey's men rushed in—he dived headforemost
on to the floor below, breaking his neck and dying
instantly.

"The story goes on to say," continued Mr.
Williams, with a diffident cough, "that even
while the butchery began in the room below—for
most of the Protestants were unarmed—the poor
girl collapsed in the gallery, and shortly afterwards the child was born. A girl baby, who
survived, though the mother died. One likes to
think that if she had indeed misjudged her
husband, it was a merciful act on the part of
the Almighty to let her join him so soon. Thank
you, I will have another cup of tea. One lump,
please."

"A most fascinating story, Mr. Williams,"
said Phyllis. "Thank you so much for having
told us. Can you make anything out of it,
Tom ? "

I laughed.

"The criminal reserves his defence. But it's
most interesting, Padre, most interesting, as Mrs.
Drage says. If I may, I'd like to come and see
that manuscript."

" I shall be only too delighted," he murmured with old-fashioned courtesy. " Whenever you like."

And then the conversation turned on things parochial until he rose to go. The others had still not returned, and for a while we two sat on talking as the spirit moved us in the darkening room. At last the servants appeared to draw the curtains, and it was then that we heard Jack and Bill in the hall.

I don't know what made me make the remark ; it seemed to come without my volition.

" If I were you, Phyllis," I said, " I don't think I'd tell the story of the dining-room to Bill."

She looked at me curiously.

" Why not ? "

" I don't know—but I wouldn't." In the brightly lit room his fears of the morning seemed ridiculous ; yet, as I say, I don't know what made me make the remark.

" All right ; I won't," she said gravely. " Do you think——"

But further conversation was cut short by the entrance of Bill and her husband.

" Twelve miles if an inch," growled Drage, throwing himself into a chair. " You awful fellow."

Sibton laughed.

" Do you good, you lazy devil. He's getting too fat, Phyllis, isn't he ? "

I glanced at him as he, too, sat down : in his

eyes there remained no trace of the terror of the morning.

III

And now I come to that part of my story which I find most difficult to write. From the story-teller's point of view pure and simple, it is the easiest; from the human point of view I have never tackled anything harder. Because, though the events I am describing took place months ago—and the first shock is long since past—I still cannot rid myself of a feeling that I was largely to blame. By the cold light of reason I can exonerate myself; but one does not habitually have one's being in that exalted atmosphere. Jack blames himself; but in view of what happened the night before—in view of the look in Bill's eyes that Sunday morning—I feel that I ought to have realised that there were influences at work which lay beyond my ken— influences which at present lie not within the light of reason. And then at other times I wonder if it was not just a strange coincidence and an—accident. God knows: frankly, I don't.

We spent that evening just as we had spent the preceding one, save that in view of shooting on Monday morning we went to bed at midnight. This time I fell asleep at once—only to be roused by someone shaking my arm. I sat up blinking: it was Jack Drage.

"Wake up, Tom," he whispered. "There's

11

a light in the dining-room, and we're going down to investigate. Dick is getting Bill."

In an instant I was out of bed.

" It's probably Bill himself," I said. " I found him down there last night walking in his sleep."

" The devil you did ! " muttered Jack, and at that moment Dick Armytage came in.

" Bill's room is empty," he announced ; and I nodded.

" It's Bill right enough," I said. " He went back quite quietly last night. And, for Heaven's sake, you fellows, don't wake him. It's very dangerous."

Just as before the dining-room door was open, and the light filtered through into the passage as we tiptoed along it. Just as before we saw Bill standing by the table—his hand outstretched.

Then came the same words as I had heard last night.

" You lie, Sir Henry !—you lie ! "

" What the devil——" muttered Jack ; but I held up my finger to ensure silence.

" He'll come to bed now," I whispered. " Keep quite still."

But this time Bill Sibton did not come to bed ; instead, he turned and stared into the shadows of the musicians' gallery. Then, very slowly, he walked away from us and commenced to mount the stairs. And still the danger did not strike us.

Dimly we saw the tall figure reach the top and

walk along the gallery, as if he saw someone at the end—and at that moment the peril came to the three of us.

To Dick and Jack the rottenness of the balustrade; to me—*the end of the vicar's story.* What they thought I know not; but to my dying day I shall never forget my own agony of mind. In that corner of the musicians' gallery—though we could see her not—stood Lady Wrothley; to the man walking slowly towards her the door was opening slowly—the door which had remained shut the night before—the door behind which lay the terror.

And then it all happened very quickly. In a frenzy we raced across the room to get at him—but we weren't in time. There was a rending of wood—a dreadful crash—a sprawling figure on the floor below. To me it seemed as if he had hurled himself against the balustrade, had literally dived downwards. The others did not notice it—so they told me later. But I did.

And then we were kneeling beside him on the floor.

" Dear God! " I heard Drage say in a hoarse whisper. " He's dead; he's broken his neck."

. . . . .

Such is my story. Jack Drage blames himself for the rottenness of the woodwork, but I feel it was my fault. Yes—it was my fault. I ought to have known, ought to have done something. Even if we'd only locked the dining-room door.

And the last link in the chain I haven't

mentioned yet. The vicar supplied that—though to him it was merely a strange coincidence.

The baby-girl—born in the gallery—a strange, imaginative child, so run the archives, subject to fits of awful depression and, at other times, hallucinations—married. She married in 1551, on the 30th day of October, Henry, only son of Frank Sibton and Mary his wife.

God knows: I don't. It may have been an accident.

I

" But, Bill, I don't understand.   How much did
you borrow from this man ? "

Sybil Daventry looked at her brother, sitting
huddled up in his chair, with a little frown.

" I borrowed a thousand," he answered,
sulkily.   " And like a fool I didn't read the
thing he made me sign—at least, not carefully.
Hang it, I've only had the money six months,
and now he's saying that I owe him over two.   I
saw something about twenty-five per cent., and
now I find it was twenty-five per cent. a month.
And the swine is pressing for payment unless
——"   He broke off and stared into the fire
shamefacedly.

" Unless what ? " demanded his sister.

" Well, you see, it's this way."   The boy
stammered a little, and refused to look at her.
" I was jolly well up the spout when this blighter
told me what I owed him, and I suppose I must
have showed it pretty clearly.   Anyway, I was
propping up the bar at the Cri., getting a cocktail,
when a fellow standing next me started gassing.
Not a bad sort of cove at all ; knows you very
well by sight."

" Knows me ? " said the girl, bewildered.
" Who was he ? "

" I'm coming to that later," went on her
brother. " Well, we had a couple more and
then he suggested tearing a chop together. And
I don't know—he seemed so decent and all that
—that I told him I was in the soup. Told him
the whole yarn and asked his advice sort of
business. Well, as I say, he was bally sporting
about it all, and finally asked me who the bird
was who had tied up the boodle. I told him,
and here's the lucky part of the whole show—
this fellow Perrison knew him. Perrison was
the man I was lunching with."

He paused and lit a cigarette, while the girl
stared at him gravely.

" Well," she said at length, " go on."

" It was after lunch that he got busy. He
said to me : ' Look here, Daventry, you've made
a bally fool of yourself, but you're not the first.
I'll write a note to Messrs. Smith and Co.'—
those are the warriors who gave me the money—
' and try and persuade them to give you more
time, or even possibly reduce the rate of interest.'
Of course, I was all on this, and I arranged to
lunch with him again next day, after Smith and
Co. had had time to function. And sure enough
they did. Wrote a letter in which they were all
over me ; any friend of Mr. Perrison's was
entitled to special treatment, and so on and so
forth. Naturally I was as bucked as a dog with
two tails, and asked Perrison if I couldn't do

something more material than just thank him.
And—er—he—I mean it was then he told me
he knew you by sight."

He glanced at his sister, and then quickly
looked away again.

" He suggested—er—that perhaps I could
arrange to introduce him to you ; that it would
be an honour he would greatly appreciate, and
all that sort of rot."

The girl was sitting very still. " Yes," she
said, quietly, " and you—agreed."

" Well, of course I did. Hang it, he's quite a
decent fellow. Bit Cityish to look at, and I
shouldn't think he knows which end of a horse
goes first. But he's got me out of the devil of
a hole, Sybil, and the least you can do is to be
moderately decent to the bird. I mean it's
not asking much, is it ? I left the governor
looking at him in the hall as if he was just going
to tread on his face, and that long slab—your
pal—is gazing at him through his eyeglasses as if
he was mad."

" He's not my pal, Bill." Sybil Daventry's
colour heightened a little.

" Well, you asked him here, anyway," grunted
the boy. Then with a sudden change of tone he
turned to her appealingly. " Syb, old girl—for
the Lord's sake play the game. You know what
the governor is, and if he hears about this show
—especially as it's—as it's not the first time—
there'll be the deuce to pay. You know he said
last time that if it happened again he'd turn me

out of the house. And the old man is as stub-
born as a mule. I only want you to be a bit
decent to Perrison."

She looked at him with a grave smile. " If
Mr. Perrison is satisfied with my being decent to
him, as you put it, I'm perfectly prepared to play
the game. But——" She frowned and rose abruptly. " Come on, and I'll have a look at him."

In silence they went downstairs. Tea had
just been brought in, and the house-party was
slowly drifting into the hall. But Sybil barely
noticed them ; her eyes were fixed on the man
talking to her father. Or rather, at the moment,
her father was talking to the man, and his
remark was painfully audible.

" There is a very good train back to London
at seven-thirty, Mr.—ah—Mr.——"

Her brother stepped forward. " But I say,
Dad," he said, nervously, " I asked Perrison to
stop the night. I've just asked Sybil, and she
says she can fix him up somewhere."

" How do you do, Mr. Perrison ? " With a
charming smile she held out her hand. " Of
course you must stop the night."

Then she moved away to the tea-table,
feeling agreeably relieved ; it was better than
she had expected. The man was well-dressed ;
perhaps, to her critical eye, a little too well-
dressed—but still quite presentable.

" You averted a catastrophe, Miss Daventry."
A lazy voice beside her interrupted her thoughts,
and with a smile she turned to the speaker.

" Dad is most pestilentially rude at times, isn't he ? And Bill told me he left *you* staring at the poor man as if he was an insect."

Archie Longworth laughed.

" He'd just contradicted your father flatly as you came downstairs. And on a matter concerning horses. However—the breeze has passed. But, tell me," he stared at her gravely, " why the sudden invasion ? "

Her eyebrows went up a little. " May I ask why not ? " she said, coldly. " Surely my brother can invite a friend to the house if he wishes."

" I stand corrected," answered Longworth, quietly. " Has he known him long ? "

" I haven't an idea," said the girl. " And after all, Mr. Longworth, I hadn't known you very long when I asked you."

And then, because she realised that there was a possibility of construing rather more into her words than she had intended, she turned abruptly to speak to another guest. So she failed to see the sudden inscrutable look that came into Archie Longworth's keen blue eyes—the quick clenching of his powerful fists. But when a few minutes later she again turned to him, he was just his usual lazy self.

" Do you think your logic is very good ? " he demanded. " You might have made a mistake as well."

" You mean that you think my brother has ? " she said, quickly.

"It is visible on the surface to the expert eye," he returned, gravely. "But, in addition, I happen to have inside information."

"Do you know Mr. Perrison, then?"

He nodded. "Yes, I have—er—met him before."

"But he doesn't know you," cried the girl.

"No—at least—er—we'll leave it at that. And I would be obliged, Miss Daventry, in case you happen to be speaking to him, if you would refrain from mentioning the fact that I know him." He stared at her gravely.

"You're very mysterious, Mr. Longworth," said the girl, with an attempt at lightness.

"And if I may I will prolong my visit until our friend departs," continued Longworth.

"Why, of course," she said, bending over the tea-tray. "You weren't thinking of going— going yet, were you?"

"I was thinking after lunch that I should have to go to-morrow," he said, putting down his tea-cup.

"But why so soon?" she asked, and her voice was low. "Aren't you enjoying yourself?"

"In the course of a life that has taken me into every corner of the globe," he answered, slowly, "I have never dreamed that I could be so utterly and perfectly happy as I have been here. It has opened my mind to a vista of the Things that Might Be—if the Things that Had Been were different. But as you grow older, Sybil,

you will learn one bitter truth : no human being
can ever be exactly what he seems. Masks?
just masks! And underneath—God and that
being alone know."

He rose abruptly, and she watched him bending over Lady Granton with his habitual lazy
grace. The indolent smile was round his lips—
the irrepressible twinkle was in his eyes. But
for the first time he had called her Sybil; for
the first time—she *knew*. The vague forebodings
conjured up by his words were swamped by that
one outstanding fact; she *knew*. And nothing
else mattered.

II

It was not until Perrison joined her in the
conservatory after dinner that she found herself
called on to play the part set her by her
brother.

She had gone there—though nothing would
have induced her to admit the fact—in the hope
that someone else would follow : the man with
the lazy blue eyes and the eyeglass. And then
instead of him had come Perrison, with a shade
too much deference in his manner, and a shade
too little control of the smirk on his face. With
a sudden sick feeling she realised at that moment
exactly where she stood. Under a debt of
obligation to this man—under the necessity of a
tête-à-tête with him, one, moreover, when, if she
was to help Bill, she must endeavour to be extra
nice.

For a while the conversation was common-place, while she feverishly longed for someone to come in and relieve the tension. But Bridge was in progress, and there was Snooker in the billiard-room, and at length she resigned herself to the inevitable. Presumably she would have to thank him for his kindness to Bill; after all he undoubtedly had been very good to her brother.

"Bill has told me, Mr. Perrison, how kind you've been in the way you've helped him in this—this unfortunate affair." She plunged valiantly, and gave a sigh of relief as she cleared the first fence.

Perrison waved a deprecating hand. "Don't mention it, Miss Daventry, don't mention it. But—er—of course, something will have to be done, and—well, there's no good mincing matters —done very soon."

The girl's face grew a little white, but her voice was quite steady.

"But he told me that you had arranged things with these people. Please smoke, if you want to."

Perrison bowed his thanks and carefully selected a cigarette. The moment for which he had been playing had now arrived, in circumstances even more favourable than he had dared to hope.

"Up to a point that is quite true," he remarked, quietly. "Messrs. Smith and Co. have many ramifications of business—money-lending

being only one of the irons they have in the fire.
And because I have had many dealings with the
firm professionally—over the sale of precious
stones, I may say, which is my own particular
line of work—they were disposed to take a
lenient view about the question of the loan. Not
press for payment, and perhaps—though I can't
promise this—even be content with a little less
interest. But—er—Miss Daventry, it's the
other thing where the trouble is going to occur."

The girl stared at him with dilated eyes.
" What other thing, Mr. Perrison? "

" Hasn't your brother told you ? " said
Perrison, surprised. " Oh, well, perhaps I—er
—shouldn't have mentioned it."

" Go on, please." Her voice was low. " What
is this other thing ? "

For a moment he hesitated—a well-simulated
hesitation. Then he shrugged his shoulders
slightly.

" Well—if you insist. As a matter of fact,
your brother didn't tell me about it, and I only
found it out in the course of my conversation
with one of the Smith partners. Apparently
some weeks ago he bought some distinctly valuable jewellery—a pearl-necklace, to be exact—
from a certain firm. At least, when I say he
bought it—he did not pay for it. He gave your
father's name as a reference, and the firm considered it satisfactory. It was worth about
eight hundred pounds, this necklace, and your
very stupid brother, instead of giving it to the

lady whom, presumably, he had got it for,
became worse than stupid. He became criminal."

" What do you mean ? " The girl was looking
at him terrified.

" He pawned this necklace which he hadn't
paid for, Miss Daventry, which is, I regret to say,
a criminal offence. And the trouble of the
situation is that the firm he bought the pearls
from has just found it out. He pawned it at a
place which is one of the ramifications of Smith
and Co., who gave him, I believe, a very good
price for it—over five hundred pounds. The
firm, in the course of business, two or three days
ago—and this is the incredibly unfortunate part
of it—happened to show this self-same necklace,
while they were selling other things, to the man
it had originally come from. Of course, being
pawned, it wasn't for sale—but the man recognised it at once. And then the fat was in the
fire."

" Do you mean to say," whispered the girl,
" that—that they might send him to prison ? "

" Unless something is done very quickly, Miss
Daventry, the matter will certainly come into
the law courts. Messrs. Gross and Sons "—a
faint noise from the darkness at the end of the
conservatory made him swing round suddenly,
but everything was silent again—" Messrs. Gross
and Sons are very difficult people in many ways.
They are the people it came from originally, I
may tell you. And firms, somewhat naturally,
differ, like human beings. Some are disposed to

be lenient—others are not. I'm sorry to say Gross and Sons are one of those who are not."

"But couldn't you see them, or something, and explain?"

"My dear Miss Daventry," said Perrison, gently, "I must ask you to be reasonable. What can I explain? Your brother wanted money, and he adopted a criminal method of getting it. That I am afraid—ugly as it sounds—is all there is to it."

"Then, Mr. Perrison—can nothing be done?" She bent forward eagerly, her hands clasped, her lips slightly parted; and once again came that faint noise from the end of the conservatory.

But Mr. Perrison was too engrossed to heed it this time; the nearness, the appeal of this girl, who from the time he had first seen her six months previously at a theatre had dominated his life, was making his senses swim. And with it the veneer began to drop; the hairy heel began to show, though he made a tremendous endeavour to keep himself in check.

"There is one thing," he said, hoarsely. "And I hope you will understand that I should not have been so precipitate—except for the urgency of your brother's case. If I go to Messrs. Gross and say to them that a prosecution by them would affect me personally, I think I could persuade them to take no further steps."

Wonder was beginning to dawn in the girl's eyes. "Affect you personally?" she repeated.

"If, for instance, I could tell them that for

family reasons—urgent, strong family reasons—
they would be doing me a great service by letting
matters drop, I think they would do it.''

She rose suddenly—wonder replaced by horror.
She had just realised his full meaning.

'' What on earth are you talking about, Mr.
Perrison ? '' she said, haughtily.

And then the heel appeared in all its hairiness.
'' If I may tell them,'' he leered, '' that I am
going to marry into the family I'll guarantee they
will do nothing more.''

'' Marry you ? '' The biting scorn in her tone
changed the leer to a snarl.

'' Yes—marry me, or see your brother jugged.
Money won't save him—so there's no good going
to your father. Money will square up the Smith
show—it won't square the other.'' And then
his tone changed. '' Why not, little girl ? I'm
mad about you ; have been ever since I saw you
at a theatre six months ago. I'm pretty well
off even for these days, and——'' He came
towards her, his arms outstretched, while she
backed away from him, white as a sheet. Her
hands were clenched, and it was just as she had
retreated as far as she could, and the man was
almost on her, that she saw red. One hand
went up ; hit him—hit the brute—was her only
coherent thought. And the man, realising it,
paused—an ugly look in his eyes.

Then occurred the interruption. A strangled
snort, as of a sleeper awakening, came from
behind some palms, followed by the creaking of

a chair. With a stifled curse Perrison fell back and the girl's hand dropped to her side as the branches parted and Archie Longworth, rubbing his eyes, stepped into the light.

"Lord save us, Miss Daventry, I've been asleep," he said, stifling a yawn. "I knew I oughtn't to have had a third glass of port. Deuced bad for the liver, but very pleasant for all that, isn't it, Mr.—Mr. Perrison?"

He smiled engagingly at the scowling Perrison, and adjusted his eyeglass.

"You sleep very silently, Mr. Longworth," snarled that worthy.

"Yes—used to win prizes for it at an infant school. Most valuable asset in class. If one snores it disconcerts the lecturer."

Perrison swung round on his heel. "I would like an answer to my suggestion by to-morrow, Miss Daventry," he said, softly. "Perhaps I might have the pleasure of a walk where people don't sleep off the effects of dinner."

With a slight bow he left the conservatory, and the girl sat down weakly.

"Pleasant type of bird, isn't he?" drawled Longworth, watching Perrison's retreating back.

"He's a brute—an utter brute," whispered the girl, shakily.

"I thought the interview would leave you with that impression," agreed the man.

She sat up quickly. "Did you hear what was said?"

12

" Every word. That's why I was there." He smiled at her calmly.

" Then why didn't you come out sooner ? " she cried, indignantly.

" I wanted to hear what he had to say, and at the same time I didn't want you to biff him on the jaw—which from your attitude I gathered you were on the point of doing."

" Why not ? I'd have given anything to have smacked his face."

" I know. I'd have given anything to have seen you do it. But—not yet. In fact, to-morrow you've got to go for a walk with him."

" I flatly refuse ! " cried Sybil Daventry.

" More than that," continued Longworth, calmly, " you've got to keep him on the hook. Play with him ; let him think he's got a chance."

" But why ? " she demanded. " I loathe him."

" Because it is absolutely essential that he should remain here until the day after to-morrow at the earliest."

" I don't understand." She looked at him with a puzzled frown.

" You will in good time." It seemed to her his voice was just a little weary. " Just now it is better that you shouldn't. Do you trust me enough to do that, Sybil ? "

" I trust you absolutely," and she saw him wince.

" Then keep him here till I come back."

" Are you going away, Archie ? " Impulsively she laid her hand on his arm.

" To-morrow, first thing. I shall come back as soon as possible."

For a moment or two they stood in silence, then, with a gesture strangely foreign to one so typically British, he raised her hand to his lips. And the next instant she was alone.

A little later she saw him talking earnestly to her brother in a corner ; then someone suggested billiard-fives. An admirable game, but not one in which it is wise to place one's hand on the edge of the table with the fingers over the cushion. Especially if the owner of the hand is not paying attention to the game. It was Perrison's hand, and the agony of being hit on the fingers by a full-sized billiard ball travelling fast must be experienced to be believed. Of course it was an accident : Longworth was most apologetic. But in the middle of the hideous scene that followed she caught his lazy blue eye and beat a hasty retreat to the hall. Unrestrained mirth in such circumstances is not regarded as the essence of tact.

III

It was about ten o'clock on the morning of the next day but one that a sharp-looking, flashily-dressed individual presented himself at the door of Messrs. Gross and Sons. He was of the type that may be seen by the score any day of the week propping up the West-end bars and discoursing on racing form in a hoarse whisper.

" Mornin'," he remarked. " Mr. Johnson here yet ? "

" What do you want to see him about ? " demanded the assistant.

" To tell him that your hair wants cutting," snapped the other. " Hop along, young fellah ; as an ornament you're a misfit. Tell Mr. Johnson that I've a message from Mr. Perrison."

The youth faded away, to return in a minute or two with a request that the visitor would follow him.

" Message from Perrison ? What's up ? " Mr. Johnson rose from his chair as the door closed behind the assistant.

The flashy individual laughed and pulled out his cigarette-case.

" He's pulled it off," he chuckled. " At the present moment our one and only Joe is clasping the beauteous girl to his bosom."

" Strike me pink—he hasn't, has he ? " Mr. Johnson slapped his leg resoundingly and shook with merriment.

" That's why I've come round," continued the other. " From Smith, I am. Joe wants to give her a little present on account." He grinned again, and felt in his pocket. " Here it is—and he wants a receipt signed by you—acknowledging the return of the necklace which was sent out— on approval." He winked heavily. " He's infernally deep, is Joe." He watched the other

man as he picked up the pearls, and for a moment
his blue eyes seemed a little strained. " He
wants to give that receipt to the girl—so as to
clinch the bargain."

" Why the dickens didn't he 'phone me
direct ? " demanded Johnson, and once again
the other grinned broadly.

" Strewth ! " he said, " I laughed fit to burst
this morning. The 'phone at his girl's place is
in the hall, as far as I could make out, and Joe
was whispering down it like an old woman with
lumbago. ' Take 'em round to Johnson,' he
said. ' Approval—approval—you fool.' And
then he turned away and I heard him say—
' Good morning, Lady Jemima.' Then back he
turns and starts whispering again. ' Do you get
me, Bob ? ' ' Yes,' I says, ' I get you. You
want me to take round the pearls to Johnson and
get a receipt from him. And what about the
other thing—you know, the money the young
boob borrowed ? ' ' Put it in an envelope and
send it to me here, with the receipt,' he says.
' I'm going out walking this morning.' Then he
rings off, and that's that. Lord ! think of Joe
walking."

The grin developed into a cackling laugh, in
which Mr. Johnson joined.

" He's deep—you're right," he said, admir-
ingly. " Uncommonly deep. I never thought
he'd pull it off. Though personally, mark
you, I think he's a fool. They'll fight like
cat and dog." He rang a bell on his desk

then opening a drawer he dropped the necklace inside.

"Bring me a formal receipt form," he said to the assistant. "Have you got the other paper?" he asked, as he affixed the firm's signature to the receipt, and the flashy individual produced it from his pocket.

"Here it is," he announced. "Put 'em both in an envelope together and address it to Joe. I'm going along; I'll post it."

"Will you have a small tiddley before you go?" Mr. Johnson opened a formidable-looking safe, disclosing all the necessary-looking ingredients for the manufacture of small tiddleys.

"I don't mind if I do," conceded the other. "Here's the best—and to the future Mrs. Joe."

A moment or two later he passed through the outer office and was swallowed up in the crowd. And it was not till after lunch that day that Mr. Johnson got the shock of his life—when he opened one of the early evening papers.

"DARING ROBBERY IN WELL-KNOWN CITY FIRM.

"*A most daring outrage was carried out last night at the office of Messrs. Smith and Co., the well-known financial and insurance brokers. At a late hour this morning, some time after work was commenced, the night watchman was discovered bound and securely gagged in a room at the top of the premises. Further investigation revealed that*

*the safe had been opened—evidently by a master
hand—and the contents rifled. The extent of the
loss is at present unknown, but the police are
believed to possess several clues."*

And at the same time that Mr. Johnson was
staring with a glassy stare at this astounding
piece of news, a tall, spare man with lazy blue
eyes, stretched out comfortably in the corner of a
first-class carriage, was also perusing it.

" Several clues," he murmured. " I wonder !
But it was a very creditable job, though I say it
myself."

Which seemed a strange soliloquy for a well-
dressed man in a first-class carriage. And what
might have seemed almost stranger, had there
been any way of knowing such a recondite fact,
was that in one of the mail bags reposing in the
back of the train, a mysterious transformation
had taken place. For a letter which had
originally contained two documents and had
been addressed to J. Perrison, Esq., now contained three and was consigned to Miss Sybil
Daventry. Which merely goes to show how
careful one should be over posting letters.

IV

" Good evening, Mr. Perrison. All well, and
taking nourishment, so to speak ? "

Archie Longworth lounged into the hall,
almost colliding with the other man

"You look pensive," he continued, staring at him blandly. "*Agitato, fortissimo*. Has aught occurred to disturb your masterly composure?"

But Mr. Perrison was in no mood for fooling: a message he had just received over the telephone had very considerably disturbed his composure.

"Let me have a look at that paper," he snapped, making a grab at it.

"Tush! Tush!" murmured Archie. "Manners, laddie, manners! You've forgotten that little word."

And then at the far end of the hall he saw the girl, and caught his breath. For the last two days he had almost forgotten her in the stress of other things; now the bitterness of what had to come rose suddenly in his throat and choked him.

"There is the paper. Run away and play in a corner."

Then he went forward to meet her with his usual lazy smile.

"What's happened?" she cried, a little breathlessly.

"Heaps of things," he said, gently. "Heaps of things. The principal one being that a very worthless sinner loves a very beautiful girl—as he never believed it could be given to man to love." His voice broke and faltered: then he went on steadily. "And the next one—which is really even more important—is that the very beautiful girl will receive a letter in a long envelope by to-night's mail. The address will be

typed, the postmark Strand. I do not want the
beautiful girl to open it except in my presence.
You understand ? ''

" I understand," she whispered, and her eyes
were shining.

" Have you seen this ? " Perrison's voice—
shaking with rage—made Longworth swing
round.

" Seen what, dear lad ? " he murmured, taking
the paper. " Robbery in City—is that what you
mean ? Dear, dear—what dastardly outrages
do go unpunished these days ! Messrs. Smith and
Co. Really ! Watchman bound and gagged.
Safe rifled. Work of a master hand. Still,
though I quite understand your horror as a law-
abiding citizen at such a thing, why this thus-
ness ? I mean—altruism is wonderful, laddie ;
but it seems to me that it's jolly old Smith and
Co. who are up the pole."

He burbled on genially, serenely unconscious
of the furious face of the other man.

" I'm trying to think where I've met you
before, Mr. Longworth," snarled Perrison.

" Never, surely," murmured the other.
" Those classic features, I feel sure, would have
been indelibly printed on my mind. Perhaps in
some mission, Mr. Perrison—some evangelical
revival meeting. Who knows ? And there, if I
mistake not, is the mail."

He glanced at the girl, and she was staring at
him wonderingly. Just for one moment did he
show her what she wanted to know—just for one

moment did she give him back the answer which was to him the sweetest and at the same time the most bitter in the world. Then he crossed the hall and picked up the letters.

"A business one for you, Miss Daventry," he murmured, mildly. "Better open it at once, and get our business expert's advice. Mr. Perrison is a wonderful fellah for advice."

With trembling fingers she opened the envelope, and, as he saw the contents, Perrison, with a snarl of ungovernable fury, made as if to snatch them out of her hand. The next moment he felt as if his arm was broken, and the blue eyes boring into his brain were no longer lazy.

"You forgot yourself, Mr. Perrison," said Archie Longworth, gently. "Don't do that again."

"But I don't understand," cried the girl, bewildered. "What are these papers?"

"May I see?" Longworth held out his hand, and she gave them to him at once.

"They're stolen." Perrison's face was livid. "Give them to me, curse you."

"Control yourself, you horrible blighter," said Longworth, icily. "This," he continued, calmly, "would appear to be a receipt from Messrs. Gross and Sons for the return of a pearl necklace—sent out to Mr. Daventry on approval."

"But you said he'd bought it and pawned it." She turned furiously on Perrison.

"So he did," snarled that gentleman. "That's a forgery."

" Is it ? " said Longworth. " That strikes me as being Johnson's signature. Firm's official paper. And—er—he has the necklace, I—er—assume."

" Yes—he has the necklace. Stolen last night by—by——" His eyes were fixed venomously on Longworth.

" Go on," murmured the other. " You're being most entertaining."

But a sudden change had come over Perrison's face—a dawning recognition. " By God ! " he muttered, " you're—you're——"

" Yes. I'm—who ? It'll come in time, laddie—if you give it a chance. And in the meantime we might examine these other papers. Now, this appears to my inexperienced eye to be a transaction entered into on the one part by Messrs. Smith and Co. and on the other by William Daventry. And it concerns filthy lucre. Dear, dear. Twenty-five per cent. per month. Three hundred per cent. Positive usury, Mr. Perrison. Don't you agree with me ? A rapacious bloodsucker is Mr. Smith."

But the other man was not listening : full recollection had come to him, and with a cold look of triumph he put his hands into his pockets and laughed.

" Very pretty," he remarked. " Very pretty indeed. And how, in your vernacular, do you propose to get away with the swag, Mr. Flash Pete ? I rather think the police—whom I propose to call up on the 'phone in one minute—

will be delighted to see such an old and elusive
friend."

He glanced at the girl, and laughed again at
the look on her face.

"What's he mean, Archie?" she cried,
wildly. "What's he mean?"

"I mean," Perrison sneered, "that Mr.
Archie Longworth is what is generally described
as a swell crook with a reputation in certain
unsavoury circles extending over two or three
continents. And the police, whom I propose
to ring up, will welcome him as a long-lost
child."

He walked towards the telephone, and with a
little gasp of fear the girl turned to Archie.

"Say it's not true, dear—say it's not true."

For a moment he looked at her with a whimsical smile ; then he sat down on the high fender
round the open fire.

"I think, Mr. Perrison," he murmured, gently,
"that if I were you I would not be too precipitate
over ringing up the police. The engaging
warrior who sent this letter to Miss Daventry
put in yet one more enclosure."

Perrison turned round : then he stood very
still.

"A most peculiar document," continued the
man by the fire, in the same gentle voice, "which
proves very conclusively that amongst their
other activities Messrs. Smith and Co. are not
only the receivers of stolen goods, but are mixed
up with illicit diamond buying."

In dead silence the two men stared at one another; then Longworth spoke again.

"I shall keep these three documents, Mr. Perrison, as a safeguard for your future good behaviour. Mr. Daventry can pay a certain fair sum or not as he likes—that is his business : and I shall make a point of explaining exactly to him who and what you are—and Smith—and Gross. But should you be disposed to make any trouble over the necklace—or should the idea get abroad that Flash Pete was responsible for the burglary last night—it will be most unfortunate for you— most. This document would interest Scotland Yard immensely."

Perrison's face had grown more and more livid as he listened, and when the quiet voice ceased, unmindful of the girl standing by, he began to curse foully and hideously. The next moment he cowered back, as two iron hands gripped his shoulders and shook him till his teeth rattled.

"Stop, you filthy swine," snarled Longworth, " or I'll break every bone in your body. Quite a number of men are blackguards, Perrison— but you're a particularly creeping and repugnant specimen. Now—get out—and do it quickly. The nine-thirty will do you nicely. And don't forget what I've just said : because, as there's a God above, I mean it."

"I'll be even with you for this some day, Flash Pete," said the other venomously over his shoulder. " And then——"

"And then," said Longworth, contemptuously, "we will resume this discussion. Just now—get out."

V

"Yes: it is quite true." She had known it was—and yet, womanlike, she had clung to the hope that there was some mistake—some explanation. And now, alone with the man she had grown to love, the faint hope died. With his lazy smile, he stared down at her—a smile so full of sorrow and pain that she could not bear to see it.

"I'm Flash Pete—with an unsavoury reputation, as our friend so kindly told you, in three continents. It was I who broke open the safe at Smith's last night, I who got the receipt from Gross. You see, I spotted the whole trick from the beginning; as I said, I had inside information. And Perrison is Smith and Co.; moreover he's very largely Gross as well—and half a dozen other rotten things in addition. The whole thing was worked with one end in view right from the beginning: the girl your brother originally bought the pearls for was in it; it was she who suggested the pawning. Bill told me that the night before last." He sighed and paced two or three times up and down the dim-lit conservatory. And after a while he stopped in front of her again, and his blue eyes were very tender.

"Just a common sneak-thief—just a common

worthless sinner. And he's very, very glad that
he has been privileged to help the most beautiful
girl in all the world. Don't cry, my dear, don't
cry : there's nothing about that sinner's that's
worth a single tear of yours. You must forget
his wild presumption in falling in love with that
beautiful girl : his only excuse is that he couldn't
help it. And maybe, in the days to come, the
girl will think kindly every now and then of a
man known to some as Archie Longworth—
known to others as Flash Pete—known to himself as—well, we won't bother about that."

He bent quickly and raised her hand to his
lips ; then he was gone almost before she had
realised it. And if he heard her little gasping
cry—" Archie, my man, come back—I love you
so ! " he gave no sign.

For in his own peculiar code a very worthless
sinner must remain a very worthless sinner to
the end—and he must run the course alone.

I

" WHAT a queer little place, Jimmy ! " The
girl glanced round the tiny restaurant with frank
interest, and the man looked up from the menu
he was studying with a grin.

" Dont let François hear you say that, or
you'll be asked to leave." The head-waiter was
already bearing down on them, his face wreathed
in an expansive smile of welcome. " To him it
is the only restaurant in London."

" Ah, m'sieur ! it is long days since you were
here." The little Frenchman rubbed his hands
together delightedly. " And mam'selle—it is
your first visit to Les Coquelins, n'est-ce-pas ? "

" But not the last, I hope, François," said the
girl with a gentle smile.

" Ah, mais non ! " Outraged horror at such
an impossible idea shone all over the head-
waiter's face. " My guests, mam'selle, they
come here once to see what it is like—and they
return because they know what it is like."

Jimmy Lethbridge laughed.

" There you are, Molly," he cried. " Now you
know what's expected of you. Nothing less than
once a week—eh, François ? "

" Mais oui, m'sieur. There are some who come
every night." He produced his pencil and stood

waiting. " A few oysters," he murmured.
" They are good ce soir : real Whitstables. And
a bird, M'sieur Lethbridge—with an omelette aux
fines herbes——"

" Sounds excellent, François," laughed the
man. " Anyway, I know that once you have
decided—argument is futile."

" It is my work," answered the waiter, shrug-
ging his shoulders. " And a bottle of Corton—
with the chill just off. Toute de suite."

François bustled away, and the girl looked
across the table with a faintly amused smile in
her big grey eyes.

" He fits the place, Jimmy. You must bring
me here again."

" Just as often as you like, Molly," answered
the man quietly, and after a moment the girl
turned away. " You know," he went on steadily,
" how much sooner I'd bring you to a spot like
this, than go to the Ritz or one of those big places.
Only I was afraid it might bore you. I love it :
it's so much more intimate."

" Why should you think it would bore me ? "
she asked, drawing off her gloves and resting her
hands on the table in front of her. They were
beautiful hands, ringless save for one plain signet
ring on the little finger of her left hand. And,
almost against his will, the man found himself
staring at it as he answered :

" Because I can't trust myself, dear ; I can't
trust myself to amuse you," he answered slowly.
" I can't trust myself not to make love to you—

13

and it's so much easier here than in the middle
of a crowd whom one knows."

The girl sighed a little sadly.

"Oh, Jimmy, I wish I could! You've been
such an absolute dear. Give me a little longer,
old man, and then—perhaps——"

"My dear," said the man hoarsely, "I don't
want to hurry you. I'm willing to wait years for
you—years. At least "—he smiled whimsically
—" I'm not a little bit willing to wait years—
really. But if it's that or nothing—then, believe
me, I'm more than willing."

"I've argued it out with myself, Jimmy."
And now she was staring at the signet ring on
her finger. "And when I've finished the argument, I know that I'm not a bit further on. You
can't argue over things like that. I've told
myself times out of number that it isn't fair to
you——"

He started to speak, but she stopped him with
a smile.

"No, dear man, it is not fair to you—whatever
you like to say. It isn't fair to you even though
you may agree to go on waiting. No one has a
right to ask another person to wait indefinitely,
though I'm thinking that is exactly what I've
been doing. Which is rather like a woman," and
once again she smiled half sadly.

"But I'm willing to wait, dear," he repeated
gently. "And then I'm willing to take just as
much as you care to give. I won't worry you,
Molly; I won't ask you for anything you don't

feel like granting me. You see, I know now that
Peter must always come first. I had hoped that
you'd forget him ; I still hope, dear, that in time
you will——''

She shook her head, and the man bit his lip.

" Well, even if you don't, Molly," he went on
steadily, " is it fair to yourself to go on when you
know it's hopeless ? There can be no doubt now
that he's dead ; you know it yourself—you've
taken off your engagement ring—and is it fair
to—you ? Don't worry about me for the
moment—but what is the use ? Isn't it better
to face facts ? "

The girl gave a little laugh that was half a
sob.

" Of course it is, Jimmy. Much better. I
always tell myself that in my arguments." Then
she looked at him steadily across the table.
" You'd be content, Jimmy—would you ?—with
friendship at first."

" Yes," he answered quietly. " I would be
content with friendship."

" And you wouldn't bother me—ah, no !
forgive me, I know you wouldn't. Because,
Jimmy, I don't want there to be any mistake.
People think I've got over it because I go about ;
in some ways I have. But I seem to have lost
something—some part of me. I don't think I
shall ever be able to *love* a man again. I like
you, Jimmy—like you most frightfully—but I
don't know whether I'll ever be able to love you
in the way I loved Peter."

" I know that," muttered the man. " And I'll risk it."

" You dear ! " said the girl—and her eyes were shining. " That's where the unfairness comes in. You're worth the very best—and I can't promise to give it to you."

" You are the very best, whatever you give me," answered the man quietly. " I'd sooner have anything from you than everything from another woman. Oh, my dear ! " he burst out, " I didn't mean to worry you to-night—though I knew this damned restaurant would be dangerous —but can't you say yes ? I swear you'll never regret it, dear—and I—I'll be quite content to know that you care just a bit."

For a while the girl was silent ; then with a faint smile she looked at him across the table.

" All right, Jimmy," she said.

" You mean you will, Molly ? " he cried, a little breathlessly.

And the girl nodded.

" Yes, old man," she answered steadily. " I mean I will."

. . . . . .

It was two hours later when Molly Daventry went slowly upstairs to her room and shut the door. Jimmy Lethbridge had just gone ; she had just kissed him. And the echo of his last whispered words—" My dear ! my very dear girl ! "—was still sounding in her ears.

For a while she stood by the fireplace smiling a little sadly. Then she crossed the room and

switched on a special light. It was so placed
that it shone directly on the photograph of an
officer in the full dress of the 9th Hussars. And
at length she knelt down in front of the table on
which the photograph stood, so that the light fell
on her own face also—glinting through the red-
gold of her hair, glistening in the mistiness of her
eyes. For maybe five minutes she knelt there,
till it seemed to her as if a smile twitched round
the lips of the officer—a human smile, an under-
standing smile.

" Oh, Peter ! " she whispered, " he was your
pal. Forgive me, my love—forgive me. He's
been such a dear."

And once again the photograph seemed to smile
at her tenderly.

" It's only you, Peter, till Journey's End—
but I must give him the next best, mustn't I ?
It's only fair, isn't it ?—and you hated unfairness.
But, dear God ! it's hard."

Slowly she stretched out her left hand, so that
the signet ring touched the big silver frame.

" Your ring, Peter," she whispered, " your
dear ring."

And with a sudden little choking gasp she
raised it to her lips.

II

It was in a side-street close to High Street,
Kensington, that it happened—the unbelievable
thing. Fate decided to give Jimmy two months

of happiness; cynically allowed him to come within a fortnight of his wedding, and then——

For a few seconds he couldn't believe his eyes; he stood staring like a man bereft of his senses. There on the opposite side of the road, playing a barrel-organ, was Peter himself—Peter, who had been reported " Missing, believed killed," three years before. Peter, whom a sergeant had categorically said he had seen killed with his own eyes. And there he was playing a barrel-organ in the streets of London.

Like a man partially dazed Jimmy Lethbridge went over towards him. As he approached the player smiled genially, and touched his cap with his free hand. Then after a while the smile faded, and he stared at Jimmy suspiciously.

" My God, Peter ! " Lethbridge heard himself say, " what are you doing this for ? "

And as he spoke he saw a girl approaching— a girl who placed herself aggressively beside Peter.

" Why shouldn't I ? " demanded the player. " And who the hell are you calling Peter ? "

" But," stammered Jimmy, " don't you know me, old man ? "

" No ! " returned the other truculently. " And I don't want to, neither."

" A ruddy torf, 'e is, Bill," chimed in the girl.

" Good God ! " muttered Lethbridge, even then failing to understand the situation. " You playing a barrel-organ ! "

" Look here, 'op it, guv'nor." Peter spoke

with dangerous calmness. " I don't want no blinking scenes 'ere. The police ain't too friendly as it is, and this is my best pitch."

" But why didn't you let your pals know you were back, old man ? " said Jimmy feebly. " Your governor, and all of us ? "

" See 'ere, mister," the girl stepped forward, " 'e ain't got no pals—only me. Ain't that so, Billy ? " she turned to the man, who nodded.

"I looks after him, I do, d'yer see ? " went on the girl. " And I don't want no one coming butting their ugly heads in. It worries 'im, it does."

" But do you mean to say——" began Jimmy dazedly, and then he broke off. At last he understood, something if not all. In some miraculous way Peter had not been killed ; Peter was there in front of him—but a new Peter ; a Peter whose memory of the past had completely gone, whose mind was as blank as a clean-washed slate.

" How long have you been doing this ? " he asked quietly.

" Never you mind," said the girl sharply. " He ain't nothing to you. I looks after 'im, I do."

Not for a second did Jimmy hesitate, though deep down inside him there came a voice that whispered—" Don't be a fool ! Pretend it's a mistake. Clear off ! Molly will never know." And if for a moment his hands clenched with the strength of the sudden hideous temptation, his voice was calm and quiet as he spoke.

"That's where you're wrong." He looked at her gently. "He is something to me—my greatest friend, whom I thought was dead."

And now Peter was staring at him fixedly, forgetting even to turn the handle of the machine.

"I don't remember yer, guv'nor," he said, and Jimmy flinched at the appalling accent. "I've kind o' lost my memory, yer see, and Lizzie 'ere looks after me."

"I know she does," continued Jimmy quietly. "Thank you, Lizzie, thank you a thousand times. But I want you both to come to this house to-night." He scribbled the address of his rooms on a slip of paper. "We must think what is best to be done. You see, Lizzie, it's not quite fair to him, is it? I want to get a good doctor to see him."

"I'm quite 'appy as I am, sir," said Peter. "I don't want no doctors messing about with me."

"Yer'd better go, Bill." The girl turned to him. "The gentleman seems kind. But"—she swung round on Jimmy fiercely—"you ain't going to take 'im away from me, guv'nor? 'E's mine, yer see—mine——"

"I want you to come with him to-night, Lizzie," said Lethbridge gravely. "I'm not going to try and take him away from you. I promise that. But will you promise to come? It's for his sake I ask you to bring him."

For a while she looked at him half fearfully; then she glanced at Peter, who had apparently lost interest in the matter. And at last she muttered under her breath : " Orl right—I'll bring him. But 'e's mine—mine. An' don't yer go forgetting it."

And Jimmy, walking slowly into the main street, carried with him the remembrance of a small determined face with the look on it of a mother fighting for her young. That and Peter ; poor dazed memory-lost Peter—his greatest pal.

At first, as he turned towards Piccadilly, he grasped nothing save the one stupendous fact that Peter was not dead. Then, as he walked on, gradually the realisation of what it meant to him personally came to his mind. And with that realisation there returned with redoubled force the insidious tempting voice that had first whispered : " Molly will never know." She would never know—could never know—unless he told her. And Peter was happy ; he'd said so. And the girl was happy—Lizzie. And perhaps—in fact most likely—Peter would never recover his memory. So what was the use ? Why say anything about it ? Why not say it was a mistake when they came that evening ? And Jimmy put his hand to his forehead and found it was wet with sweat.

After all, if Peter didn't recover, it would only mean fearful unhappiness for everyone. He wouldn't know Molly, and it would break her heart, and the girl's, and—but, of course, *he* didn't count. It was the others he was thinking of—not himself.

He turned into the Park opposite the Albert Hall, and passers-by eyed him strangely, though he was supremely unaware of the fact. But when all the demons of hell are fighting inside a man, his face is apt to look grey and haggard. And as he walked slowly towards Hyde Park Corner, Jimmy Lethbridge went through his Gethsemane. They thronged him; pressing in on him from all sides, and he cursed the devils out loud. But still they came back, again and again, and the worst and most devilish of them all was the insidious temptation that by keeping silent he would be doing the greatest good for the greatest number. Everyone was happy now— why run the risk of altering things?

And then, because it is not good that man should be tempted till he breaks, the Fate that had led him to Peter, led him gently out of the Grim Garden into Peace once more. He gave a short hard laugh which was almost a sob, and turning into Knightsbridge he hailed a taxi. It was as it drew up at the door of Molly's house that he laughed again—a laugh that had lost its hardness. And the driver thought his fare's " Thank you " was addressed to him. Perhaps it was. Perhaps it was the first time Jimmy had prayed for ten years.

" Why, Jimmy, old man—you're early, I'm not dressed yet." Molly met him in the hall, and he smiled at her gravely.

" Do you mind, dear," he said, " if I cry off tonight? I've got a very important engagement—

even more important than taking you out to dinner, if possible."

The smile grew whimsical, and he put both his hands on her shoulders.

" It concerns my wedding present for you," he added.

" From the bridegroom to the bride ? " she laughed.

" Something like that," he said, turning away abruptly.

" Of course, dear," she answered. "As a matter of fact, I've got a bit of a head. Though what present you can be getting at this time of day, I can't think."

" You mustn't try to," said Jimmy. " It's a surprise, Molly—a surprise. Pray God you like it, and that it will be a success ! "

He spoke low under his breath, and the girl looked at him curiously.

" What's the matter, dear ? " she cried. " Has something happened ? "

Jimmy Lethbridge pulled himself together ; he didn't want her to suspect anything yet.

" Good heavens, no ! " he laughed. " What should have ? But I want to borrow something from you, Molly dear, and I don't want you to ask any questions. I want you to lend me that photograph of Peter that you've got—the one in full dress."

And now she was staring at him wonderingly.

" Jimmy," she said breathlessly, " does it concern the present ? "

" Yes ; it concerns the present."

" You're going to have a picture of him painted for me ? "

" Something like that," he answered quietly.

" Oh, you dear ! " she whispered, " you dear ! I've been thinking about it for months. I'll get it for you."

She went upstairs, and the man stood still in the hall staring after her. And he was still standing motionless as she came down again, the precious frame clasped in her hands.

" You'll take care of it, Jimmy ? " she said, and he nodded.

Then for a moment she laid her hand on his arm.

" I don't think, old man," she said quietly, " that you'll have to wait very long with friendship only."

The next moment she was alone with the slam of the front door echoing in her ears. It was like Fate to reserve its most deadly arrow for the end.

III

" You say he has completely lost his memory ? "

Mainwaring, one of the most brilliant of London's younger surgeons, leaned back in his chair and looked thoughtfully at his host.

" Well, he didn't know me, and I was his greatest friend," said Lethbridge.

The two men were in Jimmy's rooms, waiting for the arrival of Peter and the girl.

" He looked at me without a trace of recognition," continued Lethbridge. " And he's developed a typical lower-class Cockney accent."

" Interesting, very," murmured the surgeon, getting up and examining the photograph on the table. " This is new, isn't it, old boy; I've never seen it before ? "

" I borrowed it this afternoon," said Jimmy briefly.

" From his people, I suppose ? Do they know ? "

" No one knows at present, Mainwaring— except you and me. That photograph I got this afternoon from Miss Daventry."

Something in his tone made the surgeon swing round.

" You mean your fiancée ? " he said slowly.

" Yes—my fiancée. You see, she was—she was engaged to Peter. And she thinks he's dead. That is the only reason she got engaged to me."

For a moment there was silence, while Mainwaring stared at the other. A look of wonder had come into the doctor's eyes—wonder mixed with a dawning admiration.

" But, my God! old man," he muttered at length, " if the operation is successful——"

" Can you think of a better wedding present to give a girl than the man she loves ? " said Jimmy slowly, and the doctor turned away.

There are times when it is not good to look on another man's face.

" And if it isn't successful ? " he said quietly.

" God knows, Bill. I haven't got as far as that—yet."

And it was at that moment that there came a ring at the front-door bell. There was a brief altercation ; then Jimmy's man appeared.

" Two—er—persons say you told them——" he began, when Lethbridge cut him short.

" Show them in at once," he said briefly, and his man went out again.

" You've got to remember, Bill," said Jimmy as they waited, " that Peter Staunton is literally, at the moment, a low-class Cockney."

Mainwaring nodded, and drew back a little as Peter and the girl came into the room. He wanted to leave the talking to Jimmy, while he watched.

" Good evening, Lizzie," Lethbridge smiled at the girl reassuringly. " I'm glad you came."

" Who's that cove ? " demanded the girl suspiciously, staring at Mainwaring.

" A doctor," said Jimmy. " I want him to have a look at Peter later on."

" His name ain't Peter," muttered the girl sullenly. " It's Bill."

" Well, at Bill, then. Don't be frightened, Lizzie ; come farther into the room. I want you to see a photograph I've got here."

Like a dog who wonders whether it is safe to go to a stranger, she advanced slowly, one step

at a time; while Peter, twirling his cap awk-
wardly in his hands, kept beside her. Once or
twice he glanced uneasily round the room, but
otherwise his eyes were fixed on Lizzie as a child
looks at its mother when it's scared.

" My God, Jimmy ! " whispered the doctor,
" there's going to be as big a sufferer as you if
we're successful."

And he was looking as he spoke at the girl,
who, with a sudden instinctive feeling of
protection, had put out her hand and taken
Peter's.

Like a pair of frightened children they crept
on until they came to the photograph ; then they
stopped in front of it. And the two men came a
little closer. It was the girl who spoke first, in
a low voice of wondering awe :

" Gawd ! it's you, Bill—that there bloke in
the frame. You were a blinking orficer."

With a look of pathetic pride on her face, she
stared first at the photograph and then at the
man beside her. " An orficer ! Bill—an
orficer ! What was 'is regiment, mister ? "
The girl swung round on Jimmy. " Was 'e in
the Guards ? "

" No, Lizzie," said Lethbridge. " Not the
Guards. He was in the cavalry. The 9th
Hussars," and the man, who was holding the
frame foolishly in his hands, suddenly looked
up. " The Devil's Own, Peter," went on
Lethbridge quietly. " C Squadron of the Devil's
Own."

But the look had faded; Peter's face was blank again.

"I don't remember, guv'nor," he muttered. "And it's making me 'ead ache—this."

With a little cry the girl caught his arm, and faced Lethbridge fiercely.

"Wot's the good of all this?" she cried. "All this muckin' abaht? Why the 'ell can't you leave 'im alone, guv'nor? 'E's going to 'ave one of 'is 'eads now—'e nearly goes mad, 'e does, when 'e gets 'em."

"I think, Lizzie, that perhaps I can cure those heads of his."

It was Mainwaring speaking, and the girl, still holding Peter's arm protectingly, looked from Lethbridge to the doctor.

"And I want to examine him, in another room where the light is a little better. Just quite alone, where he won't be distracted."

But instantly the girl was up in arms.

"You're taking 'im away from me—that's wot yer doing. And I won't 'ave it. Yer don't want to go, Bill, do yer? Yer don't want to leave yer Liz?"

And Jimmy Lethbridge bit his lip; Mainwaring had been right.

"I'm not going to take him away, Lizzie," said the doctor gently. "I promise you that. You shall see him the very instant I've made my examination. But if you're there, you see, you'll distract his attention."

She took a step forward, staring at the doctor

as if she would read his very soul. And in the infinite pathos of the scene, Jimmy Lethbridge for the moment forgot his own suffering. Lizzie —the little slum girl—fighting for her man against something she couldn't understand; wondering if she should trust these two strangers. Caught in a net that frightened her; fearful that they were going to harm Bill. And at the bottom of everything the wild, inarticulate terror that she was going to lose him.

" You swear it ? " she muttered. " I can see 'im after yer've looked at 'im."

" I swear it," said Mainwaring gravely.

She gave a little sob. " Orl right, I believe yer on the level. You go with 'im, Bill. Perhaps 'e'll do yer 'ead good."

" 'E's queer sometimes at night," said Lizzie, as the door closed behind Mainwaring. " Seems all dazed like."

" Is he ? " said Jimmy. " How did you find him, Lizzie ? "

" 'E was wandering round—didn't know nuthing about 'imself," she answered. " And I took 'im in—and looked after 'im, I did. Saved and pinched a bit, 'ere and there—and then we've the barrel-organ. And we've been so 'appy, mister—so 'appy. Course 'e's a bit queer, and 'e don't remember nuthing—but 'e's orl right if 'e don't get 'is 'eadaches. And when 'e does, I gets rid of them. I jest puts 'is 'ead on me lap and strokes 'is forehead—and they goes after a while. Sometimes 'e goes to sleep when

14

I'm doing it—and I stops there till 'e wakes
again with the 'ead gone. Yer see, I under-
stands 'im. 'E's 'appy with me."

She was staring at the photograph—a pathetic
little figure in her tawdry finery—and for a
moment Jimmy couldn't speak. It had to be
done ; he had to do it—but it felt rather like
killing a wounded bird with a sledge-hammer—
except that it wouldn't be so quick.

" He's a great brain surgeon, Lizzie—the
gentleman with Bill," he said at length, and the
girl turned round and watched him gravely.
" And he thinks that an operation might cure
him and give him back his memory."

" So that 'e'd know 'e was an orficer ? "
whispered the girl.

" So that he'd know he was an officer," said
Jimmy. " So that he'd remember all his past
life. You see, Lizzie, your Bill is really Sir Peter
Staunton—whom we all thought had been killed
in the war."

" Sir Peter Staunton ! " she repeated dazedly.
" Gawd ! "

" He was engaged, Lizzie," he went on quietly,
and he heard her breath come quick— " engaged
to that lady." He pointed to a picture of Sybil
on the mantelpiece.

" No one wouldn't look at me with 'er about,"
said the girl thoughtfully.

" She loved him very dearly, Lizzie—even as
he loved her. I don't think I've ever known two
people who loved one another quite so much.

And——" for a moment Jimmy faltered, then he went on steadily : " I ought to know in this case, because I'm engaged to her now."

And because the Cockney brain is quick, she saw—and understood.

" So if yer doctor friend succeeds," she said, " she'll give yer the chuck ? "

" Yes, Lizzie," answered Jimmy gravely, " she'll give me the chuck."

" And yer love 'er ? Orl right, old sport. I can see it in yer face. Strikes me "—and she gave a little laugh that was sadder than any tears—" strikes me you 'anded out the dirty end of the stick to both of us when you come round that street to-day."

" Strikes me I did, Lizzie," he agreed. " But, you see, I've told you this because I want you to understand that we're both of us in it—we've both of us got to play the game."

" Play the game ! " she muttered. " Wot d'yer want me to do ? "

" The doctor doesn't want him excited, Lizzie," explained Lethbridge. " But he wants him to stop here to-night, so that he can operate to-morrow. Will you tell him that you want him to stop here ?—and stay here with him if you like."

" And to-morrer she'll tike 'im." The girl was staring at Sybil's photograph. " 'E won't look at me—when 'e knows. Gawd ! why did yer find 'im—why did yer find 'im ? We was 'appy, I tells yer—'appy ? "

She was crying now—crying as a child cries, weakly and pitifully, and Lethbridge stood watching her in silence.

" Poor kid ! '' he said at length. " Poor little kid ! ''

" I don't want yer pity," she flared up. " I want my man.'' And then, as she saw Jimmy looking at the photograph on the mantelpiece, in an instant she was beside him. " Sorry, old sport,'' she whispered impulsively. " Reckon you've backed a ruddy loser yourself. I'll do it. Shake 'ands. I guess I knew all along that Bill wasn't really my style. And I've 'ad my year.''

" You're lucky, Lizzie," said Jimmy gravely, still holding her hand. " Very, very lucky.''

" I've 'ad my year," she went on, and for a moment her thoughts seemed far away. " A 'ole year—and——'' she pulled herself together and started patting her hair.

" And what, Lizzie ? '' said Jimmy quietly.

" Never you mind, mister,'' she answered. " That's my blooming business.''

And then the door opened and Mainwaring came in.

" Does Lizzie agree ? '' he asked eagerly.

" Yes, Bill—she agrees,'' said Jimmy. " What do you think of him ? ''

" As far as I can see there is every hope that an operation will be completely successful. There is evidently pressure on the right side of the skull which can be removed. I'll operate early to-morrow morning. Keep him quiet to-night—and make him sleep, Lizzie, if you can."

"What d'yer think, mister?" she said scornfully. "Ain't I done it fer a year?"

Without another word she left the room, and the two men stood staring at one another.

"Will she play the game, Jimmy!" Mainwaring was lighting a cigarette.

"Yes—she'll play the game," answered Lethbridge slowly. "She'll play the game—poor little kid!"

"What terms are they on—those two?" The doctor looked at him curiously.

"I think," said Lethbridge even more slowly, "that that is a question we had better not inquire into too closely."

IV

It was successful—brilliantly successful—the operation. Lizzie made it so; at any rate she helped considerably. It was she who held his hand as he went under the anæsthetic; it was she who cheered him up in the morning, when he awoke dazed and frightened in a strange room. And then she slipped away and disappeared from the house. It was only later that Lethbridge found a scrawled pencil note, strangely smudged, on his desk:

"Let me no wot appens.—LIZZIE."

He didn't know her address, so he couldn't

write and tell her that her Bill had come to
consciousness again, completely recovered except
for one thing. There was another blank in his
mind now—the last three years. One of his
first questions had been to ask how the fight
had gone, and whether we'd broken through
properly.

And then for a day or two Lizzie was forgotten;
he had to make his own renunciation.

Molly came, a little surprised at his unusual
invitation, and he left the door open so that she
could see Peter in bed from one part of his
sitting-room.

"Where have you buried yourself, Jimmy?"
she cried. "I've been——" And then her face
grew deathly white as she looked into the bedroom. Her lips moved, though no sound came
from them; her hands were clenching and
unclenching.

"But I'm mad," he heard her whisper at
length, "quite mad. I'm seeing things, Jimmy—
seeing things. Why—dear God! it's Peter!"

She took a step or two forward, and Peter saw
her.

"Molly," he cried weakly, "Molly, my
darling——"

And Jimmy Lethbridge saw her walk forward
slowly and uncertainly to the man who had come
back. With a shaking little cry of pure joy she
fell on her knees beside the bed, and Peter put a
trembling hand on her hair. Then Jimmy shut
the door, and stared blankly in front of him.

It was Lizzie who roused him—Lizzie coming shyly into the room from the hall.

" I seed her come in," she whispered. " She looked orl right. 'Ow is 'e ? "

" He's got his memory back, Lizzie," he said gently. " But he's forgotten the last three years."

" Forgotten me, as 'e ? " Her lips quivered.

" Yes, Lizzie. Forgotten everything—barrel-organ and all. He thinks he's on sick leave from the war."

" And she's wiv 'im now, is she ? "

" Yes—she's with him, Lizzie."

She took a deep breath—then she walked to the glass and arranged her hat—a dreadful hat with feathers in it.

" Well, I reckons I'd better be going. I don't want to see 'im. It would break me 'eart. And I said good-bye to 'im that last night before the operation. So long, mister. I've 'ad me year— she can't tike that away from me."

And then she was gone. He watched her from the window walking along the pavement, with the feathers nodding at every step. Once she stopped and looked back—and the feathers seemed to wilt and die. Then she went on again—and this time she didn't stop. She'd " 'ad 'er year," had Lizzie ; maybe the remembrance of it helped her gallant little soul when she returned the barrel-organ—the useless barrel-organ.

. . . . . .

"So this was your present, Jimmy." Molly was speaking just behind him, and her eyes were very bright.

"Yes, Molly," he smiled. "Do you like it?"

"I don't understand what's happened," she said slowly. "I don't understand anything except the one big fact that Peter has come back."

"Isn't that enough?" he asked gently. "Isn't that enough, my dear? Peter's come back—funny old Peter. The rest will keep."

And then he took her left hand and drew off the engagement ring he had given her.

"Not on that finger now—Molly; though I'd like you to keep it now if you will."

For a while she stared at him wonderingly.

"Jimmy, but you're big!" she whispered at length. "I'm so sorry!" She turned away as Peter's voice, weak and tremulous, came from the other room.

"Come in with me, old man," she said. "Come in and talk to him."

But Jimmy shook his head.

"He doesn't want me, dear; I'm just—just going out for a bit——"

Abruptly he left the room—they didn't want him: any more than they wanted Lizzie.

Only she had had her year.

I

" My dear Cynthia, you haven't seen our Hermit yet. He's quite the show exhibit of the place."

Lady Cynthia Stockdale yawned and lit a cigarette. Hermits belonged undoubtedly to the class of things in which she was *not* interested; the word conjured up a mental picture of a dirty individual of great piety, clothed in a sack. And Lady Cynthia loathed dirt and detested piety.

" A hermit, Ada ! " she remarked, lazily. " I thought the brand was extinct. Does he feed ravens and things ? "

It is to be regretted that theological knowledge was not her strong point, but Ada Laverton, her hostess, did not smile. From beneath some marvellously long eyelashes she was watching the lovely girl lying back in the deck-chair opposite, who was vainly trying to blow smoke rings. A sudden wild idea had come into her brain—so wild as to be almost laughable. But from time immemorial wild ideas anent their girl friends have entered the brains of young married women, especially the lucky ones who have hooked the right man. And Ada Laverton had undoubtedly done that. She alternately bullied, cajoled,

217

and made love to her husband John, in a way
that eminently suited that cheerful and easy-
going gentleman. He adored her quite openly
and ridiculously, and she returned the com-
pliment just as ridiculously, even if not quite so
openly.

Moreover, Cynthia Stockdale was her best
friend. Before her marriage they had been
inseparable, and perhaps there was no one living
who understood Cynthia as she did. To the
world at large Cynthia was merely a much
photographed and capricious beauty. Worthy
mothers of daughters, who saw her reproduced
weekly in the society papers, sighed inwardly
with envy, and commented on the decadence of
the aristocracy : the daughters tore out the
pictures in a vain endeavour to copy her frocks.
But it wasn't the frocks that made Cynthia
Stockdale : it was she who made the frocks.
Put her in things selected haphazard from a
jumble sale—put her in remnants discarded by
the people who got it up, and she would still
have seemed the best-dressed woman in the
room. It was a gift she had—not acquired, but
natural.

Lady Cynthia was twenty-five, and looked
four years younger. Since the war she had been
engaged twice—once to a man in the Blues, and
once to a young and ambitious member of Parliament. Neither had lasted long, and on the second
occasion people had said unkind things. They
had called her heartless and capricious, and she

had scorned to contradict them. It mattered nothing to her what people said : if they didn't like her they could go away and have nothing to do with her. And since in her case it wasn't a pose, but the literal truth, people did not go away. Only to Ada Laverton did she give her real confidence : only to Ada Laverton did she show the real soul that lay below the surface.

" I'm trying," she had said, lying in that same chair a year previously, " I'm trying to find the real thing. I needn't marry if I don't want to ; I haven't got to marry for a home and a roof. And it's got to be the right man. Of course I may make a mistake—a mistake which I shan't find out till it's too late. But surely when one has found it out before it's too late, it's better to acknowledge it at once. It's no good making a second worse one by going through with it. I thought Arthur was all right "—Arthur was the member of Parliament—" I'm awfully fond of Arthur still. But I'm not the right wife for him. We jarred on one another in a hundred little ways. And he hasn't got a sense of humour. I shall never forget the shock I got when I first realised that. He seemed to think that a sense of humour consisted of laughing at humorous things, of seeing a jest as well as anyone else. He didn't seem to understand me when I told him that the real sense of humour is often closer to tears than laughter. Besides "—she had added inconsequently—" he had a dreadful trick of whistling down my neck when we danced. No

woman can be expected to marry a permanent
draught. And as for poor old Bill—well Bill's
an angel. I still adore Bill. He is, I think,
the most supremely handsome being I've ever
seen in my life—especially when he's got his full
dress on. But, my dear, I blame myself over Bill.
I ought to have known it before I got engaged to
him ; as a matter of fact I did know it. Bill is,
without exception, the biggest fool in London. I
thought his face might atone for his lack of brains;
I thought that perhaps if I took him in hand he
might do something in the House of Lords—his
old father can't live much longer—but I gave it
up. He is simply incapable of any coherent
thought at all. He can't spell ; he can't add, and
once when I asked him if he liked Rachmaninoff,
he thought it was the man who had built the
Pyramids."

This and much more came back to Ada
Laverton as she turned over in her mind the
sudden wild idea that had come to her. Above
all things she wanted to see Cynthia married ;
she was so utterly happy herself that she longed
for her friend to share it too. She knew, as no
one else did, what a wonderful wife and pal
Cynthia would make to the right man. But it
must be the right man ; it must be the real thing.
And like a blinding flash had come the thought of
the Hermit—the Hermit who had come into the
neighbourhood six months previously, and taken
the little farm standing in the hollow overlooking
the sea. For, as she frequently told John, if it

hadn't been for the fact that she was tied to a silly old idiot of a husband, she'd have married the Hermit herself.

"No, he doesn't feed ravens," she remarked at length. "Only puppies. He breeds Cairns and Aberdeens. We'll stroll up and see him after tea."

"A hermit breeding dogs!" Cynthia sat up lazily. "My dear, you intrigue me."

"Oh! he's not a bad young man," said Ada Laverton, indifferently. "Quite passable looking, D.S.O. and M.C. and that sort of thing. Been all over the world, and is really quite interesting when you can get him to talk."

"What sort of age?" asked her friend.

"Thirty to thirty-five. You shall see him. But you're not to go and turn his head; he's very peaceful and happy as he is."

Lady Cynthia smiled.

"I don't think hermits are much in my line. A man's job is to be up and doing; not to bury himself alive and breed dogs."

"You tell him so," said her hostess. "It will do him good."

II

An excited rush of puppies—fat, bouncing, lolloping puppies; a stern order: "Heel, you young blighters, heel!" in a pleasant, cheerful voice; a laughing greeting from Ada Laverton, and Lady Cynthia Stockdale found herself shaking hands with the Hermit. She shook hands

as a man shakes hands, with a firm, steady
grasp, and she looked the person she was greeting
straight in the eyes. To her that first hand-
shake meant, more often than not, the final
estimate of a stranger's character; it always
meant the first. And her first estimate of
Desmond Brooke was good. She saw a man of
clear skin and clear eye. He wore no hat, and
his brown hair, curling a little at the temples, was
slightly flecked with grey. His face was bronzed
and a faint smile hovered in the corners of the
eyes that met hers fair and square. His shirt
was open at the neck; the sleeves were rolled up,
showing a pair of muscular brown arms. He was
clean shaven, and his teeth were very white and
regular. So much, in detail, she noticed during
that first half-second; then she turned her
attention to the puppies.

"What toppers!" she remarked. "What
absolute toppers!"

She picked a fat, struggling mixture of legs
and ecstatically slobbering tongue out of the
mêlée at her feet, and the Hermit watched her
gravely. It struck him that in the course of a
fairly crowded life he had never seen a more lovely
picture than the one made by this tall slender girl
with the wriggling puppy in her arms. And
another thing struck him also, though he said
nothing. Possibly it was accidental, but the
puppy she had picked up, and which was now
making frantic endeavours to lick her face, was
out and away the best of the litter. Almost

angrily he told himself that it *was* an accident,
and yet he could not quite banish the thought
that it was an accident which would happen
every time. Thoroughbred picks thoroughbred ;
instinctively the girl would pick the best. His
mouth set a little, giving him a look of sternness,
and at that moment their eyes met over the
puppy's head.

" Is he for sale ? " asked the girl.

Undoubtedly he was for sale ; Desmond
Brooke, though he was in no need of money, did
not believe in running anything save on business
lines. But now something that he did not stop to
analyse made him hesitate. He felt a sudden
inconsequent distaste against selling the puppy
to her.

" You've picked the best, I see," he said
quietly.

" Of course," she answered, with the faintest
trace of hauteur. Insensibly she felt that this
man was hostile to her.

" I am afraid that that one is not for sale,"
he continued. " You can have any of the
others if you like."

Abruptly she restored the puppy to its mother.

" Having chosen the best, Mr. Brooke," she
said, looking him straight in the face, " I don't
care about taking anything second-rate."

For a second or two they stared at one
another. Ada Laverton had wandered away and
was talking shop to the gardener ; the Hermit
and Lady Cynthia were alone.

" You surprise me," said the Hermit, calmly.

" That is gratuitously rude," answered the girl quietly. " It is also extremely impertinent. And lastly it shows that you are a very bad judge of character."

The man bowed.

" I sincerely hope that your ' lastly ' is true. Am I to understand, then, that you do not care to buy one of the other puppies ? "

And suddenly the girl laughed half-angrily.

" What do you mean by daring to say such a thing to me ? Why, you haven't known me for more than two minutes."

" That is not strictly true, Lady Cynthia. Anyone who is capable of reading and takes in the illustrated papers can claim your acquaintance weekly."

" I see," she answered. " You disapprove of my poor features being reproduced."

" Personally not at all," he replied. " I know enough of the world, and am sufficiently broad-minded, I trust, to realise how completely unimportant the matter is. Lady Cynthia Stockdale at Ascot, at Goodwood, in her motor-car, out of her motor-car, by the fire, by the gas stove, in her boudoir, out of her boudoir, in the garden, not in the garden—and always in a different frock every time. It doesn't matter to me, but there are some people who haven't got enough money to pay for the doctor's bill when their wives are dying. And it's such a comfort to them to see you by the fire. To know that half the money you paid for your frock would save the life of the woman they love."

" You're talking like a ranting tub-thumper," she cried, furiously. " How dare you say such things to me ? And, anyway, does breeding dogs in the wilderness help them with their doctors' bills ? "

" *Touché*," said the man, with a faint smile. " Perhaps I haven't expressed myself very clearly. You can't pay the bills, Lady Cynthia— I can't. There are too many thousands to pay. But it's the bitter contrast that hits them, and it's all so petty." For a while he paused, seeming to seek for his words. " Come with me, Lady Cynthia, and I'll show you something."

Almost violently he swung round on his heel and strode off towards the house. For a moment she hesitated, then she followed him slowly. Anger and indignation were seething in her mind ; the monstrous impertinence of this complete stranger was almost bewildering. She found him standing in his smoking-room unlocking a drawer in a big writing-desk.

" Well," she said uncompromisingly from the doorway.

" I have something to show you," he remarked quietly. " But before I show it to you, I want to tell you a very short story. Three years ago I was in the back of beyond in Brazil. I'd got a bad dose of fever, and the gassing I got in France wasn't helping matters. It was touch and go whether I pulled through or not. And one day

15

one of the fellows got a two-month-old *Tatler*.
In that *Tatler* was a picture—a picture of the
loveliest girl I have ever seen.   I tore it out, and
I propped it up at the foot of my bed.   I think
I worshipped it; I certainly fell in love with it.
There is the picture."

He handed it to her, and she looked at it in
silence.   It was of herself, and after a moment or
two she raised her eyes to his.

" Go on," she said gently.

" A few months ago I came back to England.
I found a seething cauldron of discontent; men
out of work—strikes—talk of revolution.   And
this was the country for which a million of our
best had died.   I also found—week after week—
my picture girl displayed in every paper, as if no
such thing as trouble existed.   She, in her motor-
car, cared for none of these things."

" That is unjust," said the girl, and her voice
was low.

" I knew it was unjust," answered the man,
" but I couldn't help it.   And if I couldn't help
it—I who loved her—what of these others ?   It
seemed symbolical to me."

" Nero fiddling," said the girl, with a faint
smile.   " You're rather a strange person, Mr.
Brooke.   Am I to understand that you're in love
with me ? "

" You are not.   I'm in love with the you of
that picture."

" I see.   You have set up an image.   And
supposing that image is a true one."

" Need we discuss that ? " said the man, with faint sarcasm.

The girl shrugged her shoulders.

" The supposition is at least as possible as that you are doing any vast amount of good for the seething cauldron of discontent, I think you called it, by breeding Aberdeens in the country. I'm afraid you're a crank, Mr. Brooke, and not a very consistent one at that. And a crank is to my mind synonymous with a bore."

The man replaced the picture in his desk.

" Then perhaps we had better join Mrs. Laverton," he remarked. " I apologise for having wearied you."

In silence they went out into the garden, to find Ada Laverton wandering aimlessly round looking for them.

" Where have you two been ? " she demanded, as she saw them approaching.

" Mr. Brooke has been showing me a relic of his past," said Lady Cynthia. " Most interesting and touching. Are you ready to go, Ada ? "

Mrs. Laverton gave a quick glance at their two faces, and wondered what had happened. Not much, surely, in so short a time—and yet with Cynthia you never could tell. The Hermit's face, usually so inscrutable, showed traces of suppressed feeling ; Cynthia's was rather too expressionless.

" Are you coming to the ball to-morrow night, Hermit ? " she asked.

" I didn't know there was one on, Mrs. Laverton," he answered.

" The cricket ball, my good man," she exclaimed. " It's been advertised for the last month."

" But surely Mr. Brooke doesn't countenance anything so frivolous as dancing ? " remarked Lady Cynthia. " After the lecture he has just given me on my personal deportment the idea is out of the question."

" Nevertheless I propose to come, Lady Cynthia," said Brooke quietly. " You must forgive me if I have allowed my feelings to run away with me to-day. And perhaps to-morrow you will allow me to find out if the new image is correct—or a pose also."

" What do you mean ? " asked the girl, puzzled.

" ' Lady Cynthia Stockdale—possibly the best dancer in London,' " he quoted mockingly ; " I forget which of the many papers I saw it in."

" Do you propose to pass judgment on my dancing ? " she asked.

" If you will be good enough to give me a dance."

For a moment words failed her. The cool, the sublime impertinence of this man literally choked her. Then she nodded briefly.

" I'll give you a dance if you're there in time. And then you can test for yourself, if you're capable of testing."

He bowed without a word, and stood watching them as they walked down the lane.

" I think, Ada, that he's the most detestable man I've ever met," remarked Lady Cynthia furiously, as they turned into the main road.

And Ada Laverton said nothing, but wondered the more.

III

She saw him as soon as she got into the ballroom. It was the last day but one of the local cricket week, and the room was crowded. A large number of the men she knew—men she had danced with in London who had come down to play—and within half a minute she was surrounded. It was a chance of getting a dance with her which was not to be missed ; in London she generally danced with one or at the most two men for the whole evening—men who were absolutely perfect performers. For dancing was a part of Lady Cynthia's life—and a big part.

The humour of the situation had struck her that day. For this dog-breeding crank to presume to judge her powers of dancing seemed too sublimely funny for annoyance. But he deserved to be taught a very considerable lesson. And she proposed to teach him. After that she proposed to dismiss him completely from her mind.

She gave him a cool nod as he came up, and frowned slightly as she noticed the faint glint of laughter in his eyes. Really Mr. Desmond

Brooke was a little above himself. So much the worse for him.

"I don't know whether you'll find one or not," she remarked carelessly, handing him her programme.

He glanced at it without a word, and quietly erased someone's name.

"I've made special arrangements with the band for Number 9, Lady Cynthia," he remarked coolly. "A lot of people will be in at supper then, so we ought to have the floor more to ourselves."

The next instant he had bowed and disappeared, leaving her staring speechlessly at her programme.

"A breezy customer," murmured a man beside her. "Who is he?"

"A gentleman who is going to have the biggest lesson of his life," she answered ominously, and the man laughed. He knew Lady Cynthia—and he knew Lady Cynthia's temper when it was roused. But for once he was wrong in his diagnosis; the outward and visible were there all right—the inward and mental state of affairs in keeping with them was not. For the first time in her life Lady Cynthia felt at a loss. Her partners found her *distraite* and silent; as a matter of fact she was barely conscious of their existence. And the more she lashed at herself mentally, the more confused did she get.

It was preposterous, impossible. Why should she cut Tubby Dawlish to dance with a crank who

kept dogs? A crank, moreover, who openly
avowed that his object was to see if she could
dance. Every now and then she saw him loung-
ing by the door watching her. She knew he was
watching her, though she gave no sign of being
aware of his existence. And all the while
Number 9 grew inexorably nearer.

Dance indeed! She would show him how she
could dance. And as a result she fell into the
deadly fault of trying. No perfect dancer ever
tries to dance; they just dance. And Lady
Cynthia knew that better than most people.
Which made her fury rise still more against the
man standing just outside the door smoking a
cigarette. A thousand times—no; she would
not cut Tubby.

And then she realised that people were moving
in to supper; that the 8 was being taken down
from the band platform—that 9 was being
put up. And she realised that Desmond Brooke
the Hermit was crossing the room towards
her; was standing by her side while Tubby—
like an outraged terrier—was glaring at him
across her.

" This is mine, old thing," spluttered Tubby.
" Number 9."

" I think not," said the Hermit quietly. " I
fixed Number 9 especially with Lady Cynthia
yesterday."

She hesitated—and was lost.

" I'm sorry, Tubby," she said a little weakly.
" I forgot."

Not a trace of triumph showed on the Hermit's face, as he gravely watched the indignant back of his rival retreating towards the door : not a trace of expression showed on his face as he turned to the girl.

" You've been trying to-night, Lady Cynthia," he said gravely. " Please don't—this time. It's a wonderful tune this—half waltz, half tango. It was lucky finding Lopez conducting : he has played for me before. And I want you just to forget everything except the smell of the passion flowers coming in through the open windows, and the thrumming of the guitars played by the natives under the palm-trees." His eyes were looking into hers, and suddenly she drew a deep breath. Things had got beyond her.

It was marked as a fox-trot on the programme, and several of the more enthusiastic performers were waiting to get off on the stroke of time. But as the first haunting notes of the dance wailed out—they paused and hesitated. This was no fox-trot ; this was—but what matter what it was ? For after the first bar no one moved in the room : they stood motionless watching one couple—Lady Cynthia Stockdale and an unknown man.

" Why, it's the fellow who breeds dogs," muttered someone to his partner, but there was no reply. She was too engrossed in watching.

And as for Lady Cynthia, from the moment she felt Desmond Brooke's arm round her, the world had become merely movement—such movement

as she had never thought of before. To say that
he was a perfect dancer would be idle : he was
dancing itself. And the band, playing as men
possessed, played for them and them only.
Everything was forgotten : nothing in the world
mattered save that they should go on and on and
on—dancing. She was utterly unconscious of
the crowd of onlookers : she didn't know that
people had left the supper-room and were
thronging in at the door : she knew nothing save
that she had never danced before. Dimly she
realised at last that the music had stopped :
dimly she heard a great roar of applause—but
only dimly. It seemed to come from far away—
the shouts of " Encore " seemed hazy and dream-
like. They had left the ballroom, though she
was hardly conscious of where he was taking her,
and when he turned to her and said, " Get a wrap
or something : I want to talk to you out in
God's fresh air," she obeyed him without a word.
He was waiting for her when she returned,
standing motionless where she had left him. And
still in silence he led the way to his car which had
been left apart from all the others, almost as if
he had expected to want it before the end. For
a moment she hesitated, for Lady Cynthia,
though utterly unconventional, was no fool.

" Will you come with me ? " he said gravely.

" Where to ? " she asked.

" Up to the cliffs beyond my house. It will
take ten minutes—and I want to talk to you with
the sound of the sea below us."

" You had the car in readiness ? " she said quietly.

" For both of us—or for me alone," he answered. " If you won't come, then I go home. Will you come with me ? " he repeated.

" Yes ; I will come."

He helped her into the car and wrapped a rug round her ; then he climbed in beside her. And as they swung out of the little square, the strains of the next dance followed them from the open windows of the Town Hall.

He drove as he danced—perfectly ; and in the dim light the girl watched his clear-cut profile as he stared ahead into the glare of the head-lights. Away to the right his farm flashed by, the last house before they reached the top of the cliffs. And gradually, above the thrumming of the engine, she heard the lazy boom of the big Atlantic swell on the rocks ahead. At last he stopped where the road ran parallel to the top of the cliff, and switched off the lights.

" Well," she said, a little mockingly, " is the new image correct or a pose ? "

" You dance divinely," he answered gravely. " More divinely than any woman I have ever danced with, and I have danced with those who are reputed to be the show dancers of the world. But I didn't ask you to come here to talk about dancing ; I asked you to come here in order that I might first apologise, and then say Good-bye."

The girl gave a little start, but said nothing.

" I talked a good deal of rot to you yesterday,"

he went on, after a moment. "You were justified in calling me a ranting tub-thumper. But I was angry with myself, and when one is angry with oneself one does foolish things. I know as well as you do just how little society photographs mean : that was only a peg to hang my inexcusable tirade on. You see, when one has fallen in love with an ideal—as I fell in love with that picture of you, all in white in the garden at your father's place—and you treasure that ideal for three years, it jolts one to find that the ideal is different to what you thought. I fell in love with a girl in white, and sometimes in the wilds I've seen visions and dreamed dreams. And then I found her a lovely being in Paquin's most expensive frocks ; a social celebrity : a household name. And then I met her, and knew my girl in white had gone. What matter that it was the inexorable rule of Nature that she must go : what matter that she had changed into an incredibly lovely woman ? She had gone : my dream girl had vanished. In her place stood Lady Cynthia Stockdale—the well-known society beauty. Reality had come—and I was angry with you for having killed my dream— angry with myself for having to wake up.

"Such is my apology," he continued gravely. "Perhaps you will understand : I think you will understand. And just because I was angry with you, I made you dance with me to-night. I said to myself : 'I will show Lady Cynthia Stockdale that the man who loved the girl in

white can meet her successor on her own ground.'
That's the idea I started with, but things went
wrong half-way through the dance. The anger
died; in its place there came something else
Even my love for the girl in white seemed to
become a bit hazy; I found that the successor
had supplanted her more completely than I
realised. And since the successor has the world
at her feet—why, the breeder of dogs will efface
himself, for his own peace of mind. So, good-bye,
Lady Cynthia—and the very best of luck. If it
won't bore you I may say that I'm not really a
breeder of dogs by profession. This is just an
interlude; a bit of rest spent with the most
wonderful pals in the world. I'm getting back
to harness soon: voluntary harness, I'm glad to
say, as the shekels don't matter. But anything
one can do towards greasing the wheels, and
helping those priceless fellows who gave everything without a murmur during the war, and
who are up against it now—is worth doing."

And still she said nothing, while he backed the
car on to the grass beside the road, and turned
it the way they had come. A jumble of strange
thoughts were in her mind; a jumble out of
which there stuck one dominant thing—the
brown tanned face of the man beside her. And
when he stopped the car by his own farm and
left her without a word of apology, she sat quite
motionless staring at the white streak of road in
front. At last she heard his footsteps coming
back along the drive, and suddenly a warm

wriggling bundle was placed in her lap—a bundle which slobbered joyfully and then fell on the floor with an indignant yelp.

" The puppy," he said quietly. " Please take him." And very softly under his breath he added : " The best to the best."

But she heard him, and even as she stooped to lift the puppy on to her knees, her heart began to beat madly. She knew : at last, she knew.

" I'll take you back to the dance," he was saying, " and afterwards I'll deposit that young rascal at Mrs. Laverton's house."

And then for the first time she spoke.

" Please go to Ada's house first. Afterwards we'll see about the dance."

He bowed and swung the car left-handed through the lodge gates.

" Will you wait for me ? " she said, as he pulled up at the front door.

"As long as you like," he answered courteously.

" Because I may be some time," she continued a little unevenly. " And don't wait for me here : wait for me where the drive runs through that little copse, half-way down to the lodge."

The next instant she had disappeared into the house, with the puppy in her arms. Why by the little copse ? wondered the man as he slowly drove the car down the drive. The butler had seen them already, so what did it matter ? He pulled up the car in the shadow of a big oak tree, and lit a cigarette. Then, with his arms resting on the steering wheel, he sat staring in front of him. He had done a mad thing, and she'd taken it wonderfully well. He always had done mad things all his life ; he was made that way. But this was the maddest he had ever done. With a grim smile he pictured her infuriated partners, waiting in serried rows by the door, cursing him by all their gods. And then the smile faded, and he sighed, while his knuckles gleamed white on the wheel. If only she wasn't so gloriously pretty ; if only she wasn't so utterly alive and wonderful. Well—it was the penalty of playing with fire ; and it had been worth it. Yes ; it had been worth it—even if the wound never quite healed.

" *A fool there was, and he made his prayer. . . .* "

He pitched his cigarette away, and suddenly he stiffened and sat motionless, while something seemed to rise in his throat and choke him, and the blood hammered hotly at his temples. A girl in white was standing not five feet from him on the fringe of the little wood : a girl holding a puppy in her arms. And then he heard her speaking.

" It's not the same frock—but it's the nearest I can do."

She came up to the car, and once again over the head of the puppy their eyes met.

" I've been looking," she said steadily, " for the real thing. I don't *think* I've found it—I *know* I have."

" My dear ! " he stammered hoarsely. " Oh ! my dear dream girl."

" Take me back to the cliff, Desmond," she whispered. " Take me back to our cliff."

And an outraged puppy, bouncing off the running-board on to a stray fir-cone, viewed the proceedings of the next five minutes with silent displeasure.

"It's as easy as shelling peas to be a detective in fiction," grunted the Barrister. "He's merely the author of the yarn disguised as a character, and he knows the solution before he starts."

"But the reader doesn't, if the story is told well," objected the Doctor. "And that's all that matters."

"Oh! I grant you that," said the Barrister, lighting a cigar. "I'm not inveighing against the detective story—I love 'em. All I'm saying is that in life a detective's job is a very different matter to—well, take the illustrious example— to that of Sherlock Holmes. He's got to make the crime fit to the clues, not the clues fit into the crime. It's not so terribly difficult to reconstruct the murder of the Prime Minister from a piece of charred paper discovered in the railway refreshment-room at Bath—in fiction; it's altogether a different matter in reality."

The Soldier thoughtfully filled his pipe.

"And yet there have been many cases when the reconstruction has been made on some clue almost equally 'flimsy,'" he murmured.

"A few," conceded the Barrister. "But nine out of ten are built up with laborious care. The structure does not rest on any one fact—but on a whole lot of apparently unimportant and trivial ones. Of course it's more spectacular to bring a man to the gallows because half a brick was found lying on the front door-step, but in practice it doesn't happen."

" It does—sometimes," remarked a quiet, sandy-haired man who was helping himself to a whisky-and-soda. " It does sometimes, you man of law. Your remarks coupled with my present occupation remind me of just such a case."

" Your present occupation appears to be drinking whisky," said the Doctor, curiously.

" Precisely," returned the other. " Almost as prosaic a thing as our legal luminary's half-brick." He settled himself comfortably in a chair, and the others leaned forward expectantly. " And yet on that very ordinary pastime hinged an extremely interesting case : one in which I was lucky enough to play a principal part."

" The night is yet young, old man," said the Barrister. " It's up to you to prove your words, and duly confound me."

The sandy-haired man took a sip of his drink : then he put the glass on the table beside him and began.

" Well, if it won't bore you, I'm agreeable. I'll tell you the whole thing exactly as it took place, only altering the names of the people involved. It happened before the war—in that hot summer of 1911, to be exact. I'd been work-

16

ing pretty hard in London, and about the end of July I got an invitation to go down and stop with some people in Devonshire. I will call them the Marleys, and they lived just outside a small village on the north coast. The family consisted of old Marley, who was a man rising sixty, and his two daughters, Joan and Hilda. There was also Jack Fairfax, through whom, as a matter of fact, I had first got to know them.

"Jack was about my own age—thirty odd, and we'd been up at Cambridge together. He was no relation to old Marley, but he was an orphan, and Marley was his guardian, or had been when Jack was a youngster. And from the very first Jack and the old man had not got on.

"Marley was not everybody's meat, by a long way—rather a queer-tempered, secretive blighter; and Jack Fairfax had the devil of a temper at times. When he was a boy he had no alternative except to do as his guardian told him, but even in those early days, as I gathered subsequently, there had been frequent storms. And when he came down from Cambridge there were two or three most unholy rows which culminated in Jack leaving the house for good.

"It was apparently this severance from the two girls, whom he had more or less regarded as sisters, which caused the next bust-up. And this one, according to Jack, was in the nature of a volcanic eruption The two girls had come up to London to go through the season with some aunt, and Jack had seen a good deal of them with the net result that he and Joan had fallen in love with each other. Then the fat was in the fire. Jack straightway had gone down to Devonshire to ask old Marley's consent: old Marley had replied in terms which, judging from Jack's account of the interview, had contained a positive profusion of un-Parliamentary epithets. Jack had lost his temper properly—and, well, you know, the usual thing. At any rate, the long and the short of it was that old Marley had recalled both his daughters from London, and had sworn that if he ever saw Jack near the house again he'd pepper him with a shot-gun. To which Jack had replied that only his grey hairs and his gout saved Mr. Marley from the biggest hiding he'd ever had in his life—even if not the biggest he deserved. With which genial exchange of playful badinage I gathered the interview ended. And that was how matters stood when I went down in July, 1911.

" For some peculiar reason the old man liked me, even though I was a friend of Jack's. And in many ways I quite liked him, though there was always something about him which defeated me. Of course, he had a foul temper—but it wasn't altogether that. He seemed to me at times to be in fear of something or somebody; and yet, though I say that now, I don't know that I went as far as thinking so at the time. It was an almost indefinable impression—vague and yet very real.

" The two girls were perfectly charming,

though they were both a little afraid of their
father. How long it would have taken Joan to
overcome this timidity, and go to Jack without
her father's consent, I don't know. And incidentally, as our legislators say, the question did
not arise. Fate held the ace of trumps, and proceeded to deal it during my visit."

The sandy-haired man leant back in his
chair and crossed his legs deliberately.

" I think it was about the fourth day after I
arrived (he went on, after a while) that the
tragedy happened. We were sitting in the
drawing-room after dinner—a couple of men
whose names I forget, and a girl friend of Hilda's.
Hilda herself was there, and Joan, who seemed
very preoccupied, had come in about a quarter
of an hour previously. I had noticed that Hilda
had looked at her sister inquiringly as she
entered, and that Joan had shrugged her
shoulders. But nothing had been said, and
naturally I asked no questions with the others
there, though from the air of suppressed excitement on Joan's face I knew there was something
in the wind.

" Old Marley himself was not with us : he was
in his study at the other end of the house. The
fact was not at all unusual : he frequently retired
to his own den after dinner, sometimes joining
the rest of the party for a few minutes before going
to bed, more often not appearing again till the
following morning. And so we all sat there
talking idly, with the windows wide open and the

light shining out on to the lawn. It must have been somewhere about ten to a quarter past when suddenly Hilda gave a little scream.

" ' What do you want ? ' she cried. ' Who are you ? '

" I swung round in my chair, to find a man standing on the lawn outside, in the centre of the light. He was facing us, and as we stared at him he came nearer till he was almost in the room. And the first thing that struck me was that he looked a little agitated.

" ' You will excuse me appearing like this,' he said, ' but——' He broke off and looked at me. ' Might I have a word with you alone, sir ? '

" I glanced at the others : obviously he was a stranger. No trace of recognition appeared on anyone's face, and I began to feel a little suspicious.

" ' What is it ? ' I cried. ' What can you possibly want to speak to me about that you can't say now ? '

" He shrugged his shoulders slightly. ' As you will,' he answered. ' My idea was to avoid frightening the ladies. In the room at the other end of the house a man has been murdered.'

" For a moment everyone was too thunderstruck to reply ; then Hilda gave a choking cry.

" ' What sort of a man ? ' she said, breathlessly.

" ' An elderly man of, I should think, about sixty,' returned the other, gravely, and Hilda buried her face in her hands.

" ' I will come with you at once, sir,' I said,
hurriedly, and the two other men rose. Instinctively, I think, we all knew it must be old
Marley : there was no one else it could be. But
the sudden shock of it had dazed us all. I
glanced at Joan. She was staring at the man
like a girl bereft of her senses, and I put my hand
reassuringly on her shoulder. And then she
looked up at me, and the expression in her eyes
pulled me together. It was like a cold douche,
and it acted instantaneously. Because it wasn't
horror or dazed stupefaction that I read on her
face : it was terror—agonised terror. And
suddenly I remembered her air of suppressed
excitement earlier in the evening."

Once again the sandy-haired man paused
while the others waited in silence for him to
continue.

" It was old Marley right enough (he went on
quietly). We walked round the front of the
house until we came to the window of his study,
and there instinctively we paused. The window
was open, and he was sitting at his desk quite
motionless. His head had fallen forward, and
on his face was a look of dreadful fear.

" For a while none of us moved. Then, with
an effort, I threw my leg over the window-sill
and entered.

" ' He's quite dead,' I said, and I felt my voice
was shaking. ' We'd better send for the police.'

" The others nodded, and in silence I picked
up the telephone.

" ' Mr. Marley's been killed,' I heard myself saying. ' Will you send someone up at once ? '

" And then for the first time I noticed the poker lying beside the chair, and saw the back of the old man's head. It wasn't a pretty sight, and one of the other men staying in the house— a youngster—turned very white, and went to the window.

" ' Pretty obvious how it was done,' said the stranger, quietly. ' Well, gentlemen, nothing ought to be touched in this room until the police arrive. I suggest that we should draw the curtains and go somewhere else to wait for them.'

" I don't think any of us were sorry to fall in with his suggestion. I also don't think I've ever drunk such a large whisky-and-soda as I did a few minutes later. Discovering the body had been bad enough : breaking the news to the two girls was going to be worse.

" It was Joan who met me in the hall—and we stared at one another in silence. Then I nodded my head stupidly.

" ' It's father,' she whispered. ' Oh, my God ! '

" I put out my hand to steady her, and she was looking at me with a fixed stare.

" ' Don't you understand ? ' she muttered, hoarsely, and swallowing all the time. ' Don't you understand ? Jack has been here to-night.'

" ' Jack ! ' I looked at her foolishly. ' Jack ! '

" And then her full meaning struck me.

" ' How did that man find out ? ' she whispered. ' And who is he ? '

" ' I don't know. I'll go and ask him.' I was still trying to adjust this new development—and her next words seemed to come from a great distance.

" ' Do something. For God's sake—do something.'

" Then she turned and left me, and I watched her go up the stairs, walking stiffly and clinging to the banisters.

" So Jack had been there ! And old Marley was dead ! Murdered ! Hit on the head with a poker. And Jack had been there. It's only in romantic fiction that the reader is expected to assume the impossibility of the hero committing a crime, owing to the extreme beauty of his nature. And this wasn't romantic fiction. It was hard, brutal reality. The two facts stood there, side by side, in all their dazzling simplicity. Jack's nature was not supremely beautiful. He was an ordinary man, with the devil of a temper when it was roused.

" Mechanically I started to walk back to the room where I had left the other three men. They were sitting in silence when I entered, and after a while the stranger got up.

" ' A dreadful thing to happen,' he said, gravely.

" ' May I ask, sir,' I began, ' how you came to discover it ? '

" ' Very simply,' he answered. ' I was strolling along the road, going back to the village inn where I have been stopping for two or three nights, when I saw the window of the room through the trees. The light was shining out, and I could see someone sitting at the desk. More out of idle curiosity than anything else, I paused for a moment or two, and then something began to arouse my suspicions. The man at the desk seemed so motionless. I thought perhaps he had fainted, or was ill, and after a little hesitation I went in at the gate and looked through the window. To my horror I saw he was dead— and I at once came round to the other room from which the light was shining, and where I found you.'

" ' There is a point which may have some bearing on the crime,' he continued, after a pause. ' On my way up from the inn a man passed me. He was coming from this direction, and seemed to me to be in a very excited condition. It was his obvious agitation that made me notice him at the time, though in the dim light I couldn't see his face very clearly. But he was swinging his stick in the air, and muttering to himself. At the moment I didn't think much about it. But now——' He shrugged his shoulders slightly. ' Of course, I may be completely wrong, but I think it is a thing worth mentioning to the police.'

" ' Would you know the man again ? ' I asked, trying to speak quite normally.

" ' Well, he was tall—six feet at least—and broad. And he was clean-shaven.' He spoke thoughtfully, weighing his words. ' I might know him again—but I wouldn't swear to it. One has to be doubly careful if a man's life is at stake.'

" I turned away abruptly. Jack was tall and broad and clean-shaven. Strive as I would, the deadly suspicion was beginning to grip me that Jack, in a fit of ungovernable passion, had killed the old man. And at such moments, whatever may be the legal aspect of the matter, one's main idea is how best to help a pal. If Jack had indeed done it, what was the best thing to do ?

" I rang the bell, and told the scared-looking maid to bring the whisky and some glasses. Then, with a muttered apology, I left the room. I felt I wanted to talk to Joan about it. I found her dry-eyed and quite composed, though she was evidently holding herself under control with a great effort. And briefly I told her what the stranger had said.

" She heard me out in silence : then she spoke with a quiet assurance that surprised me.

" ' If Jack did it,' she said, ' he doesn't know he's done it. He doesn't know he's killed— father.' She faltered a bit over the last word, and I didn't interrupt. ' What I mean is this,' she went on after a moment. ' I know Jack— better than anyone else. I know those rages of his—when he sees red. But they're over in a minute. He's capable of anything for a second or two, but if he'd done it, Hugh, if he'd hit father—and killed him—his remorse would have

been dreadful. He wouldn't have run away:
I'm certain of that. That's why I say that if
Jack did it he doesn't know—he killed him.'

" I said nothing : there was no good telling
her that it wasn't one blow, nor yet two or three,
that had been used. There was no good telling
her that it was no accidental thing done unwittingly in the heat of the moment—that it was
an absolute impossibility for the man who had
done it to be in ignorance of the fact. And yet,
though I realised all that, her simple conviction
put new hope into me. Illogical, I admit, but I
went downstairs feeling more confident.

" I found that the local police had arrived—a
sergeant and an ordinary constable—and had
already begun their investigations. The principal evidence, of course, came from the stranger,
and he repeated to them what he had already
told me. His name apparently was Lenham—
Victor Lenham—and the police knew he had
been stopping at the local inn.

" ' You saw the body through the window,
sir,' said the sergeant, ' and then went round to
the drawing-room ? '

" ' That is so, sergeant.'

" ' You didn't go into the room ? '

" ' Not until later—with these gentlemen.
You see,' he added, ' I've seen death too often
not to recognise it. And as, in a way, you will
understand, it was no concern of mine, I thought
it advisable to have some member of the house
itself with me before entering the room.'

"'Quite, sir, quite.' The sergeant nodded portentously. 'Is there anything else you can tell us?'

"'Well,' said Lenham, 'there is a point, which I have already mentioned to this gentleman.' He glanced at me, and then, turning back to the sergeant, he told him about the man he had passed on the road. And it was when he came to the description that suddenly the constable gave a whistle of excitement. The sergeant frowned on him angrily, but the worthy P.C., whose only experience of crime up-to-date had been assisting inebriated villagers home, had quite lost his head.

"'Mr. Fairfax, sergeant,' he exploded. ''E was down here to-night. Caught the last train, 'e did. Jenkins at the station told me—sure thing.'

"'Good heavens, sergeant!' I said angrily, 'what the devil is the man talking about? He surely doesn't suppose that Mr. Fairfax had anything to do with it?'

"But the mischief was done. The sergeant formally told off his indiscreet subordinate, but it was obvious that it was merely an official rebuke. In a village like that everybody knows everybody else's private affairs, and the strained relations between the dead man and Jack Fairfax were common property. I could see at a glance that the sergeant regarded the matter as solved already.

"'Would you recognise this man again, sir?'

he demanded, and Lenham gave him the same
guarded reply as he had already given to me.
He might—but he wouldn't swear to it. It was
impossible to be too careful in such a case, he
repeated, and it was practically dark when he
had passed the man.

"It was all duly noted down, and then we
adjourned to the room of the tragedy. The constable—a ruddy-faced young man—turned pale
when he saw the body; then he pulled himself
together and assisted the sergeant in his formal
examination. I didn't blame him—we were all
feeling the strain, somewhat naturally. Lenham
seemed the least concerned, but it wasn't a
personal matter with him as it was with us,
especially with me. All the time I was fidgeting
round the room, subconsciously watching the
stolid sergeant making notes, but with only one
thought dominating my brain—how best to help
Jack. Not that I had definitely made up my
mind that he'd done it, but even at that stage of
the proceedings I realised that appearances were
against him. And Joan's words were ringing in
my head—'For God's sake—do something.'

"After a while I crossed the room to a small
table on which a tantalus of whisky and two
glasses were standing. I looked at the tray with
unseeing eyes—an Indian silver one, which old
Marley had been very proud of. And then
mechanically I picked up the glasses. I don't
know why I did so; the action was, as I say,
mechanical. They had been used—both of

them : they had been used for whisky—one
could tell that by the smell. And when I put
the glasses down again on the tray, the sergeant
was approaching with his note-book."

The sandy-haired man paused, with a reminis-
cent smile.

" Ever noticed how extraordinarily dense you
can be at times, even with a plain fact staring
you straight in the face ?   There was one staring
at me for ten minutes that night before my grey
matter began to stir."

" Just hold on a minute," interrupted the
Barrister.   " Is this plain fact staring us in the
face now ? "

" No, it isn't," conceded the narrator.   " At
the moment you are in the position of the other
people in that room.   Mind you, I've left out
nothing in order to mystify you ; the story, as I
have given it to you, is a plain unvarnished
account of what took place.   But I'm out to
disprove your half-brick theory, lawyer-man, and
to do so with such little story-telling ability as I
happen to posesss.

" Now, I won't weary you with what happened
during the next week, beyond saying that an
inquest and a burglary took place.   And the
latter, at any rate, was very successful.   The
former moved along obvious lines, and resulted
in Jack Fairfax being arrested for the wilful
murder of his guardian, Roger Marley.   The
evidence was purely circumstantial, but it was
about as damning as it could be.   Jack admitted

to having had an interview with Marley that
night ; he admitted that they had had an appalling quarrel. What was even worse was that he
admitted to having struck the old man in a
furious fit of rage, but beyond that he denied
everything. He absolutely swore that the blow
he struck Marley could not have killed him ;
further, that he had never handled the poker.
And then, a finger-print expert proved that he
had. That was the worst shock of the lot, and
his explanation given afterwards that, now he
came to think of it, he had picked up the poker
to ram the tobacco down in his pipe convinced no
one. He indignantly denied that his action in
going up to London by the last train was in any
sense running away ; he had intended all along
to go up by that train. And his reason for
leaving the house after the interview without
attempting to see his *fiancée* was that he was in
such a rage with her father that he couldn't
trust himself to speak to her for fear of what he
might say.

" So much for Jack Fairfax's case—pretty
black, as you will agree. In fact, I don't
think I should be exaggerating if I said
that there were only two people in England
convinced of his innocence. And he was one
of them. Even Joan's faith was shaken, a
little.

" It was on the tenth day after the inquest
that I rang up the inspector who had come over
from Exeter to look into the case, with a request

that he would come up to the house. I told him
that I had certain information which might
interest him and suggested that he might care to
hear it. I also rang up Lenham at the inn, and
asked him if he would mind coming along at the
same time. I told him I'd discovered the burglar.
By the way, I didn't tell you that it was his room
that had been burgled.

"In about half an hour they arrived, and the
local sergeant as well.

"'What's this about my burglar?' laughed
Lenham. 'A funny fellow—because as far as I
can see he didn't take anything.'

"'All in good time,' I answered, smiling.
'I've found out a lot of strange things in
town.'

"Lenham looked at me quickly. Oh! have
you been to London?' he inquired.

"'Yes,' I answered, 'for two days. Most
entertaining.'

"And then the inspector chipped in, im-
patiently :

"'Well, sir, what is it you want to say to me?'
He looked at his watch suggestively.

"'First of all, inspector,' I said, quietly,
'I want to ask you a question. Have you ever
heard the legal maxim, *Falsus in uno, falsus
in omne*?'

"I could see that he hadn't the faintest idea
what I was driving at. I could also see that
Lenham's eyes had suddenly become strained.

"'It means,' I went on, 'that if a witness—

let us say—is proved to have told one lie, there is strong presumptive evidence that he has told several. At any rate, the value of his statement is greatly diminished. Do you agree ? '

" ' Certainly,' he answered. ' But I don't see——'

" ' You will shortly, inspector,' I remarked. ' Now who would you consider the principal witness against Mr. Fairfax ? '

" ' Mr. Fairfax himself,' said the inspector, promptly.

" ' And leaving him out ? ' I asked.

" ' Well—I suppose—this gentleman here.' He nodded towards Lenham, who was sitting quite motionless, watching me.

" ' Precisely,' I murmured. ' Then why was it necessary for Mr. Lenham to state that his name was Lenham, and further to swear that he had never seen Mr. Marley before—when both those statements were lies ? '

" ' What the devil do you mean ? ' snarled Lenham, rising from his chair. ' What do you mean by saying my name is not Lenham ? '

" ' You wanted to know about the burglar who took nothing, didn't you ? ' I said, grimly. ' Well—I was the burglar, and I took something very valuable—an address.'

" ' What on earth——' began the inspector, and then he glanced at Lenham. ' I think you'd better sit still, Mr. Lenham,' he said, quietly, ' until we have heard what this gentleman has to say.'

17

" Lenham sat back in his chair with a venomous look at me.   Then he laughed harshly.

" ' By all means, inspector,' he remarked. ' Only it is a little disconcerting to be cross-examined suddenly by a man who admits he is a thief.'

" As a matter of fact the man didn't know how much I knew—or how little ; and between ourselves it was deuced little.   But, watching him closely, I knew I was right, and my only hope was to bluff him into some admission.

" ' Shall we endeavour to reconstruct the events of the night when Mr. Marley was murdered, Mr. Lenardi ? ' I began, quietly. ' That is your name, is it not ?—and you are a Corsican.'

" ' Well,' he said, ' what if I am ?   I had a very good reason for changing my name.'

" ' Doubtless,' I agreed. ' Let us hope your reason will prove satisfactory to the inspector. May I suggest, however, unless you can supply a better one, that your reason was to avoid the notoriety which would inevitably arise if a foreigner came to stay in a small village like this ?   And you were particularly anxious to avoid any possibility of Mr. Marley knowing that a Corsican was in the neighbourhood.'

" He laughed sarcastically. ' I think that I have already stated that I have never even seen Mr. Marley,' he sneered.

" ' Oh ! ' I remarked. ' Then might I ask you, inspector, to have a look at this photograph ? It is old and faded, but the faces are still clear.'

" I handed the photograph to the inspector, and with a sudden curse the Corsican whipped out a knife and sprang at me. He realised even then that the game was up, and his one thought was to revenge himself on me. But I'd been expecting some such move, and I'd got a revolver handy. Incidentally, revolver shooting is one of the few things I can do, and I plugged him through the forearm before he could do any damage.

" He stood there glaring at me sullenly, and then the inspector took a hand.

" ' Stand by that window, sergeant. Now, Mr. whatever-your-name-is, no monkey tricks. Do you still deny that you knew Mr. Marley ? "

" ' I refuse to answer,' snarled the man.

" ' Because this photograph is of you and Marley and a woman. Taken abroad somewhere.'

" ' Naples, to be exact, inspector,' I said. ' I found it in his rooms in Berners Street, the address of which I got as the result of my burglary here."

" The Corsican stood there like a beast at bay, and the inspector's face was stern.

" ' What explanation have you got to give ? ' he rapped out. ' Why did you lie in evidence ? '

" ' I refuse to answer,' repeated the man.

" ' Since he is so uncommunicative,' I remarked, ' perhaps you will allow me to reconstruct the crime. Much of it, of necessity, is guess-work. For instance, Lenardi, what was your motive in murdering Mr. Marley ? ' I rapped the question out at him, and though he'd have killed me willingly if he could have got at me he didn't deny it.

" ' Well,' I continued, ' it doesn't matter. Let us assume it was the girl in that photograph. You tracked Marley to earth here—in this village—that is all that concerns us. And having tracked him, you bided your time. Vengeance is the sweeter for delay. Each evening you walked up here, watching him through the window—gloating over what was to come. And then one night you found another man with him— Jack Fairfax—and they were quarrelling. At once you saw that this was your opportunity. However skilfully you hid your traces under ordinary circumstances, there was always a grave risk ; but here, ready to hand, was a marvellous stroke of luck. Perhaps you crept nearer the window in the darkness, secure in the fact that the room was in a remote part of the house. You saw Jack Fairfax leave, blind with rage, and then, skulking out of the night, you entered the room yourself.'

" ' It's a lie ! ' shouted the Corsican, but his lips were white.

" ' And then old Marley saw you, and the rage on his face was replaced by a dreadful terror. He knew what you had come for. I don't think you wasted much time, Lenardi. You picked up the poker with a gloved hand—oh ! you were taking no chances—and you battered his head in.

And then, Lenardi—and then you drank a whisky-and-soda. You drank a whisky-and-soda, and then you decided on a very bold move : you came and alarmed the rest of the house. It was clever of you, but——"

The sandy-haired man smiled thoughtfully.

" We sprang forward together—the inspector and I ; but we were too late. The Corsican had swallowed poison before we could stop him. He was dead in half a minute and he never spoke again. So I can only assume that my imagination was not far off the rails."

" Yes, but hang it, man," said the Barrister, peevishly, " the whole thing was a pure fluke on your part."

" I've never laid any claim to being a detective," murmured the sandy-haired man, mildly, rising and helping himself to some more whisky. " All that I said was that there are times when you can build an entire case from your half-brick or its equivalent. And when you find two glasses both smelling strongly of whisky in a room, you assume that two people have drunk whisky. Which was where the Corsican tripped up. You see, he distinctly swore he hadn't entered the room till he came in with us."

The Barrister raised protesting hands to the ceiling.

" The man is indubitably mad," he remarked to no one in particular. " Was not Fairfax in the room most of the evening ? "

The sandy-haired man looked even more mild.

" I think that perhaps I ought to have mentioned one fact sooner, but I was afraid it would spoil the story. The cat has an aversion to water; the fish have an aversion to dry land. But both these aversions pale into total insignificance when compared to Jack Fairfax's aversion to whisky."

He gazed thoughtfully at his glass.

" A strange flaw in an otherwise fine character Thank heavens the symptom is not common ! "

" Yes ; she's a beautiful woman. There's no doubt about that. What did you say her name was ? "

" I haven't mentioned her name," I returned. " But there's no secret about it. She is Lady Sylvia Clavering."

" Ah ! Sylvia. Of course, I remember now."

He drained his glass of brandy and sat back in his chair, while his eyes followed one of the most beautiful women in London as she threaded her way through the tables towards the entrance of the restaurant. An obsequious head-waiter bent almost double as she passed ; her exit, as usual, befitted one of the most be-photographed women of Society. And it was not until the doors had swung to behind her and her escort that the man I had been dining with spoke again.

" I guess that little bow she gave as she passed here was yours, not mine," he said, with the suspicion of a smile.

" Presumably," I answered a little curtly. " Unless you happen to know her. I have that privilege."

His smile grew a trifle more pronounced though his eyes were set and steady. " Know her ? " He beckoned to the waiter for more brandy

" No, I can't say I know her.   In fact, my sole
claim to acquaintanceship is that I carried her for
three miles in the dark one night, slung over my
shoulder like a sack of potatoes.   But I don't
know her."

" You did what ? " I cried, staring at him in
amazement.

" Sounds a bit over the odds, I admit."   He
was carefully cutting the end off his cigar.
" Nevertheless it stands."

Now when any man states that he has carried
a woman for three miles, whether it be in the dark
or not, and has followed up such an introduction
so indifferently that the woman fails even to
recognise him afterwards, there would seem to be
the promise of a story.   But when the woman is
one of the Lady Sylvia Claverings of this world,
and the man is of the type of my dinner com-
panion, the promise resolves itself into a
certainty.

Merton was one of those indefinable characters
who defy placing.   You felt that if you landed in
Yokohama, and he was with you, you would
instinctively rely on him for information as to the
best thing to do and the best way to do it.   There
seemed to be no part of the globe, from the
South Sea Islands going westward to Alaska,
with which he was not as well acquainted as the
ordinary man is with his native village.   At the
time I did not know him well.   The dinner
was only our third meeting, and during the meal
we confined ourselves to the business which had

been the original cause of our running across one
another at all. But even in that short time I had
realised that Billy Merton was a white man.
And not only was he straight, but he was essentially a useful person to have at one's side in a
tight corner.

" Are you disposed to elaborate your somewhat
amazing statement ? " I asked, after a pause.

For a moment or two he hesitated, and his eyes
became thoughtful.

" I don't suppose there's any reason why I
shouldn't," he answered slowly. " It's ancient
history now—ten years or so."

" That was just about the time she was
married," I remarked.

He nodded. " She was on her honeymoon
when it happened. Well, if you want to hear the
yarn, come round to my club."

" Why, certainly," I said, beckoning for the
bill. " Let's get on at once ; I'm curious."

" Do you know Africa at all ? " he asked me,
as we pulled our chairs up to the fire. We had
the room almost to ourselves ; a gentle snoring
from the other fireplace betokened the only other
occupant.

" Egypt," I answered. " Parts of South Africa.
The usual thing : nothing out of the ordinary."

He nodded. " It was up the West Coast that
it happened," he began, after his pipe was going
to his satisfaction. " And though I've been in
many God-forsaken spots in my life, I've never
yet struck anything to compare with that place.

Nwambi it was called—just a few shacks stretching in from the sea along a straggling, dusty street—one so-called shop and a bar. It called itself an hotel, but Lord help the person who tried to put up there. It was a bar pure and simple, though no one could call the liquor that. Lukewarm gin, some vile substitute for whisky, the usual short drinks, and some local poisons formed the stock; I ought to know—I was the bartender.

" For about three miles inland there stretched a belt of stinking swamp—one vast malaria hot-bed—and over this belt the straggling street meandered towards the low foot-hills beyond. At times it almost lost itself : but if you didn't give up hope, or expire from the stench, and cast about you'd generally find it again leading you on to where you felt you might get a breath of God's fresh air in the hills. As a matter of fact you didn't; the utmost one can say is that it wasn't quite so appalling as in the swamp itself. Mosquitoes! Heavens! they had to be seen to be believed. I've watched 'em there literally like a grey cloud."

Merton smiled reminiscently.

" That—and the eternal boom of the sea on the bar half a mile out, made up Nwambi. How any white man ever got through alive if he had to stop there any length of time is beyond me ; to be accurate, very few did. It was a grave, that place, and only the down-and-outers went there. At the time I was one myself.

" The sole reason for its existence at all was that the water alongside the quay was deep enough for good-sized boats to come in, and most of the native produce from the district inland found its way down to Nwambi for shipment. Once over the belt of swamp and a few miles into the hills the climate was much better, and half a dozen traders in a biggish way had bungalows there. They were Dagos most of them—it wasn't a British part of the West Coast—and I frankly admit that my love for the Dago has never been very great. But there was one Scotchman, McAndrew, amongst them—and he was the first fellow who came into the bar after I'd taken over the job. He was down for the night about some question of freight.

" ' You're new,' he remarked, leaning against the counter. ' What's happened to the other fellow ? Is he dead ? '

" ' Probably,' I returned. ' What do you want ? '

" ' Gin—double tot. What's your name ? '

" I told him, and he pondered the matter while he finished his drink.

" ' Well,' he said at length, ' I warned your predecessor, and I'll warn you. Don't fall foul of my manager down here. Name of Mainwaring —I do *not* think. Don't give him advice about keeping off the drink, or he'll kill you. He's killing himself, but that's his business. I'm tough—you look tough, but he's got us beat to a frazzle. And take cover if he ever gets mixed up with any of the Dagos—the place isn't healthy.'

" It was just at that moment that the door swung open and a tall, lean fellow lounged in. He'd got an eyeglass screwed into one eye, and a pair of perfectly-fitting polo boots with some immaculate white breeches encased his legs. His shirt was silk, his sun-helmet spotless ; in fact, he looked like the typical English dude of fiction.

" ' My manager, Mainwaring,' said McAndrew, by way of introduction.

" Mainwaring stared at me for a moment or two—then he shrugged his shoulders.

" ' You look sane ; however, if you come here you can't be.   Double gin—and one for yourself.'

" He spoke with a faint, almost affected drawl, and as I poured out the drinks I watched him covertly.   When he first came in I had thought him a young man ; now I wasn't so sure.   It was his eyes that made one wonder as to his age—they were so utterly tired.   If he was indeed drinking himself to death, there were no traces of it as yet on his face, and his hand as he lifted his glass was perfectly steady.   But those eyes of his—I can see them now.   The cynical bitterness, the concentrated weariness of all Hell was in them.   And it's not good for any man to look like that ; certainly not a man of thirty-five, as I afterwards discovered his age to be."

Merton paused and sipped his whisky-and-soda, while from the other side of the room came indications that the sleeper still slept.

" I never found out what his real name was," he continued, thoughtfully. " Incidentally, it doesn't much matter. We knew him as Mainwaring, and the J. which preceded it in his signature was assumed to stand for James or Jimmy. Anyway, he answered to it, which was the main point. As far as I know, he never received a letter and he never read a paper, and I guess I got to know him better than anyone else in that hole. Every morning, punctual to the second at eleven o'clock, he'd stroll into the bar and have three double-gins. Sometimes he'd talk in his faint, rather pleasant drawl; more often he'd sit silently at one of the rickety tables, staring out to sea, with his long legs stretched out in front of him. But whichever he did—whatever morning it was—you could always see your face in his boots.

" I remember once, after I'd been there about a month, I started to pull his leg about those boots of his.

" ' Take the devil of a long time cleaning them in the morning, don't you, Jimmy ? ' I said, as he lounged up to the bar for his third gin.

" ' Yes,' he answered, leaning over the counter so that his face was close to mine. ' Got anything further to say about my appearance ? '

" ' Jimmy,' I replied, ' your appearance doesn't signify one continental damn to me. But as the only two regular British *habitués* of this first-class American bar, don't let's quarrel.'

" He grinned—a sort of slow, lazy grin.

" ' Think not ? ' he said.   ' Might amuse one.
However, perhaps you're right.'

" And so it went on—one sweltering day after
another, until one could have gone mad with the
hideous boredom of it.   I used to stand behind
the bar there sometimes and curse weakly and
foolishly like a child, but I never heard Mainwaring do it.   What happened during those
steamy nights in the privacy of his own room,
when he—like the rest of us—was fighting for
sleep, is another matter.   During the day he
never varied.   Cold, cynical, immaculate, he
seemed a being apart—above our little worries
and utterly contemptuous of them.   Maybe he
was right—maybe the thing that had downed him
was too big for foolish cursing.   Knowing what
I do now, a good many things are clear which one
didn't realise at the time.

" Only once, I think, did I ever get in the
slightest degree intimate with him.   It was latish
one evening, and the bar was empty save for us
two.   I'd been railing against the fate that had
landed me penniless in such an accursed spot,
and after a while he chipped in, in his lazy
drawl :

" ' Would a thousand be any good to you ? '

" I looked at him speechless.   ' A thousand
pounds ? '   I stammered.

" ' Yes ;   I think I can raise that for you.'
He was staring in front of him as he spoke.
' And yet I don't know.   I've got more or less

used to you and you'll have to stop a bit longer.
Then we'll see about it.'

" ' But, good heavens ! man,' I almost shouted,
' do you mean to say that you stop here when you
can lay your hand on a thousand pounds ? '

" ' It appears so, doesn't it ? '   He rose and
stalked over to the bar.   ' It doesn't much matter
where you stop, Merton, when you can't be in the
one place where you'd sell your hopes of Heaven
to be.   And it's best, perhaps, to choose a place
where the end will come quickly.'

" With that he turned on his heel, and I
watched him with a sort of dazed amazement as
he sauntered down the dusty road, white in the
tropical moon, towards his own shack.   A
thousand pounds ! The thought of it rang in
my head all through the night.   A thousand
pounds !   A fortune !   And because, out in
death-spots like that, men are apt to think
strange thoughts—thoughts that look ugly by the
light of day—I found myself wondering how long
he could last at the rate he was going.   Two—
sometimes three—bottles of gin a day: it
couldn't be long.   And then—who knew ?   It
would be quick, the break-up ; all the quicker
because there was not a trace of it now.   And
perhaps when it came he'd remember about that
thousand.   Or I could remind him."

Merton laughed grimly.

" Yes, we're pretty average swine, even the
best of us, when we're up against it, and I lay no
claims to be a plaster saint.   But Fate had

decreed that Jimmy Mainwaring was to find the
end which he craved for quicker than he had
anticipated. Moreover—and that's what I've
always been glad about—it had decreed that he
was to find it before drink had rotted that iron
constitution of his; while his boots still shone
and his silk shirts remained spotless. It had
decreed that he was to find it in the way of all
others that he would have chosen, had such a wild
improbability ever suggested itself. Which is
going ahead a bit fast with the yarn—but no
matter.

"It was after I'd been there about three
months that the incident happened which was
destined to be the indirect cause of his death. I
told you, didn't I, that there were several Dago
traders who lived up in the foot-hills, and on the
night in question three of them had come down
to Nwambi on business of some sort—amongst
them one Pedro Salvas, who was as unpleasant
a specimen of humanity as I have ever met.
A crafty, orange-skinned brute, who indulged,
according to common knowledge, in every known
form of vice, and a good many unknown ones too.
The three of them were sitting at a table near the
door when Mainwaring lounged in—and Mc-
Andrew's words came back to me. The Dagos
had been drinking; Jimmy looked in his most
uncompromising mood. He paused at the door,
and stared at each of them in turn through his
eyeglass; then he turned his back on them and
came over to me.

" I glanced over his shoulder at the three men, and realised there was trouble coming. They'd been whispering and muttering together the whole evening, though at the time I had paid no attention. But now Pedro Salvas, with an ugly flush on his ugly face, had risen and was coming towards the bar.

" ' If one so utterly unworthy as I,' he snarled, ' may venture to speak to the so very exclusive Englishman, I would suggest that he does not throw pictures of his lady-loves about the streets.'

" He was holding something in his hand, and Jimmy swung round like a panther. His hand went to his breast pocket ; then I saw what the Dago was holding out. It was the miniature of a girl. And after that I didn't see much more ; I didn't even have time to take cover. It seemed to me that the lightning movement of Jimmy's left hand as he grabbed the miniature, and the terrific upper-cut with his right, were simultaneous. Anyway, the next second he was putting the picture back in his breast pocket, and the Dago, snarling like a mad dog, was picking himself out of a medley of broken bottles. That was phase one. Phase two was equally rapid, and left me blinking. There was the crack of a revolver, and at the same moment a knife stuck out quivering in the wall behind my head. Then there was a silence, and I collected my scattered wits.

" The revolver, still smoking, was in Jimmy's
18

hand : Salvas, his right arm dripping with blood, was standing by the door, while his two pals were crouching behind the table, looking for all the world like wild beasts waiting to spring.

" ' Next time,' said Jimmy, ' I shoot to kill.'

" And he meant it.   He was a bit white round the nostrils, which is a darned dangerous sign in a man, especially if he's got a gun and you're looking down the business end of it.   And no one knew it better than those three Dagos.   They went on snarling, but not one of them moved an eyelid.

" ' Put your knives on that table, you scum,' ordered Jimmy.

" The other two obeyed, and he laughed contemptuously.

" ' Now clear out.   You pollute the air.'

" For a moment or two they hesitated : then Salvas, with a prodigious effort, regained his self-control.

" ' You are brave, Señor Mainwaring, when you have a revolver and we are unarmed,' he said, with a sneer.

" In two strides Jimmy was at the table where the knives were lying.   He picked one up, threw me his gun, and pointed to the other knife.

" ' I'll fight you now, Salvas,' he answered, quietly.   ' Knife to knife, and to a finish.'

" But the Dago wasn't taking any, and 'pon my soul I hardly blamed him.   For if ever a man was mad, Jimmy Mainwaring was mad that night : mad with the madness that knows no fear and is absolutely blind to consequences.

" ' I do not brawl in bars with drunken Englishmen,' remarked Salvas, turning on his heel.

" A magnificent utterance, but ill-advised with Jimmy as he was. He gave a short laugh and took a running kick, and Don Pedro Salvas disappeared abruptly into the night. And the other two followed with celerity.

" ' You'll be getting into trouble, old man,' I said, as he came back to the bar, ' if you start that sort of game with the Dagos.'

" ' The bigger the trouble the more I'll like it,' he answered, shortly. ' Give me another drink. Don't you understand yet, Merton, that I'm beyond caring ? '

" And thinking it over since, I've come to the conclusion that he spoke the literal truth. It's a phrase often used, and very rarely meant; in his case it was the plain, unvarnished truth. Rightly or wrongly he had got into such a condition that he cared not one fig whether he lived or died ; if anything he preferred the latter. And falling foul of the Dago colony was a better way than most of obtaining his preference.

" Of course, the episode that night had shown me one thing : it was a woman who was at the bottom of it all. I didn't ask any questions; he wasn't a man who took kindly to crossexamination. But I realised pretty forcibly that if the mere handling of her picture by a Dago had produced such a result, the matter must be

serious.   Who she was I hadn't any idea, or what
was the trouble between them—and, as I say,
I didn't ask.

" And then one day a few weeks later I got
the answer to the first question.   Someone left
a month-old *Tatler* in the bar, and I was glanc-
ing through it when Mainwaring came in.   I
reached up for the gin bottle to give him his usual
drink, and when I turned round to hand it to him
he was staring at one of the pictures with the
look of a dead man on his face.   I can see him
now with his knuckles gleaming white through the
sunburn of his hands, and his great powerful
chest showing under his shirt.   He stood like
that maybe for five minutes—motionless ; then,
without a word, he swung round and left the bar.
And I picked up the paper."

Merton paused and drained his glass.

" Lady Sylvia's wedding ? " I asked, unnecessarily, and he nodded.

" So the first part of the riddle was solved,"
he continued, quietly.   " And when two days
passed by without a sign of Mainwaring, I began
to be afraid that he had solved his own riddle in
his own way.   But he hadn't ; he came into the
bar at ten o'clock at night, and leaned up against
the counter in his usual way.

" ' What have you been doing with yourself ? '
I said, lightly.

" ' I've been trying to get drunk,' he answered
slowly, letting one of his hands fall on my arm
with a grip like steel.   ' And, dear God ! I can't.'

" It doesn't sound much—told like this in the smoking-room of a London club. But though I've seen and heard many things in my life that have impressed me—horrible, dreadful things that I shall never forget—the moment of all others that is most indelibly stamped on my brain is that moment when, leaning across the bar, I looked into the depths of the soul of the man who called himself Jimmy Mainwaring— the man who could not get drunk."

Once again he paused, and this time I did not interrupt him. He was back in that steaming night, with the smell of stale spirits in his nostrils and the sight of strange things in his eyes. And I felt that I, too, could visualise that tall, immaculate Englishman leaning against the counter—the man who was beyond caring.

" But I must get on with it," continued Merton, after a while. " The club will be filling up soon and I've only got the finish to tell you now. And by one of those extraordinary coincidences which happen far more frequently in life than people will allow, the finish proved a worthy one.

" It was about two days later. I was in the bar polishing the glasses when the door swung open and two men came in. They were obviously English, and both of them were dressed as if they were going to a garden-party.

" ' Thank heavens ! Tommy, here's a bar, at any rate,' said one of them. ' I say, barman, what have you got ? '

" Well, I had a bit of a liver, and I disliked being called barman.

" ' Several bottles of poison,' I answered, ' and the hell of a temper.'

" The second one laughed, and after a moment or two the other joined in.

" ' I don't wonder at the latter commodity,' he said. ' This is a ghastly hole.'

" ' I wouldn't deny it,' I answered. ' What, if I may ask, has brought you here ? '

" ' Oh, we've had a small breakdown, and the skipper came in here to repair it. We've just come ashore to have a look round.'

" I glanced through the window, and noticed for the first time that a steam yacht was lying off the shore. She was a real beauty—looked about a thousand tons—and I gave a sigh of envy.

" ' You're not in want of a barman, by any chance, are you ? ' I said. ' If so, I'll swim out and chance the sharks.'

" ' 'Fraid we've got everything in that line,' he answered. ' But select the least deadly of your poisons, and join us.'

" And it was as I was pulling down the gin and vermouth that Jimmy Mainwaring came into the bar. He got about half-way across the floor, and then he stopped dead in his tracks. And I guess during the next two seconds you could have heard a pin drop.

" ' So this is where you've hidden yourself,' said the smaller of the two men—the one who had done most of the talking. ' I don't think we'll trouble you for those drinks, barman.'

" Without another word he walked out of the place—and after a moment or two the other man started to follow him. He hesitated as he got abreast of Jimmy, and then for the first time Mainwaring spoke :

" ' Is she here ? '

" ' Yes,' answered the other. ' On board the yacht. There's a whole party of us.'

" And with that he stepped into the street and joined his pal. With a perfectly inscrutable look on his face Jimmy watched them as they walked through the glaring sun and got into the small motor-boat that was waiting alongside the quay. Then he came up to the bar.

" ' An artistic touch, doubtless, on the part of Fate,' he remarked, quietly. ' But a little unnecessary.'

" And I guess I metaphorically took off my hat to him at that moment. What he'd done, why he was there, I neither knew nor cared ; all that mattered to me was the way he took that last rotten twist of the surgeon's knife. Not by the quiver of an eyelid would you have known that anything unusual had happened : he drank his three double-gins at exactly the same rate as every other morning. And then he too swung out of the bar, and went back to his office in McAndrew's warehouse, leaving me to lie down on my bed and sweat under the mosquito curtains, while I wondered at the inscrutable working out of things. Was it blind, the Fate that moved the pieces; or was there some definite pattern beyond our ken? At the moment it seemed pretty blind and senseless; later on—well, you'll be able to form your own opinion.

"You know how quickly darkness falls in those latitudes. And it was just before sunset that I saw a boat shoot away from the side of the yacht and come full speed for the shore. I remember I wondered casually who was the mug who would leave a comfortable yacht for Nwambi, especially after the report of it that must have been given by our two morning visitors. And then it struck me that, whoever it might be, he was evidently in the deuce of a hurry. Almost before the boat came alongside a man sprang out and scrambled up the steps. Then at a rapid double he came sprinting towards me as I stood at the door of the bar. It was the smaller of the two men who had been ashore that morning, and something was evidently very much amiss.

"'Where is she?' he shouted, as soon as he came within earshot. 'Where's my wife, you damned scoundrel?'

"Seeing that he was quite beside himself with worry and alarm, I let the remark go by.

"'Steady!' I said, as he came gasping up to me. 'I haven't got your wife; I haven't even seen her.'

"'It's that card-sharper!' he cried. 'By God! I'll shoot him like a dog, if he's tried any monkey-tricks!'

" ' Dry up, and pull yourself together,' I said angrily. ' If you're alluding to Jimmy Mainwaring——'

" And at that moment Jimmy himself stepped out of his office and strolled across the road.

" ' You swine, you cursed card-cheat—where's Sylvia ? '

" ' What the devil are you talking about ? ' said Jimmy, and his voice was tense.

" ' She came ashore this afternoon, saying she would return in an hour,' said the other man. ' I didn't know it at the time, Mr.—er—Mainwaring, I believe you call yourself. The boat came back for her, and she was not there. That was four hours ago. Where is she ? '

" He was covering Jimmy with his revolver as he spoke.

" ' Four hours ago, Clavering ! Good heavens ! man—put down your gun. This isn't a time for amateur theatricals.' He brushed past him as if he was non-existent and came up to me. ' Did you see Lady Clavering ? '

" ' Not a trace,' I answered, and the same fear was in both of us.

" ' Did she say what she was coming on shore for ? ' He swung round on the husband.

" ' To have a look round,' answered Clavering, and his voice had altered. No longer was he the outraged husband ; he was a frightened man relying instinctively on a bigger personality than himself.

" ' If she's not about here, she must have gone

inland,' said Jimmy, staring at me. 'And it'll be dark in five minutes.'

"'My God!' cried Clavering, 'what are we to do? She can't be left alone for the night. Lost—in this cursed country! She may have hurt herself—sprained her ankle.'

"For a moment neither of us answered him. Even more than he did we realise the hideous danger of a white woman alone in the bush inland. There were worse dangers than snakes and wild animals to be feared. And it was as we were standing there staring at one another, and afraid to voice our thoughts, that one of McAndrew's native boys came down the street. He was running and out of breath; and the instant he saw Jimmy he rushed up to him and started gabbling in the local patois. He spoke too fast for me to follow him, and Clavering, of course, couldn't understand a word. But we both guessed instinctively what he was talking about and we both watched Jimmy's face. And as we watched it I heard Clavering catch his breath sharply.

"At last the boy finished, and Jimmy turned and looked at me. On his face was a look of such cold malignant fury that the question which was trembling on my lips died away, and I stared at him speechlessly.

"'The Dagos have got her,' he said, very softly. 'Don Pedro Salvas is, I fear, a foolish man.'

"Clavering gave a sort of hoarse cry, and Jimmy's face softened.

" ' Poor devil,' he said. ' Your job is going to be harder than mine. Go back to your yacht— get all your men on shore that you can spare— and if I'm not back in four hours, wait for dawn and then strike inland over the swamp. Find Pedro Salvas's house—and hang him on the highest tree you can find.'

" Without another word he swung on his heel and went up the street at a long, steady lope. Twice Clavering called after him, but he never turned his head or altered his stride—and then he started to follow himself. It was I who stopped him, and he cursed me like a child— almost weeping.

" ' Do what he told you,' I said. ' You'd never find your way ; you'd be worse than useless. I'll go with him : you get back and bring your men ashore."

" And with that I followed Jimmy. At times I could see him, a faint white figure in the darkness, as he dodged through that fever-laden swamp ; at times I found myself marvelling at the condition of the man, bearing in mind his method of living. Steadily, tirelessly, he forged ahead, and when he came to the foot-hills I hadn't gained a yard on him.

" And then I began wondering what was going to happen when he reached Salvas's bungalow, and by what strange mischance the girl had met the owner. That it was revenge I was certain ; he had recognised her from the picture, and I remember thinking how bitter must have been his

hatred of Mainwaring to have induced him to run
such an appalling risk. For the risk was appalling, even in that country of strange happenings.

" I don't think that Jimmy troubled his head
over any such speculations. In his mind there
was room for only one thought—an all-sufficient
thought—to get his hands on Pedro Salvas. I
don't think he even knew that I was behind him,
until after it was over and the curtain was falling
on the play. And then he had no time for me."

Merton gave a short laugh that had in it a
touch of sadness.

" A good curtain it was, too," he continued,
quietly. " I remember I made a frantic endeavour to overtake him as he raced up to the
house, and then, because I just couldn't help
myself, I stopped and watched—fascinated.
The window of the big living-room was open, and
the light blazed out. I suppose they had never
anticipated pursuit that night. Leaning up
against the wall was the girl, with a look of frozen
horror on her face, while seated at the table
were Pedro Salvas and three of his pals. And
they were drinking.

" It all happened very quickly. For one
second I saw Jimmy Mainwaring framed in the
window—then he began shooting. I don't think
I've mentioned that he could shoot the pip out
of the ace of diamonds nine times out of ten at
twenty yards, and his madness did not interfere
with his aim. And that night he was stark,
staring mad. I heard three shots—so close

together that only an artist could have fired them out of the same revolver and taken aim ; I saw the three friends of Pedro Salvas collapse limply in their chairs. And then there was a pause ; I think Jimmy wanted to get at *him* with his hands.

" But it was not to be. Just for a moment the owner of the bungalow had been so stupefied at the sudden appearance of the man he hated that he had simply sat still, staring ; but only for a moment. The movement of his arm was so quick that I hardly saw it ; I only noticed what seemed to be a streak of light which shot across the room. And then I heard Jimmy's revolver again—the tenth, the hundredth of a second too late. He'd drilled Pedro Salvas through the heart all right— I watched the swine crumple and fall with the snarl still on his face—but this time the knife wasn't sticking in the wall.

" She got to him first," went on Merton, thoughtfully. " His knees were sagging just as I got to the window, and she was trying to hold him up in her arms. And then between us we laid him down, and I saw that the end was very near. There was nothing I could do ; the knife was clean into his chest. The finish of the journey had come to the man who could not get drunk. And so I left them together, while I mounted guard by the window with a gun in each hand. It wasn't a house to take risks in.

" He lived, I think, for five minutes, and of those five minutes I would rather not speak.

There are things which a man may tell, and things which he may not. Sufficient be it to say that he may have cheated at cards or he may not—she loved him. If, indeed, he had committed the unforgivable sin amongst gentlemen all the world over, he atoned for it. And she loved him. Let us leave it at that.

"And when it was over, and the strange, bitter spirit of the man who called himself Jimmy Mainwaring had gone out on the unknown road, I touched her on the shoulder. She rose blindly and stumbled out into the darkness at my side. I don't think I spoke a word to her, beyond telling her to take my arm. And after a while she grew heavier and heavier on it, until at last she slipped down—a little unconscious heap of sobbing girlhood."

Merton paused and lit a cigarette with a smile.

"So that is how it was ordained that I should carry the Lady Sylvia Clavering, slung over my shoulder like a sack of potatoes, for three miles. I remember staggering into the village to find myself surrounded by men from the yacht. I handed her over to her distracted husband, and then I rather think I fainted myself. I know I found myself in my own bar, with people pouring whisky down my throat. And after a while they cleared off, leaving Clavering alone with me. He began to stammer out his thanks, and I cut him short.

"'No thanks are due to me,' I said. 'They're due to another man whom you called a card-cheat—but who was a bigger man than either you or I are ever likely to be.'

" ' Was ? ' he said, staring at me.

" ' Yes,' I answered. ' He's dead.'

" He stood there silently for a moment or two ; then with a queer look on his face he took off his hat.

" ' You're right,' he said. ' He was a bigger man than me.' "

Merton got up and pressed the bell.

" I've never seen him from that day to this," he said, thoughtfully. " I never saw his wife again until to-night. And I've never filled in the gaps in the story. Moreover, I don't know that I want to."

A waiter came over to his chair.

" You'll join me ? Two whiskies-and-sodas, please, waiter—large ones."